The 1

by

Lacey Wolfe

The Hot Bods Series

Fool Me Once: copyright © 2011, Lacey Wolfe

More Than Useful: copyright © 2012, Lacey Wolfe

Accidental Love: copyright © 2012, Lacey Wolfe

Opposites Attract: copyright © 2013, Lacey Wolfe

Edited by Pamela Tyner

Cover Art by Razzle Dazzle Design

ISBN: 978-1-937325-67-1

Published in the United States of America by Beachwalk Press, Incorporated

www.beachwalkpress.com

Dedication

To my family, thank you for helping me make my dreams come true.

Acknowledgements

There are so many people who've helped me along while writing The Hot Bods series. From beta readers to my editor and wonderful publisher, you've all helped make this series sparkle. Writing a book is a team effort, and I've got a fabulous team working with me.

Thank you to my readers who have wanted more and made this series what it is. I love hearing from you and your thoughts on these stories. You guys are what makes this so much fun.

Fool Me Once

Fool me once, shame on you. Fool me twice…

Drew is the last person Skylar wanted to see across from her at a local bar. A month ago he'd wined and dined her all weekend, leaving her feeling fully in love, but then she awoke alone in an empty hotel room and she hadn't heard from him since.

The weekend Drew spent with Skylar was phenomenal. There had never been anyone who made him feel as complete as she did. He shouldn't have disappeared, he should have called, but his feelings for her scared him, so he distanced himself. But when he saw her again, he knew he couldn't stay away any longer.

Skylar's determined not to give Drew another chance to hurt her, but he's just as determined to win her back. Although it won't be easy, he's up to the challenge, and he's willing to do whatever it takes to accomplish his goal.

Content Warning: Explicit Sex

Chapter 1

Skylar's eyes met his across the bar. *Shit*. Those were the last pair of eyes she wanted to see. She had hoped to never see him again. The last time she'd seen Drew was the amazing weekend they had spent together. He'd wined and dined her for two nights straight.

Her lips knew every part of his body, her tongue knew every taste. He was an amazing lover and had magic fingers that could send her over the edge in just a few strokes. When she awoke on the last morning they were to share together, she had expected to have a wild morning quickie, instead she found an empty hotel room. That was a month ago, and she hadn't seen or heard a word from him since then, until now.

She blinked her eyes and pushed the memory away. A blonde woman was attached to his arm, and she looked like the type who could have whomever she chose, unlike Skylar. The woman was so busy gabbing with people around her that she hadn't realized Drew's focus was no longer on her.

Draining her drink and setting the glass on the bar, Skylar knew it would be best to look away. As she willed herself to get out of there, she saw Drew had excused himself from the blonde and was headed her way. *Hell no!* Taking a quick glimpse around the room she looked for the bathroom as an escape. She caught sight of a hallway to her left and walked toward it.

"Skylar!" she heard him call.

She picked up her pace and ducked into the darkened hallway, expecting to see bathrooms, but instead all she saw was an exit door. "Shit."

She pushed the door open and found herself in an alley behind the building. This was the last place she wanted to be. The sound of the door opening again echoed, and she knew she was no longer alone.

"Skylar, why did you take off?" Drew's voice was just as she remembered, deep with a slight southern drawl.

Spinning around, she came face to face with him. He was hot. No, he was downright drool worthy. She stared at him a moment, taking him in, remembering what it was about him that she'd found so attractive—green eyes, dark blond hair, perfect body, muscles in all the right places. She almost wanted to feel herself in his arms once again, but she couldn't deal with the heartache of him leaving her.

"Sky," he repeated.

"What do you want, Drew?" she finally said.

"I wanted to see you."

Letting out a sarcastic laugh, she said, "I find that hard to believe. If I recall, the last time I saw you, we were tangled up in bed sheets, sweaty and calling out each other's name. And then you just left. No word. No call. No note. What the hell?"

"I had an emergency. I had to leave. Something happened at work, and I had to go."

"You couldn't leave a note?"

"I planned to call you."

"You didn't though," she snapped.

He inched toward her. She stepped back, but bumped into the wall behind her. "Why didn't you call?"

He slid his hands through his hair. "I don't know."

"You don't know! Why are you wasting my time here?" She pushed forward, trying to get around him, but he moved in closer.

He leaned in and whispered near her ear. "I want you. I've wanted you since I laid eyes on you."

Shivers went through her body, desired stirred. *Fuck.*

"What about Barbie in there? Do you want her too?"

"Who?" he said with confusion.

"Your date, I assume?" Her eyes met his.

Her stomach began to flutter. He was so close to her.

Inhaling, she smelled his aftershave, an all too familiar smell. An urge came over her to lean forward and bite into his neck. He had enjoyed bites the last time they were together.

"Francesca—she is no one."

Skylar could see he shared the same longing for her that she had for him. She now wished she had pants on instead of this skirt. As her pussy grew wet, her inner thighs felt sticky. She wiggled a little, trying to rub the moistness off.

"I bet she doesn't feel that way," Sky said.

"She loves any attention from any man. She probably doesn't even know I'm gone." He leaned in, his lips close to hers.

"Have you fucked her?" Skylar whispered.

Drew's hands tugged at her waist and pulled her hard against him, his erection pushing into her. "No one fucks as well as you."

She pressed her lips against his and dug her nails into the back of his neck, bringing him even closer. Her lips opened, and his tongue thrust inside.

"You taste so good," she moaned into his mouth.

She was smooshed against the wall, and his hips moved against her. All the right places were being rubbed.

She opened her legs wide enough to allow him access if he chose to take the cue, which he did. He drove his fingers into her, his action rough. And she loved it.

"God, Skylar, no panties."

A slight, flirty giggle escaped her mouth. "I missed those fingers." She bit into his neck as his fingers moved even faster inside her.

"I missed your bites."

The feeling of his big digits entering her two at a time sent pleasure rippling through her body. Her knees began to weaken.

"I'm about to come. Oh my God, I'm about to come!" She bit down on his shoulder, holding in the scream that longed to be released.

"Wait," he said softly in her ear.

He went to his knees. Pulling her skirt up a little, he moved his head underneath it. His warm mouth met her center. Taking in a deep breath, trying to hold back from screaming, she enjoyed just what that tongue could do as she attempted to grip the rough walls.

"You can come now."

His fingers pushed into her as his tongue swirled around her clit. As if on cue, she let out a loud moan as she chanted his name. Her walls tightened around his fingers.

After licking up every drop of liquid, he rose and took her lips again in a long, slow, passionate kiss, making sure to share her taste. She ended the kiss with a small nibble on his bottom lip.

"Wow, you really know how to make a girl come."

"I want to make you come every day, Sky."

Skylar threw her head back and laughed. "As if."

Drew's expression turned serious. "I mean it."

"You expect me to believe that shit? All I heard that weekend was how much you wanted me. Then you fuck the hell out of me and I never hear from you again."

Drew stepped back, and she took that opportunity to move past him. Straightening her skirt, she turned to look at him. "See ya around—maybe."

She walked down the alley, heading toward the parking lot, fully expecting to never see Drew again.

Chapter 2

"Yes, he finger fucked me right there in the alley," Skylar gushed to her roommate as she dressed for work.

"Why did you let him?"

Skylar paused a moment, letting her shirt stop midway as she pulled it over her head. "I don't know."

Amy laughed. "You don't know?"

"One minute I was fighting with him, and the next all I could do was kiss him."

"Did you, um, pleasure him?"

"Nope, I didn't. I told you, after he gave me an amazing orgasm, I just walked away. It felt good to get the last word this time. He's out of my system now, really."

Amy fell back across Skylar's bed. "I don't believe you."

"Seriously, chances are he isn't going to call. I just left him there, blue balls and all. I'm sure I royally pissed him off. And you know what, I hope like hell I did." Skylar looked at the clock. "Shit, I'm late!"

"That's nothing new."

* * * *

Pissed was an understatement, Drew was so furious he

was having a hard time concentrating as he sat staring at the computer monitor on his desk. Of all the days to be distracted. He had a big presentation due and all he could think about was Skylar.

In fact, all he'd thought about for the past month was leaving her in that hotel room. He regretted that, and wasn't even sure why he'd never called her. When he saw her again last night, he knew he had to win her back. Having her again in the alley was heaven for him, and her walking away as if he was just a fuck left him livid.

After she'd left him, standing there with an erection needing relief, he'd stormed back into the bar. Francesca took no time to find him. She was drunk and begged him to take her back to her place. When they arrived at Francesca's, she pulled him inside. He went in knowing it was a mistake. Francesca was all over him, grabbing at his pants. As horny as he was, fighting her was tough, but being with her wasn't an option. Disgusted with himself for even being in her apartment, he set the drunk girl on the couch and left without looking back.

He was angry with himself for going to her place. He should have chased Skylar down, proclaimed his love for her, and if he was lucky he would have spent the evening with her in his bed.

Frustration was taking him over. He threw his pen down, then called his secretary over the intercom and told her he was heading to the gym. The company had just changed gyms, something about better rates since they paid for it, and he had yet to visit. Right about now a run on the treadmill seemed like what he needed.

The gym wasn't far, only a block away. He almost wished he had walked there. Next time. Grabbing his gym bag from the trunk, he headed toward the entrance. As he entered, he took the view in. It was spacious. There were mirrors everywhere. To his left was a small daycare room and to his right was the reception area. He went over to the right.

"Welcome to Hot Bods Fitness!" the upbeat brunette said.

"Hi. Drew Jones, my company has an account here."

He watched as she typed something into the computer.

"Gotcha! Do you mind stepping over just a little so I can take your picture? Next time you visit we'll have an ID tag for you and you can just swipe it as you come in."

Drew did as she said and then asked where the locker rooms were. She directed him to the hallway right past the desk. Thanking her, he went to change.

After changing, he returned to the front where the

annoyingly perky brunette was. As he headed into the main gym area, he heard her calling to him to have a fantastic workout. She was definitely an enthusiastic one.

Taking a momentary look around the small but well organized gym, he found the cardio area. It was easy to spot. He picked a treadmill away from the women who were running. The last thing he wanted was to engage in any conversation. Placing his feet on the sides of the machine, he programmed his workout. He stepped on and started out with a light jog.

As he was wishing he had his iPod to drown out the boring talk show on the TV, he thought he heard *her* voice. He shook his head. *I must be going mad.*

"Pick up those knees, ladies. If you want those hot thighs, you need to step it up!"

He swore it sounded like her.

"Work it, ladies. Feel the burn. Feel the burn!"

Drew stopped the treadmill and followed the sound of the voice. He came to a room in the back of the gym. There she was, he would recognize that ass anywhere. She was wearing gray workout pants, a black sports bra, and had her long red hair pulled back into a high ponytail. She bounced up and down, encouraging her class to feel the burn. Everyone started doing squat jumps and her breasts bounced up and down, up and down. He watched intently.

When the jumping stopped, his eyes rose to her face and she was looking at him across the room. *Déjà vu*, he thought. He watched as she tried to collect herself to finish teaching the class. He walked away so he wouldn't disturb her further. Now he really needed to run to fight the ache he was feeling in his gym shorts.

* * * *

What the hell was he doing there? Skylar was finished with her aerobics class. Grabbing a bottle of water and squirting some in her mouth, she checked her schedule. She had an hour before her next class. That meant she had an hour to figure out what *he* was doing at this gym.

Taking a towel, she wrapped it around her neck and wiped off the sweat. She headed out of the room, intent on finding him. He was easy to spot. He was in the cardio area, in the back row like a typical man, watching the ladies' butts jiggle as they worked out. Rolling her eyes, she started his way.

"Hi, Drew," she said sweetly.

He turned off his machine and grabbed his water bottle. She watched as he touched it to his full lips, taking in a long sip.

"If you're done, do you mind following me so we can

talk a minute?" she asked. She knew a confrontation in the middle of the gym wouldn't look good for either her or the business.

"Sure."

Spinning around, she headed toward the staff only break room. Once there she stepped aside so he could come in. Luckily the place was empty. She shut the door and locked it.

"What are you doing here?" She placed her hands on her hips, trying to portray she was irritated by him, when all she really wanted was to feel his mouth on her again.

"Honestly, I had no idea you would be here."

"Yeah, and I should believe that. I haven't seen you in a month until last night and then today you show up at my work place."

He took a seat, clearly worn out from his run. "My company just switched gyms. I was having a tough morning, so I wanted to blow off some steam by taking a run."

"Sounds convenient," she retorted.

"Shit, I didn't know you would be here. It's a plus though." He eyed her belly, and she imagined his tongue there, licking her sweat off.

Silence filled the room. She didn't know whether to

believe him or not. His explanation sounded logical, and she would hate to think fate worked this out. Fate was what she first thought brought him into her life to begin with. He seemed so perfect for her. When they made love, it was so hot it almost seemed like sparks were flying off their bodies. At least at the time she considered it making love. Now she knew it was just sex to him, nothing more.

"Come here." He motioned to her.

She snickered. "I don't think so."

"Please, I just want to feel you again."

"Ain't happening, buddy. You had your chance." She knew all she had to do was resist him; that was the hardest part.

He reached out, grabbed her arm, and pulled her to him. Yanking away from him, she took a step backward.

"Come on, Sky, I know you still have feelings for me."

"Oh, I definitely have feelings for you, just not the ones you're hoping for."

He chuckled. "You know, there's a thin line between love and hate."

"That line is pretty thick for me."

"I'm not so sure."

"I am." At least she hoped.

He stood, closing in on her. As he stepped toward her,

she found herself once again flat against the wall. *Shit, how does this keep happening?* His mouth was too close for comfort. Her eyes drifted to it for just a second, knowing it was a mistake.

"This is not a good idea," she whispered. Desire stirred in her.

"I want to have you. I need to have you. You're all I have wanted."

Placing her hands on his toned chest, she pushed him back. "You're not doing this to me again, got it?"

"I will win you back," he said.

Knock knock.

"Hey, who's in there?" came a familiar voice through the door.

"Hold on!" Skylar called, giving Drew a final shove. "Stay away from me."

She jogged toward the door and opened it, seeing Jane, the receptionist.

"Everything okay, Skylar?" Jane asked, peeking around her.

"Peachy." She brushed past her, wanting to get as far away from Drew as possible.

Chapter 3

Finally, Skylar's shift was over. She was ready to blow out of this place, get home, and figure out what the hell was wrong with her. Maybe she was going insane. Each time she got around that man, she craved him. Now he was going to be a presence in her work place. A strong margarita was in order.

Closing her locker, she decided to skip the shower today. She went to the reception area to clock out.

"I have something for you, Miss Skylar." Jane handed her an envelope addressed to her.

"What's this?"

"That totally hot guy you had in the employees' break room left it."

"Okay. Well, I'll see you tomorrow." Skylar spun around, ready to leave.

"Wait, are you involved with him?" Jane called.

Skylar paused a moment. "Nope, you can have him."

She pushed her way out the building. Home, that was where she wanted to be.

When she arrived at her apartment, she was happy to see Amy wasn't there. She loved Amy, but she didn't have a silent bone in her body, and right now Skylar needed quiet.

She headed straight to her room, tossing her gym bag on the floor beside the bed. The envelope fell from the side pocket. Groaning, she leaned down and picked it up. Might as well see what he had to say.

Sky,
There is no denying the chemistry
between us. Meet me tonight at the coffee
shop near your apartment.
Drew

Rolling her eyes, she flung the letter down on the comforter beside her. There was no way in hell she was going to the coffee shop to meet him. Somehow they would end up alone together and she knew exactly what would happen then. It wouldn't be long before their clothes were scattered on the floor. No, going would be a mistake. A nap was in store instead.

* * * *

Drew was so furious his blood was boiling. He'd been stood up the night before. Not only had she left him with a massive erection each time he'd seen her, she was now a no-show. Going to the gym to get rid of his frustration was not an option today. If he saw her, he wasn't going to be able to hold his tongue.

He had to see her though. Rubbing his hand across his chin, he racked his brain. He knew where she lived. No one would be there to interrupt. They could fight it out, tear each other's clothes off. She couldn't walk away from him at her own place. It might work.

Leaning back in his office chair, his thoughts drifted to their weekend together. From the moment he had met Skylar, he'd wanted her. They had met at a club, and the connection was there instantly. When he left that evening he couldn't believe he'd parted without her number. Taking a chance, he went back to that same club the next weekend, and she was there. He couldn't believe his luck. That time he made sure to get her number. After two weeks of pleas to her, she finally agreed to go away with him.

That one weekend they'd spent together was phenomenal. They took a trip out of town to Charleston and stayed in a very nice hotel. Room service was their best friend. Dressing was optional. Sexually, there wasn't anything they didn't try.

He smiled as he remembered how she'd tied him up, then danced above him, performing a strip tease. When just her panties were left, she dropped them to his face, covering his eyes and nose. He still remembered her scent. She sucked him while he savored the scent. Her tongue was wicked. She took his entire cock into her mouth, and when he was ready to come, she brought his dick in farther and let him erupt right down her throat.

She was perfect. Not just for her skills in bed, but in every way. Even when they weren't getting dirty, the conversation flowed between them. She seemed to just get him.

So why didn't he call her after that weekend? He still searched his brain for the answer. He should have called, but his feelings for her scared him. At thirty years old, he wasn't ready to settle down yet. At least he thought he wasn't until he met Sky.

Anger filled him again. She had to feel the same way. There was no way with what they shared she wouldn't. Hell, every time they saw each other, they were all over one another.

Getting her in bed again, that was what he needed to do. It was the only way to remind Skylar that what they had was good. He wouldn't walk away from her again. He just had to show her.

* * * *

Stepping onto the cool tile after a refreshing shower, Skylar wrapped herself up in a plush white towel. After working out all day for her living, she always treated herself to a spa feeling when she got home. Inhaling deeply, the scent of lavender took hold of her, relaxing her. Towel drying her hair quickly, she stepped into her favorite slippers that were made from memory foam. They knew her tired feet well.

Heading through the apartment, she went straight for the kitchen. She took her mug out of the microwave, added some sugar, and was ready to just chill. Now all she needed was her take-out. Looking at the clock, she saw that it would be arriving anytime now.

Taking a seat on the couch, she sipped her tea slowly. Her body was sore. She had taught several kickboxing classes today, and that was always a work out.

The sound of a knock echoed through the quiet apartment.

"Finally," she mumbled as she pulled her towel tighter around her.

Grabbing a twenty out of her purse, she opened the door, using it to shield her from the delivery guy. She expected to see some young kid, but instead Drew stood there holding her food.

"Surprise. I met the delivery boy at the door. Paid him, and I'm sure glad he didn't get to see you this way. Do you often answer your door in just a towel?" He stepped inside, not even waiting for her to invite him in.

"What are you doing here? I feel like I'm being stalked." She pushed the door shut. "What do I owe you for the food?"

"Whatever you have under that towel." His gaze took in every inch of her.

She rolled her eyes, unable to stop the grin that spread across her face. "I'm going to go change."

"Don't change on my account."

"Do you think I'm crazy, Drew? The longer I stand here in this towel, the more you're going to get the idea that you just might get to see me out of it."

"Why don't you at least eat first? I promise I won't do anything you don't want me to." He took a seat on the couch and patted the cushion next to him.

"There is no way I'm sitting here half naked and eating take-out with you."

"Just sit. Look, I'll even move all the way over." He scooted to the very end of the couch. "See, I can't even reach you." When she didn't sit, he added, "I think maybe you're worried that *you* can't behave yourself around me."

The heat rose in her cheeks. How dare he think she couldn't control herself? She wasn't at all worried if she could keep her hands to herself. Letting out a groan, she clutched the top of the towel and took a seat on the opposite end of the couch.

"You had better keep your hands to yourself," she warned. "I mean it."

She was crazy and she knew it. If she were smart, she would be in her room, changing. Not sitting here in a towel about to share Chinese take-out with him.

She grabbed a pair of chopsticks and dug in. Until the food hit her lips, she didn't realize how famished she was. In fact, she heard moans coming from her mouth at how good the food tasted.

"I'm going to get hard listening to you eat. My cock is quite jealous."

Licking her lips, she sucked the chopstick deep into her mouth. "This sauce is really, really good." Her tongue swirled around the stick.

Drew groaned. The look on his face was envious.

"Okay, so what do you want?" she asked, returning to her food as normal.

"No more cock tease performance? I was enjoying it."

She rolled her eyes. "You're two seconds away from

me kicking your sweet ass out."

"Why didn't you meet me last night?"

"I didn't want to. I told you to leave me alone."

"Why?" he asked, resting his fork in the dish.

"I just told you, I didn't want to."

"I don't want to play games. I'm serious about making this work. Why can't you give this another shot?"

"Yeah, and for how long?" She dropped her take-out onto the coffee table. "A weekend, or maybe this time a week?"

"No, longer."

"Are you talking forever?" Turning to him, she studied his face.

He was silent. She waited for an answer, but one didn't come. She didn't know what the hell he wanted, but she didn't have time for this.

"Look, I'm ready for a relaxing evening. No stress. Today was a long day. I just want to veg out and rest. I'm feeling sore, and I'd like to lay down for a bit. Can we do this charade another time?"

"Turn around," he said.

"What, why?"

"Just turn around with your back to me."

"I don't think so. I told you no hanky-panky," Skylar

snapped.

"And I told you I wouldn't do anything you didn't want. Turn around, I just want to massage your shoulders."

A massage did sound good to her aching body. "Don't try anything," she warned him as she turned around.

He gripped her shoulders tightly. She whimpered at how heavenly his strong hands felt on her sore muscles. His thumbs began to make small circles on the middle of her back.

"That feels so good." She sighed.

He leaned forward, and she felt his breath on the back of her neck. She expected to feel his lips on her neck, but he kept his distance.

Her head fell forward as his hands seemed to be putting her under a spell.

"Lower the towel some," he whispered in her ear.

She turned her head, looking at him over her shoulder. He grasped her shoulders, really working his thumbs.

"Oh God!" She untied the towel and let it drop slightly in the back.

His fingers moved over the top of her chest, pulling the towel free. She gasped and started to reach for the towel to cover herself. Shivers erupted through her body as his fingers lightly rubbed just above her breasts. She knew she was in trouble now as she found herself silently praying he would touch her breasts. He didn't though. He concentrated on her lower back, still working on all the tender areas. Moaning again, her head fell back. He scooted closer so she was leaning against him. His hands lingered on her belly, slowly moving up and down. He teased her, stopping just below her breasts and then right above her pelvis.

"You're the tease now," she said softly.

"I don't have to be." His kissed her earlobe, slowly sucking in. "Just say the word."

"Fuck me," she demanded.

Lifting her up, he carried her to her room.

Chapter 4

The seconds it took Drew to get to her room melted away as Skylar found the mattress at her back. There was passion blazing in his beautiful eyes as he gazed at her. She reached up, gripping his neck and forcing his mouth to hers. She instantly opened up with a desire and need that only he could quench. The kiss was hard and forceful, yet just how she liked it.

His mouth left hers. "Are you sure?"

She nodded.

His lips nipped just under her ear. Flutters swept through her body as light kisses were placed in the spot he knew would drive her over the edge. Moaning, she felt a primal need go off in her body.

She grabbed his shoulders and pushed him off of her. He looked somewhat confused, which made her smile. She sat up and pushed him down so his back was now flat against the mattress. Crawling on top of him, she began ripping at his clothes. Grabbing his shirt in her fists, she yanked it up over his head.

"You have too much on, I need to see you." Her eyes darted to his jeans, and she began to rapidly unbutton them.

"All of you."

He helped her move things along by wiggling and kicking as she pulled his jeans and tight little blue boxer briefs down his legs, letting them drop to a mound on the floor.

"Much better." Eyeing his bare chest, she rubbed her hands on his pecs.

Her mouth met his again, and she wrapped her hand around his cock, moving slowly up and down his long, thick shaft.

"Does this feel good?" she asked.

"Yes." His voice was raspy.

She pressed her lips along his collarbone, giving light kisses. As she fondled him, enjoying the feel of his cock in her hand, liquid formed between her legs.

"Touch me," she whispered in his ear. "Put those long fingers deep inside me."

Thrusting her off him and spinning her around, he stood behind her. He forced her forward onto the bed, rubbing his hands across her ass. His palms trailed up her back, along her spine. Her body quivered with the need to be filled. Feeling light touches on her lower back, she anticipated his fingers entering her. She waited. Once again his hands teased her as he rubbed the entire length of her back. She was dripping from her pussy.

His hands left her body altogether. Sighing, she was about to beg him to touch her when suddenly his hand came down, spanking her. Her head spun around toward him in shock. *Oh my God, he spanked me!* Before she could say anything he slapped her ass again. She let out a slight yelp, amazed that the vibration from the spanking was almost enough to send her over the edge. His hand came down once more before rubbing her where he had caused pain.

"Did you like that?" he asked, his finger finally sliding into her pussy. "It feels like it. You're very wet."

"Yes," she cried out.

He began a familiar rhythm that always sent her over the top fast. His name was a whisper on her lips as her climax built. Her body began to grind onto his fingers. She was just about there when he suddenly stopped.

"Son of a bitch!" she yelled. "What the fuck?"

"Patience."

She heard the sound of a wrapper being opened.

"You don't need to come just yet," Drew instructed.

"Who are you to tell me when I can come? Damn it, get your cock in me now."

He laughed. His hands spread her legs open more.

"How bad do you want my dick?"

"I want it bad, very bad. Please," she begged.

"Only since you asked nicely." He slammed into her with such force that she shrieked, shoving her face into the mattress.

One of his hands tangled into her hair, pulled her head back. The other hand rubbed her butt, one finger slowly dipping in between the cheeks. Biting her lip, she imagined where she wanted that finger to go. She hoped he remembered.

"Please," she pleaded.

His finger slid into her ass. She bit into the comforter as the sensations grew more rapid on her body. He grinded into her faster, his finger moving in and out at an almost even speed.

"Oh my God, Drew! Oh my, oh my!"

His breathing picked up. Pumping harder and faster, they began to say each other's name. She gripped the sheets as her body exploded and the orgasm surged through her.

As soon as he released her hair, she fell limp onto the bed, his body on top of hers. Panting and rolling over, he pulled her to him. Her head rested on her pillow, her eyes closed.

Skylar had forgotten just how magical it could be between them. If only this could actually last. His arm tightened around her, tugging her to his chest. Resting her head on it, she felt her eyes moisten. She willed the tears away. There was no way she was going to get gushy over him. She would enjoy this for just a few minutes, no longer. Just a few moments of feeling his strong arms around her.

She was so relaxed and comfortable, her eyes began to close. A short nap would be okay, she told herself. Just as her eyes drifted shut she heard Amy.

"Sky, are you in there?" The door knob jiggled. Thank God it was locked.

Demanding her eyes to open and prying herself out of Drew's big arms, she grabbed a robe and put it on. She glanced back at the tangled sheets wrapped around Drew, one leg falling off the side of the bed, his eyes closed, his hair a tousled mess. She knew by his breathing he was pretending to be asleep, which was good. It would be time to send him home soon.

"Hold on, Amy." Unlocking the door, she covered the open space with her body, praying Amy wouldn't see the man in her bed.

"Is someone in there?" Amy asked, trying her best to peer around her.

"Let's go out here." Skylar squeezed out the door, shutting it behind her.

On Sky's heels, Amy questioned, "Who's in there? You have to tell me."

Rolling her eyes, Sky plopped down on the couch. "I don't have to tell you anything."

Amy placed her hands on her hips and said, "Sure you don't, but you will."

Sky grabbed the take-out box and ate a few bites. "Drew's in there."

Her roommate burst out laughing.

"It isn't funny. Now I have to get rid of him. He looks so mouthwatering lying there. I could probably go for seconds."

"Why not let him stay?"

Sky shot a look at Amy. "The longer he stays, the more my heart will open. Screw that. His ass needs to get out of here."

"Maybe he won't leave you again."

"You're so optimistic. It's sad."

Placing the food on the table, she leaned back, staring up at the popcorn ceiling. She wished Amy would leave, go to her room, anything but stand there and look at her.

"Excuse me, ladies."

Skylar's head snapped forward, and she saw Drew who was now fully dressed. Her heart hurt, knowing he was leaving her, again.

"Going so soon?" she asked with a bitter tone.

"You're tired, and I don't want to take any more of your time. I would like to continue our conversation soon though."

"Conversation? What conversation? Every time we try to talk, we end up in a compromising position," she replied.

"This time many." He grinned.

Her face grew warm. "Just get out of here—it's what you do best."

"I'm not leaving you."

"Sure as hell looks like that's what you're doing," she snapped.

"Do you want me to stay tonight?" Crossing his arms, he watched her, waiting.

Crap, turn it around why don't you. Biting her bottom lip, she wasn't sure how to answer him. Sure she wanted him there, but then again she didn't. She didn't know what the hell she wanted. She felt like a hypocrite judging him.

"Doesn't look like it. I'll see you soon, Skylar." He leaned forward and placed a kiss on her cheek.

He then turned and left. Skylar dropped her face into her hands. Why did this have to be so complicated?

"Good job, Skylar. It's obvious he wants you," Amy

said.

"Not now, Amy." Standing up, she headed toward her room.

"You finished with this food?"

"Yeah, eat what you want."

Closing the door behind her, she glanced at the bed. The pillows were pushed up toward the head board, the comforter was on the floor, and the sheets were all twisted. The sight of it reminded her of what had taken place not long ago.

Sitting on the bed, she rubbed her hands across the now cool sheets. Falling back, she wondered what she was going to do about Drew. He wanted to talk, so he said. They had tried several times. However, somehow sexual innuendos always began, and they'd get off track and start exploring one another's body. She licked her lips, it was a tasty body to explore at least. *Damn.* Even in her thoughts, she got off track.

Pulling the sheet up all the way to her nose, she could smell his scent. A mix of sweat and spice. A scent that eased her enough that she was able to drift off to sleep with her mind and body fully relaxed.

* * * *

Skylar finished up with her last class scheduled and

was thankful it was an early day. She couldn't concentrate. Her thoughts were all mingled with a certain guy, and her emotions were completely out of whack.

She cleaned up her stuff, getting things ready for the next instructor. She made a mental note to let Jane know two light bulbs were burnt out. Grabbing her gym bag, she switched the lights off and headed for the shower. She had errands to run when leaving here before she had the luxury of going home.

As she left the room she took a quick peek toward the cardio area, hoping to see Drew. Her heart did a flip as she saw him lost in thought, jogging on a treadmill. She noticed a blonde on the treadmill beside him. She looked familiar, but Skylar couldn't place where she had seen her. It was possible that she was a newer member of the gym and that was why the face rang a bell.

She found herself being pulled toward Drew. She should avoid him, head to the shower, but she couldn't help feeling drawn to him.

"Drew," she said as she approached him.

He looked up at her, slowing his run until he was able to stop.

He didn't speak. The memorable blonde also slowed her machine down and had a smile across her face.

"Hi, I'm Francesca." Hopping off the machine, she extended her hand.

Skylar took her hand, shaking it, all the while keeping her eyes on Drew. Her attention then turned to the woman in front of her. "Hi, Francesca. I'm Skylar."

"Were you just teaching that kickboxing class? I've always wanted to try that. It looks like a lot of fun. A real kick-your-ass workout."

"You're welcome anytime." *Not.*

"How do you know Drew?" she asked. Obviously now her curiosity had spiked as to why Sky had come over.

Looking back at Drew, she grinned, wondering how to answer. "You should probably ask Drew."

Francesca's smile faded. "Is she an ex, honey?"

Honey. Skylar felt as if her blood was about to boil right out of her body.

"No, she isn't an ex."

So he can speak.

"What are we then?" She pushed him a little further.

Their eyes locked on one another.

"Okay, well then, this is getting a bit awkward." Francesca grabbed her water bottle off the machine. "Catch you later."

Skylar watched as the woman skipped off, her ponytail

bouncing along the way.

"It isn't what it looked like," Drew started to explain.

She raised her hand in an attempt to stop him from saying whatever he now felt like he needed to say.

"Save it. You have nothing to explain to me. Francesca though, that might be a whole other story, *honey*."

Skylar turned and strutted away.

* * * *

Fuck. Fuck. Fuck.

That woman was always walking away from him before he could get a word in edgewise. Sure, she had a fine ass, but he sure as hell was tired of seeing it that way.

He couldn't believe that he'd stood there frozen like an idiot as the two women met and chatted. Hell, that must have made things ten times worse. How was he going to get himself out of this one?

Francesca didn't help. He had no idea she was even a member of the gym. She'd just plopped onto the machine next to his as he worked out. She didn't say much. He hadn't seen her since the night he'd left her in her apartment. He fully expected her to hate him, as any normal woman would have. Instead, she acted like nothing had happened. He supposed a talk was in order with her also. Shit, when did life get so complicated?

* * * *

Skylar was almost finished with her hair. Trying her hardest, she attempted to fill her mind with things she had to get done. She wasn't successful. Lately, the only thoughts she had were of a certain man, and now this other woman. Skylar couldn't help but worry there was something between them and she was being played, once again, by Drew.

Turning off the blow dryer and setting it onto the marble counter top, she picked up her brush. Combing through her straight, shoulder length red hair, she wondered how she was any competition for Francesca. She had freckles on her face. Pale skin. She was nothing compared to that Barbie. She wasn't even sure why Drew kept coming around.

Lost in thought, she hadn't realized someone was standing beside her. Turning, she saw the last person she wanted to see.

Chapter 5

"So, how do you know Drew?" Francesca inquired again.

Rolling her eyes and wondering why this day kept getting worse, Skylar answered, "I told you to ask Drew."

"Well, I don't want to. I'm asking you."

Packing her things up in her cosmetic bag, she tried to ignore the woman, hoping she would just go away. She wasn't succeeding though, the stupid girl just stood there, arms crossed, toes tapping, waiting.

"We slept together, several times." Skylar turned toward her, also crossing her arms tightly across her chest.

It was like they were suddenly having a showdown with their eyes.

"How long ago?"

"Yesterday."

The last thing she expected was for Francesca to burst into tears. All of the sudden she was a sobbing mess. Grabbing a handful of tissues off the vanity, Skylar tossed them at her. There was no way in hell she was going to comfort this girl. All she wanted was for her to shut up.

Gazing up at the ceiling she wondered if this would be

a good time to pray. Shit, this day just needed to end.

"I knew there was someone else. I just knew it!" Francesca wailed, wiping her snotty nose.

"If it's any comfort, it was one time and then a month ago. I can't be that special, he left me in a hotel room and never called."

The crying stopped abruptly. "Oh, he left you too. Well, I experienced that just the other night when we were at that new bar on Cleveland Street. First, I lost him for a while and then when we went back to my place to get cozy, he just left me on the couch. I don't remember much, I was pretty toasted." She tossed her tissues in the trash.

An odd feeling swept through Skylar. "What night was that?" she asked.

"Uh, a few nights ago."

Skylar was speechless. She felt like someone had just punched her in the gut. He was in the alley with her fooling around and then the asshole went home with another woman.

"It's been nice chatting, but I have to go." Grabbing her stuff, Skylar walked away as fast as she could. She couldn't bear to hear any more.

* * * *

Skylar paced the apartment as she waited on Amy.

According to the clock, Amy was almost thirty minutes late. She was never late. Amy was an on time, organized sort of woman. Skylar's complete opposite. She often had to wonder if she'd brushed her teeth that day.

Watching TV might be an option to pass the time, but she wasn't even sure she could sit down or concentrate. Her legs wanted to move a mile a minute. Her thoughts replayed what she had talked about with that blonde, and all she wanted was Amy to vent to.

Jumping jacks! Yes, that was a perfect way to burn her excess energy.

Right there smack dab in the middle of the living room she started doing jumping jacks. Her hands clapped loudly above her head, her heart beating fast. She was so caught up in her thoughts and movement she about fell over when she heard Amy.

"What in the world are you doing?" Amy asked as she closed the door behind her after entering the apartment.

"Where have you been?" Catching her breath, Sky collapsed onto the couch.

"I went window shopping after work. If you needed me you could have called. Did you forget about the little invention called a phone?"

"Ha ha!"

She took a seat beside Sky on the couch. "Okay, you only do jumping jacks when you're extremely angry, and I assume this has something to do with that hot man who was in your bed."

"Oh yeah. So get this," she began, "I finish up my last class and I see Drew. I decide what the hell, I'm going to talk to him. Some blonde chick is with him. She introduces herself as Francesca. The girl he was with that night at the bar, if you remember. So, I wait for his dumbass to say something. No, it's like he's mute. She asked how I know Drew and I attempt to get him to reply, but he just continues standing there, not saying a word. Finally she leaves, and then he suddenly starts talking. Only at this point, I don't want to hear what the fuck he has to say. So I left his sorry ass there and I went to take a shower. As I finished getting ready, Blondie came up to me wanting to talk."

"Oh Lord, did you get in a fight and lose your job?" Amy asked, biting her nails in anticipation of what was to come.

"No, but she just had to know how I knew Drew. So I told her, and yes, I let her know he was here last night and we had sex. The girl starts to cry! I mean full-out bawl, snot dripping out her nose and all. It was disgusting. Finally she shuts up, but get this, the same night he ate me out in the alley he went home with her! Can you believe it?"

"Wow."

"I know."

"So, is he seeing her too?" Amy asked.

"Not sure. She called him honey in the gym, but in the locker room I didn't get that impression. I don't know."

"Well, there's only one person to ask then, isn't there?"

"I don't think so. I don't want to see him again." She shook her head.

"Easier said than done, you guys just keep bumping into one another."

"Don't start that fate shit, please." Irritation grew in Skylar's voice. "I get so tired of that."

"I'm not saying anything about fate, only that you meet this great guy at a club. You talked about him all week, wishing you had exchanged numbers. You go back hoping he's there and he is."

"It's called a coincidence, Amy, not fate."

"Either way, that doesn't usually happen."

"Whatever. Yes, he started out this really great guy, but what about now?" Skylar asked.

"Has he turned into some dragon blowing fire?" Amy inquired.

"What? No." She rolled her eyes.

"Okay, so he didn't call. Did you ever stop to think he got caught up in life, forgot to call, and then was too embarrassed after a week or two went by?"

"My brain hurts—this is too much to process. Plus, you seem to be forgetting he is doing her too."

"You don't know that until you ask him. Go lay down, I'll make dinner and wake you when it's ready. Sound good?"

Leaning over she hugged Amy. "If you had a dick, you'd be perfect for me."

Amy laughed and hugged her back.

Skylar headed to her room, shutting her door. She slipped off her jeans and climbed into bed. Laying her head on the pillow Drew had used, which still smelled like him, she finally let her emotions take over. Her eyes started to get moist and a tear dropped out of one, landing on the pillow. Her walls were breaking that she had set up all around her heart to keep anyone from getting in. Since they first met, Drew had worked hard to tear those walls down. After he left her, she thought she had built them back up stronger, but she was wrong. The walls were crumbling and she was feeling all sorts of things. Closing her eyes, she let the tears fall as she drifted off.

* * * *

Humming away as she cooked, Amy put the finishing touches on the chicken alfredo. It was her best friend's favorite comfort food. Smiling, she imagined the look on Sky's face when she saw the fettuccini noodles mixed with the creamy white sauce, grilled chicken, and her favorite, mushrooms. Her stomach growled, and she snuck a taste. It was perfect.

She went to the pantry to find some sugar for the tea when a knock at the front door caught her attention. As she left the kitchen, she wondered who it could be.

Opening the door, she wasn't surprised at all by who stood there.

"Drew," she said coldly.

"Hi. Amy, right?" he asked.

"The one and only," she retorted.

"I was hoping I could see Sky."

"No, sorry." She crossed her arms and leaned against the doorjamb.

"Is she not here?" He gave her a look with one eyebrow raised.

"She is." She stepped out the door, letting it shut behind her. "What are your intentions with her?" she demanded.

"Excuse me?" he said in a baffled tone.

"Are you hard of hearing or something? What are your intentions with her?" she asked again.

"Are you her father?" She heard the irritation in his voice.

"Funny. Right now I have a best friend who is upset because of your games. Your girlfriend doesn't help this matter. Especially since you were with both of them on separate occasions in one night."

"Shit." He rubbed his hands through his hair.

"Care to explain?"

"Francesca isn't my girlfriend for one. Second, I wasn't with them on the same night. Where did you get that from?"

"Your two women had a little chat today in the locker room. Apparently you went home with Francesca the same night you were with my friend."

"Uh-uh. I took her home, yes. She was drunk, I couldn't leave her at the club. I only took her home and then got the hell out of there," he explained.

Amy bit her bottom lip. He seemed sincere, and Sky did mention it didn't seem like they were involved. "So nothing is going on between you and Francesca?"

"Nothing."

"Well, I have a best friend in there who is torn up over

what happened. You're going to have to fix this."

"Can I just see her, please? Explain this to her?"

"Still gonna have to say no. Give her some time, okay?" she said, smiling now.

"Then how do I make this better?"

"You'll figure it out."

He raked his hands through his hair, groaning.

"By the way, don't forget about one of the greatest inventions to date, it's called a phone. You could try that if you want to actually talk to her without ripping one another's clothes off. You do have her number, don't you?" she asked.

"Yeah."

"Then maybe it's about time you use it, the same way you should have after that weekend you spent together. Have a nice evening. I have a dinner to finish." Without looking back, she spun on her heels and headed inside.

Smiling to herself, she felt love was in the air and these two were just dancing around. Eventually the dance was going to end and she was going to see two very happy people. Maybe one day she would get her own Prince Charming. Hopefully, though, she wouldn't have as complicated of a time as Skylar was having getting hers.

Chapter 6

The air was chilly and the slight breeze was cool to her skin. As she rocked in the chair with a coffee mug in her hand, Skylar knew this was the only way to start her day off. Eyes closed, the sun shining on her. The balcony was her favorite place.

The world seemed to be quieter this time of day. The birds chirped, and people hustled to their cars in a mad attempt to not be late for work. Not her this morning. No rushing, just enjoying.

She told herself it was a thinking free day, if possible. She wished a certain person away and if she just didn't think about that darn name then maybe things could get uncomplicated again.

The sliding glass door opened, and Amy popped her head out. "I'm heading to work. Enjoy your day."

"You too, Ames. Thanks again for dinner last night. It was so nice not eating a sandwich or take-out again. You're going to make some man happy one day with your cooking!"

"Finding a man is the problem." She laughed. "See ya, girl."

Waving a hand, Skylar went back to her coffee. She plopped her feet up on the railing, leaning the chair back. Putting her mug to her mouth, she took a long sip. The caramel flavored coffee was just what her taste buds craved this morning. Setting the mug in her lap, her eyes slowly closed again.

Beep beep.

Her eyes opened when she heard the sound of a new text on her phone. Damn, she should have left that stupid thing on her nightstand instead of bringing it out here with her. Most likely the new instructor called in sick and they wanted her to come to work. She briefly considered ignoring it, but then she reached down and picked the phone up off the deck.

Drew: Free for lunch?

Lifting one eyebrow and puckering her lips, she tried to hold herself back from feeling any excitement that it was from him. She felt a little giddy, like a school girl, even though she should be angry. Maybe it helped that Amy had talked to him and cleared things up a little.

Skylar: Maybe

Taking her feet back down from the rails, she began to rock again, staring at her phone, waiting for the reply. Then it came.

Drew: Would like to talk, in a public place? Little Italy?

Skylar: Twelve o'clock, be there.

Drew: Wouldn't miss it.

Hitting the lock button on her phone, she decided a shower was in order and a look over her wardrobe was a must. Hopefully she and Drew could finally clear the air. Get all the baggage between them cleared up.

* * * *

Drew arrived early so he could find the perfect spot for them. There was a corner booth in the back of the dimly lit restaurant. He was thankful to see it open and requested the table. Letting the host know a beautiful redhead would be joining him, he took his seat. The place usually wasn't too busy at lunch, which was good. It would be quiet enough that they wouldn't have to yell at one another.

Hopefully, they would finally be able to talk. There was no way he was going to toss her up on the table and do her right there, or at least he assumed not. He knew when she entered his world he easily forgot where he was and the fact that there were other people around.

No one had ever made him feel the way she did. He loved her sassy attitude, her laugh, smile, the whole package. No one else understood him like her. Of course there was what she did to him physically too. He craved the sound of her moans as he tempted her body. The feel of her full breasts in his hands, soft but firm. *Shit*, he already had a hard-on and she wasn't even there.

Scooting forward so the red checkered tablecloth covered his lap, he noticed her coming toward him. She was once again dressed in a short flowing skirt, and he instantly wondered if she had on panties. He pictured her pussy free under there, rubbing against the seat. His hard-on grew bigger.

Sitting down on her side of the booth, she smiled at him. She asked the waitress to bring her a Coke and then grabbed a hold of her menu.

"Have you ordered?" she asked quietly, keeping her eyes focused on the menu.

"I was waiting on you."

"Did you want to share something?"

"Whatever sounds good to you." *You sound good to me.*

"How about the supreme?"

"That works for me."

Putting her menu down, her eyes finally met his. She studied his expression. Desire was the only thing he knew she saw in his eyes.

"Don't get any ideas, we're here to talk."

He nodded.

"I just want you to understand that even though I'm here, you're not off the hook."

He nodded again.

The waitress returned with their drinks, and they ordered a medium supreme with extra mushrooms and two side salads.

"Amy told me you came by last night and the two of you had a talk."

He laughed. "Yeah, she talked to me all right."

"Francesca isn't your girlfriend?" Just like her to get straight to the point.

"No, she's just someone I was seeing casually."

"Does she know that? I got the impression she was very interested in you. Her claws are deep," she said as she took a sip of her Coke.

"Ha, she's interested in whoever is paying her attention. She's waiting for some rich guy to sweep her up and marry her so she doesn't have to work anymore."

"And she thinks you're that person?"

"No, but she knows I have connections to rich people. If she hangs around with me, she will finally find that person, or she hopes."

The food arrived, and silence engulfed them as they ate. Biting into the pizza, Drew was glad they went with supreme, the peppers were really hitting the spot.

"Nothing happened when you took her home? She implied to me you were together."

"God, no. She was drunk and could barely stand. Even if she was sober, I wouldn't have gone there. I want you, Sky."

"So you keep saying. I'm just not sure I can trust you yet."

"I get that. I hurt you. But I promise I will make it up to you."

"Fool me once, shame on you. Fool me twice, shame on me." She smiled, taking a bite.

Looking up, he stared at her. Once again as she ate, she moaned like she was in pure ecstasy. His dick grew even harder as he imagined that pizza was him and hearing her moan as she took him, deep, telling him just how good he tasted.

"Is there something on my face?" Grabbing her napkin, she started patting her chin.

"You making those sounds as you eat, you're making me horny." He was blunt.

Dropping the napkin, she gazed at him. "Really?"

She shifted in her seat, and a grin crossed her face. "How horny?"

He felt her foot slowly move up his leg. Inhaling deeply, he asked, "What are you doing?"

"Eating." Biting into her pizza again, she let out a small mutter. Her foot found his hard cock and rubbed.

Looking down, he saw bright purple toenails. He grunted as he imagined taking them into his mouth and sucking, but that certainly wasn't appropriate in the middle of a restaurant. Then again, the way her foot was fondling him wasn't either. Scooting forward more so the waitress wouldn't see, he leaned back.

She lightly rubbed her foot up and down the bulge in his khakis. She shoved her pizza far into her mouth, biting down. A noise of pleasure erupted from her as she pulled it away, licking her lips slowly.

"I like it messy." Skylar sucked tomato sauce from her finger, letting it making a popping sound as it left her mouth.

His breathing quickened, his hands grasping the edge of the booth seat.

"Okay, you have to stop," he said.

Letting her foot drop, she shrugged. With her fork she stabbed a big black olive from her salad. She rolled her tongue around it, then took it whole in her mouth, closing her lips around it. Good God did he wish they were alone right now.

"You are a tease, Sky."

She snickered. "Don't you forget it."

"I don't think I will ever see olives the same again." He grinned. Without a doubt he knew if he was lucky enough to get her to spend the rest of her life with him, there would never be a dull moment.

* * * *

When lunch was finished, Drew walked Skylar to her car. Pressing her against it, he kissed her. He lingered a moment before he whispered, "Let me take you away for the weekend."

"I don't think so."

"Please. I promise I will leave you fully satisfied." His lips moved to her neck, giving her little love bites.

She clutched his shoulders and tried to shove him away. "Not happening. I know better."

Pressing himself into her more, his lips met hers again. Emotions ran through her as his kiss went from passion to tender. More than anything she wanted to go with him, spend a weekend together. Could she really trust him that he wouldn't just leave her yet again?

"I'm going to kiss you until you say yes."

"We might be here all day."

His lips trailed down to a sensitive spot right below her ear. He gripped the other side of her neck, tilting it so he had full access, leaving light kisses.

"That feels so good." She sighed, knowing she shouldn't be letting his lips anywhere on her.

"I could do this for hours, you know." He spoke softly into her ear.

"Okay, fine, I'll go away with you, but if you hurt me again, I will kill you."

He kissed her once more before he pulled away. "You won't be sorry." He tapped the glass on his watch. "You little tease, I'm late now."

"It's not my fault." She laughed, clutching his shirt and yanking him back to her. "You better be good to me."

"Oh, I will be."

A quick kiss on the cheek and then he spun around and headed to his car. She watched him walk away and hoped she wasn't making a mistake. If he pulled the same stunt again, she wasn't sure she was going to recover this time.

Chapter 7

The next few days flew by. Skylar found that she and Drew were starting to move in an easy groove together. A few texts during the day, light conversation at the gym, a few make out sessions in the employees break room. Her mood was upbeat, and she couldn't have wiped the grin off her face even if someone had paid her to. She was happy.

Of course there was that one small thought that remained in the back of her mind, no matter how much she tried to push it away. The worry that after this weekend he would be done with her yet again. He'd assured her several times that would not be happening. She found herself believing him and getting giddy that this might actually work. The word *fate* crossed her mind, and she didn't feel the gut wrenching need to squash it. In fact, she was starting to think that maybe a bigger hand was working in all of this.

After a little shopping for her upcoming weekend, she headed back to the apartment to pack. Drew had told her to be ready by the time he arrived. He also specified to pack very little—a bikini, sundress, and no panties. She assumed they were heading forty-five minutes north from there to the beach.

She dragged her small black suitcase out of the closet. Tossing it onto the bed, she placed her new clothes for the trip inside. She then headed to her dresser, opening the top drawer where her swimsuits and panties were kept. She picked out her favorite bikini—an itty-bitty lime string bikini. The day she'd bought it, she and Amy had laughed, wondering why anyone would want to wear that color. She'd tried it on as a joke, and they were both shocked at how well it went with her hair and made her green eyes stand out. So she got it.

She rubbed her fingers along some of her lace thongs. Biting her lip, she remembered what Drew said, but she figured if they were going out she might need them. She grabbed two, just in case, and placed them in her suitcase.

All that was left was her makeup kit and other toiletry items. Leaving her room to head to the bathroom, she bumped into Amy.

"Did I hear you humming?" Amy inquired.

"I don't know. If I was I didn't realize it."

Smiling, Amy said, "This is a nice change from the usual grumpy Sky."

"Ha ha."

An hour later, Drew arrived. Skylar snickered as Amy lectured him about not breaking her heart again. Drew nodded, most likely feeling like a teenager taking his girlfriend to the prom. Behind Amy, Sky made a gun with her fingers and pretended to shoot herself in her head in an attempt to mock Amy.

"You guys get out of here. I'm looking forward to my weekend alone," Amy said.

"Is a man coming over?" Skylar asked.

"I wish."

Hugging her best friend, Sky handed her luggage to Drew and they were out of there.

Just as she suspected, the beach was in her future. As Drew parked the car in front of a private bungalow, she felt the excitement already. Stepping out she looked toward the sunset over the water. Oranges and reds streaked the sky. It was beautiful. His arms wrapped around her and he made it perfect.

She wished they could stand there like that all night, but knew that the growing erection behind her ass was about to become priority number one.

"Here are the keys. I'm going to grab our stuff." Drew kissed her on the cheek and went toward the trunk.

She unlocked the front door and went inside. It was stunning, with dark hardwoods throughout the one room bungalow. A cherry wood bed with a white comforter nestled in the middle. Red accent pillows on top of the bedspread. Her gaze moved toward the small kitchen. Simple, white cabinets and counter tops with dark red appliances.

The place was tiny, but it was perfect. She sat on the bed and bounced a little. Her hands moved across the crisp bedspread feeling the soft satin under her fingers. She lay back, looking up at the white ceiling. There was so much white in this place, she wondered if she should have packed a bottle of bleach.

Two big hands fell next to each side of her face. She gripped Drew's biceps, rubbing small circles.

"Hello there, stranger." She giggled.

"Long time no see."

As she smiled up at him, one of her hands found its way to his pants. "Oh my, is that a pencil in there or are you just happy to see me?"

Laughing, he pushed his erection into her hand. "That definitely can*not* be compared to a pencil."

"Take it out, let me see."

She looked down and watched as he unbuttoned the pants. He lowered them and she saw he wasn't wearing any underwear.

"You bad boy," she teased.

"I said no panties, so I figured I shouldn't have any underwear either."

She thought back a second to the two thongs she'd packed and the pair she was currently wearing. Oops.

Getting back on task, she focused on his long, thick erection.

"That is no pencil." Her hands wrapped around it, feeling it. Licking her lips, she met his eyes. "I wanna taste."

Crawling on the bed, he got on his knees above her. He reached behind her and grabbed a pillow, then placed it under her head for support.

She cupped his balls as she slid his dick into her mouth, moving her tongue along the bottom of his shaft. As she found her way back to the tip, a drop of pre-cum seeped out. She licked the drop, enjoying the salty taste.

"Mmm," she murmured.

He groaned. "You're killing me."

"Shh."

Slipping his cock back into her mouth, she enjoyed the feel of it. Sucking him deeper, she placed her hands on his ass, urging his hips to grind against her. She felt a slight gag as his dick entered her throat. As big as he was, she was always amazed at how deep she could burrow him in.

His breathing was heavy. She could tell he was enjoying this. She moved her hand down and took a hold of his balls again, slightly squeezing them.

"Enough." He pulled out of her mouth.

Disappointment swept through her.

"I want to come inside of you," he said.

"I'm pretty sure you would have gotten to."

He chuckled. "You're the naughty one."

"Only for you."

His hands took a hold of her thighs, spreading them wide open. Her skirt pushed up.

"Oh dear, you have broken a rule," he said as his fingers traced along her thong. "I said no panties."

"What's my punishment?"

Gripping the top of her thong, he ripped them off. He grabbed hold of her ass, and his mouth met her pussy.

"Torture, by tongue," he replied.

"Torture me, please."

Clutching the edge of the bed, she let out a loud gasp as his tongue circled around her sensitive mound. She felt a flick of his tongue on her clit, and her eyes closed. It was pure ecstasy. As he probed her opening, her knuckles were numb. She was grabbing the edges of the bed for dear life while his tongue pleasured her to the point she couldn't think.

His fingers spread her open wider. Two fingers entered her. Arching up, a whimper broke from her lips. She murmured his name as she heard the sound of a package opening. Prying her eyes open, she watched as he rolled a condom over his massive erection. She began to scoot up toward the pillows, but he grabbed her, dragging her to the edge.

"Don't go anywhere. I have you right where I want you." Placing his hands on her inner thighs, he let the tip of his cock tease her opening.

"Please," she begged.

Smiling, he pushed forward, his tip right at her opening. She gasped as he began to enter her, slowly. She tried pushing her body into him, to get him deeper, but he held her still. As amazing as it felt, she began to feel infuriated at this tease. Jerking her hips as hard as she could, she grinded into him.

His hands grasped tighter and then he drove into her, rough.

"Oh my God, Drew!" she screamed.

Her butt was dangling off the edge of the bed. There was nowhere for her to get a good grip as the pleasure swept through her with each pump. Arching, her hands took hold of the comforter, pulling it up.

He was deep inside her, filling her completely. Noises escaped her mouth with each thrust. His breathing was heavy and she could tell he was almost there. A finger met her clit and she felt a slight pinch. The pleasure began to build and a ripple of sensation flew through her body. She opened her mouth wide and screamed out his name. One last pump and then he collapsed next to her.

She looked over and noticed that sweat had started to bead on his forehead. She took in a deep breath, smelling him, musk mixed with his aftershave. A smell she could die inhaling.

Rolling over and facing him, she grinned. "I think it just keeps getting better each time."

He smiled back. "I agree."

He leaned in and kissed her again. Giggling, she pushed him off.

"Not now, big boy. I'm feeling a bit flushed. I think a drink is in order."

As he sat up, he took her hand and pulled her up with him. "I believe I packed a bottle of wine in the cooler. How about we crack that open and watch a movie?"

"Sounds like a real romantic evening."

"You have no idea." Standing up, he turned toward

her. "Get your pretty self comfortable and I'll be right back with that wine."

Looking around, she saw there were only a few single chairs and a small bistro table. In the corner was a marble fireplace. Above it hung a widescreen television.

She fluffed the pillows. Grabbing his t-shirt, she pulled it over her head and then climbed back under the covers.

She felt like her smile had been tattooed to her face. She couldn't stop grinning. Happiness filled her and she wished more than anything that this wouldn't end. Being with Drew made her feel whole. He was sexy and did things to her no one else had ever done. They seemed to be able to talk about anything, when they were actually able to talk. He had a great job, stable she supposed since he was in marketing. She could almost see that this just might be right.

"Look at the gorgeous smile you have. I could get used to seeing it." He set a bed tray down with two wine glasses, cheese, and crackers.

"Yum." She grabbed a cracker. "So what are we going to watch?"

Pulling a movie from his bag, he said, "It's a surprise. I think you'll like it though. I hear all the women like this one."

"Ooo, is it that movie based on the Emily Giffin book?"

"You'll find out."

After getting the movie set up, he climbed back in bed. Leaning over, he planted a kiss on her cheek. "I'm so glad you're here."

* * * *

Hands caressed her shoulders and light kisses tickled the back of her neck. A moan fled Skylar's lips. Warm water surrounded her as jets massaged their bodies. Reaching over, she grabbed her glass of wine and took a small sip. Leaning her body back onto Drew's, she relaxed completely. The smell of honey and vanilla swarmed around them, making this moment perfect.

"You're spoiling me," she said softly.

"I wouldn't have it any other way."

"I could get used to this."

"I hope you do. I want you to feel this way for the rest of your life."

His hands rubbed up and down her bare arms. She hadn't been this relaxed in a long time. In fact, the last time she had was the time she had gone away with Drew before. She couldn't pinpoint what made her so incredibly happy when she was with him. She felt whole and fulfilled.

Page 65

Nothing else in the world mattered. All she cared about was being safely tucked away in his arms.

She knew her thinking was taking her into a dangerous area. The L word was crossing her mind frequently. Maybe this time it would be forever and he wouldn't abandon her again.

The feel of his erection pressed into her back. Placing her wine down, she moved one hand behind her into the water. Her hand circled his shaft and slowly began to stroke. She was able to move faster in the water and heard his breath quicken.

"Turn around and face me," he instructed.

She did as he requested. Drew reached toward the counter beside them, grabbed a condom he must have placed there earlier, and quickly put it on. His big hands lifted her slightly and his cock caressed her opening. Needing him to fill her, she started to ease down.

"You feel amazing wrapped around me." He kissed along her jaw.

He clutched her waist and directed her movement. Leaning forward a little, her lips pressed into his. Her tongue met his and her body began to move faster. Her climax was building and there was no going slow. She nibbled on his lips as she tried to hold off her orgasm.

Gazing into his eyes, she pleaded, "Come with me, please."

He thrust into her harder and faster, and she clung to his shoulders. Her back arched and she cried out as pleasure rippled through her. He pulled their bodies fully together as he drove into her several more times before her name escaped his lips and he relaxed.

With his head pressed against her breasts, feeling his rapid breathing, she twirled his hair around her fingers. One hand rubbed his back. Pulling his head up, she found his lips and kissed them gently.

"You're amazing."

"I love you," he whispered.

Skylar felt her heart beat faster, only in a different way than it had been. She could almost hear the pounding in her head.

"I love you too."

Chapter 8

"You're the perfect woman for me, Skylar."

Laughing, she punched Drew in the shoulder. "So glad the only requirement was that I was okay with eating cereal for breakfast."

"You passed with flying colors."

Rolling her eyes, she took another spoonful. "I'm just glad I'm not the only adult who still enjoys eating Lucky Charms."

"The box claims it's made with whole grain, so it's gotta be healthy."

"Keep telling yourself that." She laughed.

When she finished eating she asked, "What's on the agenda today?"

"I'm getting your hot little ass in a bikini and showing the whole damn beach that you're mine."

"I'm yours, huh?"

Taking her from the chair, he pulled her into his lap. "Damn right you are."

"If we stay in this position, we're never going to get to the beach. I can see myself flat on my back very soon," she said softly, giving him a seductive look.

"Flat on your back with your legs wrapped around my neck sounds good to me. I'm still hungry."

Excitement flooded her, and as she imagined him between her thighs, she started to feel moist. She began moving against his groin.

"I see you like that idea," he whispered.

Standing up she headed toward the bed. Since no panties were allowed all she had to do was strip her t-shirt off and she was naked. Lying down, she spread her thighs wide open. She watched as a smirk crossed his face.

"Your pussy is right there for me to feast."

"It's ready."

He crossed his arms and leaned back in the chair. "It's not ready yet. I want to see you pleasure yourself. Get it good and wet for me."

Her finger met her clit and she circled the sensitive area. As she pressed a finger into herself she also took hold of her breast and flicked her nipple. She closed her eyes and imagined it was Drew touching her. Her finger began to move faster and she murmured to herself.

A slick, hot tongue meet her opening as it urged to be inside of her. Her other hand grabbed the sheets. His tongue flicked her clitoris and swirled around, then he drew it into his mouth, sucking slightly.

"Drew!" She gasped.

She started to remove her finger from her pussy to grab his head, but he moved her hand back. She continued to pleasure herself as his tongue lavished her. Her hips grinded, her back arched, and her mouth opened wide as sounds of pleasure forced their way through her lips. The pleasure built, sending tickling sensations through her body. She couldn't resist any longer. Her orgasm erupted, and she clutched the comforter with her free hand and cried out in delight.

Her body relaxed back onto the bed. Peeking at him through her heavy lashes she watched as he gently kissed his way up her body.

With one last kiss to her collarbone, he said, "Now, go get that sexy bikini on."

Pushing up off of her, he walked toward his bag. She let out a slight laugh and knew she had gone crazy. This man was going to kill her with pleasure and she was going to let him.

* * * *

Skylar lay alone in bed, the day playing through her head. Lunch had been at a cozy little café. They ate and enjoyed getting to know one another and their plans for the future. Much of the day had been spent on the beach. It was a little more private than most since it was owned by the resort. They had small, innocent make-out sessions under the shaded umbrella, followed by more kissing in the water as they dodged the waves. She didn't think she would ever get tired of that man's lips.

Plenty of time was spent admiring him behind her sunglasses as she pretended to nap on the beach. His tanned body was shirtless and he had a real six-pack, she imagined her tongue licking each line on her way down. His bathing suit sat low enough that the top of his hips had peeked out. Hair formed around his belly button and a line of small curls disappeared into his swimming trunks. She knew right where that trail led to.

It had taken all her self-control not to take him right there on the beach. She hoped it had taken everything in him also.

Listening, she heard the shower running as he washed off from the day. Dinner was next on their agenda. He had made reservations at someplace close. One proper dinner he said, so she could feel special. If only he knew how special he already made her feel.

Sitting up, she decided she should probably get dressed. She didn't want to hold them up, being lost in her thoughts. She could lay there all day being seduced in her daydreams.

* * * *

As Drew stared across the table at Skylar, he knew he'd been right all along. He was in love with this woman.

She sat in front of him in a simple navy sundress, low cut, looking exceptionally sexy. She had pleasured him fully and left him satisfied, not only sexually but mentally too. Yet he still craved her and wanted more. He knew he would never stop yearning for her. This was knowledge he'd discovered the last time they went away. It scared him then, but now he was content with this decision. Skylar was it for him. No one else. He wanted her to be his until their lives crossed over to the other side.

Clearing his throat, he prepared to tell her. He needed to be upfront with her, and he prayed like hell she felt the same way about him.

"I have something to tell you."

She gazed back at him, confused.

"It's nothing bad. It's just, I—" he started.

"Please tell me you're not ditching me again."

"No, the opposite actually." He took a deep breath. "I know you're the one I want to spend my life with. The one I want to share my ups and downs with. Have children with. Fight with until I'm blue in the face. Make up with after the heated arguments. I want to wake up to you every morning. I want to call you when I'm having a bad day at work so just your voice can make me feel better."

She said nothing and he began to feel nervous.

Rubbing his palms together, he continued, "I knew this when we spent the last weekend together. It scared the shit out of me. Honestly, from the moment I met you, I wanted something more with you. I thought I just needed to get you out of my system, but the more I have you, the more I need you. I know I should have called. I meant to, and then too much time passed. I thought maybe other women could fill the void I felt in my heart. They couldn't. When we found each other again, I knew this was it. I can't lose you again."

"As much as I don't want to admit this, I feel the same way, Drew. I was so hurt when you just left me. Here I thought I had found this perfect man, I was getting my turn at happiness, and then you left, no note or anything. When I didn't hear from you, it really hurt." She gazed across the table into his eyes.

"I never want you to feel that way again."

"I hope you don't."

Their eyes locked on one another, and silence filled the air. He knew she had her doubts, but he would do whatever it took to show her he was serious and she was what he desired more than life itself.

"I love you, Skylar. As soon as we get this check, I plan to show you just how much."

She smiled. "I like where your mind's headed."

Laughing, he shook his head and went back to eating. He wasn't sure what he was getting into, but at least the rest of his life was going to be anything but predictable.

When they arrived back at the bungalow, he could feel the sexual tension between them. Sky's eyes were heavy with passion. Her lips appeared full and ready for him.

Tugging her to him, he spoke softly. "I want to make love to you tonight. Slowly."

Without a word from her, he lifted her dress over her head, dropping it to the floor. Stepping back, his eyes took in the view of her wearing only a black strapless bra. With one hand, he unfastened it and it fell to the floor also. She stood before him naked and downright mouthwatering sexy. Picking her up, he carried her to the bed. Gently, he lowered her onto the pillows. He wanted this time to be different. It was to be sweet and full of love.

Kissing her, he slowly pushed her lips open with his tongue. He just kissed her, leaning over her. He cupped her face with one hand, tilting her head back so his tongue could enter more deeply. The other hand found her firm breasts. As bad as he wanted to pinch her nipple—hard—he didn't. He wanted this to be light and sensual.

She pulled at his shirt, breaking the kiss to lift it over his head. She rubbed her hands down his chest and circled his belly button before taking hold of his pants. Standing straight up, he undid his pants, pulling them down. Her eyes took in his cock. More than anything he wanted to grab her by the head and let her mouth explore him the way her eyes did. He resisted though.

Climbing on the bed beside her, he drew her close to him. He kissed her collarbone and inhaled the fragrance of her flowery smell. The smell made him yearn for her more. He moved his hands down her back, grasping her ass and yanking her against him. His cock was ready to move into her moist cave. Reaching toward the nightstand, he grabbed a condom.

"Let me," she whispered, taking the package.

With her teeth, she tore open the package. She rolled the condom onto his throbbing dick. Lightly, she fondled his balls.

Rolling her onto her back, he climbed between her legs. Tilting forward, he kissed her as he entered her pussy. Her legs wrapped around his back. An urge came over him to start thrusting as fast as he could, and once again, he had to resist. He wanted them to take their time so the connection could be felt by them both.

Feeling her hands tighten in his hair, he began to push into her. Slowly he withdrew until he was almost out of her, then he pushed back fully into her. Her hands tensed in his hair.

"More," she whispered the demand.

Giving her what she wanted, he drove into her. She jerked his face into her collarbone and held him tightly as he pumped into her faster and harder. Breathing was rapid between them. Her pussy tightened around his cock, and he could tell she was almost there. His own climax was building, and he was ready to take the plunge with her. Pumping into her one final time, he cried out as his release poured out of him.

Skylar held him tightly. He relaxed on her, nuzzling his face in her neck. A yawn broke through and he knew he was spent. He was completely satisfied. Rolling to his side, he pulled her into his chest. Closing his eyes, he drifted off with her in his arms, where he hoped she would remain forever.

Chapter 9

Skylar fought to keep her eyes closed but she heard what sounded like Drew's voice speaking to someone. Not winning the battle, she opened her eyes and glanced around. It was still pretty dim in the room. The sun was just barely peeking through the clouds. Sitting up, she looked for Drew. She could hear him talking, but didn't see him.

Slipping out of bed, her toes hit the cool floor. She pulled the sheet off the bed and wrapped it around her.

"Drew," she called.

No answer.

Following his voice, she found him outside by the car, involved in a heated discussion on the phone. He hadn't noticed her, so she turned back to give him privacy. She went toward the tiny kitchen to make coffee. After she got the pot going she was still feeling not quite awake so she decided to crawl into bed and wait.

Just as she was about to drift off, she heard the door close. Footsteps came toward her.

"Sky, wake up." He sounded urgent.

"I'm up." She didn't like the tone of his voice. Something in her gut was alerting her that this wasn't going to be good.

"I have to go. I'm so sorry. I've called a cab. It should be here any moment. I'm leaving you my car to get back, and I'll have it picked up."

Skylar opened her eyes, feeling the tears beginning to build. Anger rose, and unable to contain it she snapped at him, "You're leaving me again?"

"I don't want to. Some stupid moron screwed something up, and I have to get into the office to get it fixed or it's my butt on the line."

"Are you kidding me?" she yelled.

"Wait, why are you so upset?" A look of distress crossed his face.

"Why the fuck do you think?"

"I don't know. We just spent this amazing weekend here. You have to know how I feel about you."

"This is all a little too *déjà vu*." Sitting up, she pulled the sheet close against her body.

A horn beeped outside of the bungalow.

"Damn, they are fast." He grabbed his bag, stuffing his clothes in handfuls at a time. "I will call you, I promise. I'm not leaving you."

Her lips were tight, she was biting her tongue so hard. When he leaned over to kiss her, she turned her head, only offering her cheek.

"I love you, Sky." He planted a kiss on her cheek. Reaching into his pocket, he placed his keys on the table. "I will call you, Sky. I'm going to talk to you every day for the rest of my life. I love you." One last glimpse in her direction, then he blew her a kiss and was out the door.

As the door shut behind him, tears welled up in her eyes. If he did this to her again, she didn't know if she could handle it. She would likely curl up in a hole somewhere and never come out. She felt humiliated. Played and used. But at the same time, she wanted to believe him. God did she want to. Last night she had felt such a deep connection with him, but now her heart was aching.

Inhaling a deep breath, she smelled the coffee. Did she want to get up, get a drink, and leave, or go back to sleep? She peeked down at the bed through her tears and decided to drink her coffee and get the fuck out of there. The bed smelled of sex, sweat, her perfume, and his aftershave mingled together. Another moment in this bed and she would be in the nut house. Tossing the sheet off, she hurried toward the bathroom to get cleaned up.

* * * *

Skylar arrived home early in the afternoon. Letting herself in, she took in the smell of banana bread. A smile went across her face. Amy was home and cooking.

As she dropped her suitcase by the front door, she looked toward the kitchen and saw Amy dancing by herself, ear buds in her ears, iPod attached to her arm. She stopped and pulled the banana bread out of the oven, and Skylar knew she'd hit the jackpot. At the thought of warm bread spread with butter, her stomach rumbled.

As she stepped into the kitchen, Amy finally noticed her and pulled out her ear buds. "Hey, didn't hear you come in." Looking around, she turned back toward Skylar. "Where's Drew? Figured you two would be inseparable at this point."

"Yeah, let's not talk about that right now, okay?"

"Okay?" Amy raised an eyebrow.

Grabbing a knife, Skylar started to cut into the bread.

"What are you doing? You're going to burn your fingers and tongue." Amy swatted her with an oven mitt.

"It's the best way. You know I love it warm."

"Warm yes, but not hot from the oven. Get out of here. Don't touch my bread until I say you can," Amy snapped.

Skylar stepped back, surprised by Amy's tone.

"You okay, Ames?"

"Fine," she barked.

Leaving the kitchen, Skylar decided to head to her

room and put her stuff away. No sense being out there with another grumpy person. She plopped down on the bed and pulled her phone from her purse. Sending a courtesy message to Drew seemed like the right thing to do and might ease her mind from worry.

Skylar: Home.

She sat a moment, staring at the phone. She hoped to see the phone light up with a picture of him sleeping. She smiled, remembering waking once, seeing him looking sexy as hell as he slept. Snapping a picture, she had set it as his ring ID.

Her phone beeped.

Drew: Thanks for letting me know.

She tossed the phone down and rolled her eyes. She didn't know why she had expected any more than that. Pain filled her heart. Trying her best to push it away and not feel it she busied herself sorting her clothes.

A knock on her door took her away from her task. Opening it, she found Amy standing there holding a piece of banana bread with butter dripping off, just the way she liked it.

"Sorry," Amy said.

"You're fine, why don't you tell me what's up?" Sitting down on the bed, she motioned for Amy to sit down also.

She did. "It sounds selfish, but I'm a little jealous. I want to find someone too."

"You will, trust me. And the first time you cook for him, you'll have him hooked for life."

"Yes, well, I had a date last night," she began.

"You did? That's great. How did it go?"

"Not well at all. He just sat across from me in the restaurant and talked all about himself. From his fantasy football league, to his precious maine coon cat, to his sister and her two children. I never got a word in. Any time I tried to talk about me, he always said 'oh, that reminds me of when I…' It was torture. I was so ready for the night to be over. When we parted ways, he said I was the best date he'd had in a long time. Ugh, I hope he doesn't call." Amy leaned back on the bed.

Laughing, Skylar stuffed the last piece of warm gooey bread into her mouth. "You know how to pick them."

"It isn't funny. I'm so tired of dating. They never go well. I don't know why I ever say yes."

"Where exactly did you meet this guy?"

"Outside the bakery. I was on break and he was walking by, pet carrier in hand. This creature from within was meowing as if it was being tortured. I stopped him to see if everything was okay. We started talking and conversation was pretty smooth. He was really cute too. Then again, we talked about the cat the whole time."

"That's funny."

"Glad you find it so funny." Amy rolled her eyes.

"You'll find the right one. Let him come to you. He might just pop out of nowhere for all you know."

She grunted and said, "I doubt that. I think I have been through every available man in the city. So tell me, where is your Prince Charming?"

"I really don't want to talk about it."

"I just told you my horror story of a date. Come on," she begged.

"He left me, again, in our bungalow."

Amy's jaw dropped. "You're kidding me, right?"

"I wish." Boy did she wish.

"No word again, just snuck out and left? How did you get home?"

"Well, it wasn't exactly like last time. Some emergency came up at work. He called a cab, left me his car, and promised he wasn't leaving me for good."

"Okay, and you don't believe him."

"I don't know. I don't know if I should or not. I want to. Ames, the weekend was amazing. But I can't help but have bad memories come up."

"I think it's different this time. I think it was different last time too. He loves you, I can tell. I think it just scares him."

"Like it doesn't scare me?" Skylar put her face in her hands.

"Just wait it out, he might call. Don't jump to conclusions yet, okay?"

"I'll try."

* * * *

Skylar woke from her nap feeling a bit better. Talking with Amy had made her a little less anxious. She was a pessimist and so thankful her best friend was not. Sky knew she always saw the worse in every situation. She had to keep positive thoughts, Drew would call. Hell, his car was here, he had to come get it.

Heading out of her room, she decided to get a drink and go to her favorite place—the balcony. Amy was passed out on the couch, so she quietly grabbed a Coke. The sun was now starting to set. It should be just cool enough out there, she hoped. Tiptoeing past her friend, she slid the door open. Taking her seat in her rocker, she took the sky in. It wasn't a magnificent sunset, just a usual one. The sun slightly orange as it slowly moved out of sight.

Opening her can of Coke, she glanced over at the parking lot. Drew's car was gone! Confused, she took her phone from her pocket to see if she had missed a message from him. There was nothing on her screen. She hadn't left the keys in the car, so he would have had to call her to get his keys.

She went inside and nudged Amy awake.

"Hey, did Drew stop by?" she asked uneasily.

"Uh-uh. Why?" Amy yawned.

"His car is gone, and I have the keys to it. Figured he would need the keys, ya know."

"He probably has an extra set." Sitting up, she stretched.

"Maybe, but why didn't he come up?" Her voice rose.

"Maybe he did, but we were both asleep." Amy looked around. "Geez, the sun is already going down. I'm never going back to sleep tonight now."

"He didn't come up. Wouldn't he have called or texted me?"

She shrugged. "I guess. Don't think too much about this, okay?"

"Whatever," Sky snapped.

She stormed back to her room, angry and hurt. How could he not have come up to see her? He was here, she assumed. She was tempted to call him to see why he hadn't come up. However, fear swept through her. If he was done with her, she didn't want to know.

Staring at her phone screen, she decided to send a quick text just to make sure he had picked the car up and it wasn't stolen. As she tapped in each letter, she knew deep down it hadn't been stolen. When she finished, she tossed the phone onto the pillow next to her.

She flipped on the TV in her room. Any distraction was better than sitting there, contemplating on what happened. Once again, that asshole had sucked her in, broke down her walls, and left her high and dry.

Chapter 10

Work dragged on. Skylar was itching to get this class over so she could check her phone. She just couldn't focus today. She constantly checked the gym for *him* and had been to her locker three times to check her phone. Nothing. A peek at the clock showed it was time to end class and that this day was finally over.

She instructed the class to begin their cool down by following her in some stretches. She closed her eyes and breathed deeply. Stretching her arms and legs had never felt better.

Finally, it was time to let the class go, telling everyone what a wonderful job they had done and that she hoped to see them again soon. Several members had really lost some weight and she was impressed at the time they had put in. She loved seeing people transform. It made her job worth it.

Wiping the sweat off with a white towel, she glanced in the mirror. Tightening her ponytail she headed out of the aerobics room. On her way to her locker, she noticed Jane sniffing some flowers. One of the other instructors had recently gotten engaged and her fiancé was always sending flowers. She wished one day that would happen to her.

"Jill got more flowers. Wow, two dozen reds too," Skylar said to Jane.

"These are gorgeous, aren't they?" Jane said.

"Yes, they are."

"They're for you."

"What?" she said, caught by surprise.

"You heard right, these are for you. Here's the card, open it." Jane jumped up and down excitedly.

Taking the card, Skylar opened it.

> *Had a great weekend. Sorry about how*
> *it ended.*
> *Love, Drew*

Closing the card, she held it close to her heart.

"It's from that hunk I caught you in the break room with, huh?" Jane asked.

Skylar knew her grin was wide across her face, so there was no denying it.

"Do you mind watching these while I grab my stuff?"

"God no, then I can pretend they are mine just a little bit longer. Take your time."

Laughing, Skylar hurried to collect her things. Excitement filled her that he hadn't forgotten her. Maybe this time would be different. She started to feel so restless from happiness. She was worried she was going to break out and do some jumping jacks to contain her excitement.

Taking a hold of her flowers, she handed one to Jane. "Keep one and enjoy it."

"You're so sweet. Thank you."

Waving, she headed to her car. As she was pulling her keys from her purse she noticed another rose on her windshield. Opening the door and carefully placing the vase on the floor, she grabbed the white rose and breathed in. Unable to contain herself, she threw her head back and laughed.

She slid into her car and drove home. She couldn't wait to show Amy her flowers.

She danced all the way to the door, flowers and all. She was in love and ready to shout it to the world. She was pretty sure she could shout that he loved her back too.

Letting herself in, she went into the dining room and set her flowers on the table. Keeping the white rose with her, she searched for Amy.

"Ames, are you here?" she called.

The bakery was closed on Mondays. Sometimes Amy went in and did inventory, but that was usually pretty early in the morning.

"Amy," she called again.

Nothing.

Shrugging her shoulders, she took in the scent of the rose. Grabbing her phone she decided to send a quick message to Drew, thanking him. Right after sending the message she heard a weird noise coming from her room. It was a ding similar to hers when she received a text.

Tiptoeing slowly, she noticed her door was closed. She didn't usually close her door. Amy occasionally did when she got tired of seeing the mess, but her doorway was at the end of the hall, so Amy didn't have to see in there when in the living room.

She turned the door knob and gently pushed it open. Peeking inside, she gasped. Her eyes widened as she took in the sight of rose petals on her bed and candles lit all around the room. Best of all, a hunk of a man dressed only in tight black boxer briefs laid in the middle.

Licking her lips, she said nothing. Leisurely, she walked to the bed and climbed on. She rubbed her hands across his chest, caressing his toned pecs as she looked down at him. Bending forward, she softly kissed his lips. Taking her time, she enjoyed the taste and feel of him underneath her.

"You really know how to melt a girl's heart, don't ya?"

"You're not just any girl, Sky, and you know it." He pulled her down until she rested beside him. "We need to get you out of these dirty clothes." His fingers slowly inched under her sports bra.

Without hesitating, she began to help him take her clothes off. His hands rubbed along her breasts, fingers gripped her nipples, and a low groan fled from her mouth.

"I could get used to coming home to this," she said.

He took her nipple into his mouth, sucking in deep. Her fingers curled into his hair.

"I plan to do this every day for the rest of my life." He moved to the other nipple, drawing it in. "These are all mine."

"Is that so?"

"Mmm-hmm, I will never get tired of you."

Grabbing hold of him and yanking him up to face her, she asked, "Do you mean it?"

He looked puzzled, then said, "Of course I do. I want to spend the rest of my life with you. It scares the shit out of me, but it scares me even more knowing that I might not have you."

Her heart felt warm and full.

"So, is this kind of like a proposal?"

A grin spread across his face. "I guess it sort of is.

Maybe not the official one, but it is a proposal of wanting to be with you forever. Do you accept?"

Her hands clutched the waistband of his boxer briefs. She pulled them down and tossed them across the room. A flirty smile crossed her face.

"How about I show you instead of telling you?"

With that, she slowly crept down his body, her eyes fixed on his.

"I love you, Drew, and I love that this," she said, taking his cock in her hand, "is all mine."

More Than Useful

Can she settle for just a little fun?

Every Tuesday and Thursday morning Adam stops by Amy's bakery for one of her delicious muffins…and a little flirting. When he finally asks her out, Amy is thrilled.

Adam informs her from the beginning that he isn't looking for anything serious. Just a little fun. Amy agrees, even though she isn't entirely sure that's what she wants.

She does her best to play it cool, but Adam is sending so many mixed signals he's confusing her, which she finds incredibly frustrating.

Adam is terrified by the feelings he's developing for Amy. It would be so much easier if he just backed away from her. Then there's his sister, who is insisting that Amy is not the right girl for him.

Will Adam be able to figure out what his heart desires before it's too late and he loses his chance at true happiness?

Content Warning: explicit sex

Chapter 1

Rubbing her sweaty palms across her apron, Amy kept her eye on the door. It was Tuesday. Every Tuesday *he* came in. Each time she gave herself a pep talk that this time she would have the courage to ask him out. To quit the polite flirting they did and take a risk. All he could do was say no. She groaned at the thought. That was what she was most afraid of—the rejection.

She checked that everything was stocked, coffee was fresh, creamer and sugar was full, and saw the mid-morning crowd was thinning. It would be anytime now.

Usually she was just pulling out the morning paper to catch up on local events when he arrived. It always led them to having light chit-chat about the weather or one of the latest news stories. But today, she was just too nervous. Today she would ask him out.

And there he was, like clockwork. In he walked, Mr. Sandy Blond Hair, Blue Eyed, Combo Number Nine. He ordered the same thing on each visit, black coffee and a banana nut muffin. Always something that was already prepared so no name was ever given.

Amy's stomach flipped at the sight of him. She wiped

her mouth, worried she was drooling as her eyes devoured him. He looked decadent in his police uniform. His tanned arms appeared firm and capable of being able to take on anything, his face was clean shaven, and his blue eyes sparkled. There was a slight curl to his hair, just enough that she could imagine twirling it around her fingers. He had broad shoulders that she could imagine herself clinging to as he was above her, pumping into her. God, he was a wet dream waiting to happen and maybe, just maybe, today she would finally get his number.

As he approached her, a giddy smile crossed her face. "Good morning!" She paused to catch her breath. She could smell his aftershave, and it was intoxicating. "Let me guess, combo number nine with your coffee black and a banana nut muffin?"

He gave her a slight chuckle. "You got it."

"I baked the muffins myself this morning."

"They should be extra sweet then." Digging through his wallet, he took out cash, as usual.

As she took his money from his hand, she let her fingers linger a little longer than normal, gazing into his eyes. A slight tingle journeyed up her arm and headed straight to the mound between her legs. Oh man, if no one was there she would totally let him take her right there on the counter.

As she moved her hand away, she told herself that today was the day. The connection seemed stronger as he let his hand drop slowly from hers.

She opened her mouth to speak when a blonde woman came through the bakery door, grabbing her attention.

"Adam!" the woman called.

Combo Number Nine waved to the woman.

"Oh, there you are. I'll grab us a table."

Feeling as if her heart had just been ripped out, Amy turned to get his food. He had a girlfriend. Just her freaking luck! Someone as gorgeous as him would not be single and be available to her. In fact, the blonde was probably his fiancée. She assumed he wasn't married–yet—she had checked his ring finger numerous times. Though they probably already had that house with the white picket fence, two golden labs and one cat, just waiting for the children to fill it. Damn.

"Enjoy." She spoke softly as she handed Adam—at least she knew his name now—his order.

She could feel his eyes examining her. He looked like he wanted to say something to her, but he just didn't know how. It wasn't like he had to apologize for having a girlfriend or anything; all they had was playful banter, twice a week on Tuesday and Thursday at 10:30 AM.

Sighing, she watched as he went to the table to join the blonde. She had what appeared to be a perfect body. High perky boobs, a form-fitting dress that showed she had curves in all the right places. Her hair was styled with that messy curly look that every woman was sporting nowadays.

As she pushed her bangs to the side, Amy wished, once again, that she had been blessed with more than this fine, straight, boring brown hair. It couldn't hold a curl to save her life. She kept it short, chin length, so she had an excuse to just wash, blow-dry, and go.

The amazing blonde stepped up to order. Noticing that she didn't get money from Adam gave Amy a slight hope that maybe they weren't involved. The woman ordered something that had to be specially made, of course. Taking her credit card and driver's license, Amy swiped the card and glanced at the ID. The woman's name was Francesca. Biting her bottom lip, she wondered why it sounded so familiar.

Amy handed the card back to her and went to get the food.

Why did the name Francesca sound so recognizable? Something deep down was hollering at Amy that the woman was somehow associated with her best friend

Skylar. But how? Whatever it was, she knew it was going to drive her crazy until she figured it out.

"Here ya go." Amy handed her the order. "Enjoy, and let me know if there is anything else I can get you."

Francesca gave her a polite nod and then spun around and headed to the table she shared with Adam.

Amy stayed focused on them, but tried not to be too obvious as she looked for any signs they might be anything less than boyfriend-girlfriend. They didn't sit close together. If Adam was hers, Amy would make it known to anyone watching.

Busying herself with wiping the chrome surfaces down, she couldn't brush away the feeling of knowing Francesca. In some way or another, she was tied to Skylar. The tough part would be finding the time to talk to Skylar since she was so caught up in her love life these days.

From the corner of her eye, she noticed Adam get up. Trying not to look too obvious, she watched as he tidied up his area. The two still didn't look cozy. He leaned down to where the blonde sat and gave her a slight hug, but no kiss. Before he pushed the front door open, he gazed at Amy with a flirty smile and nodded at her. Smiling, she gave a slight wave, feeling her heart speed up. As she went back to her task, she was giddy that he just might be interested.

"Excuse me," a woman called from the counter.

Amy twirled around and saw Francesca standing there with the top of her drink off.

"I need a refill."

Taking the cup, Amy remembered Francesca had ordered a specialty coffee drink. "We don't do refills on white chocolate mochas. Sorry, would you like to order another?"

"No, that's okay." Her eyes narrowed. "You have the hots for Adam, don't you?"

Dumbfounded by this woman's bluntness, she stared at her silently.

"Well, can't you speak?" Francesca said as sassy as she could.

"Uh, yeah, I can."

"Adam is a great guy, and I see the way you two looked at each other today. Hopefully you aren't like every other woman out there who goes gaga over him and then starts demanding more of his time than he's able to give them. He doesn't like clingy, so figure out your intentions before you even bother getting involved with him."

"Um, okay. I'm not even seeing him." Amy crossed her arms. *The nerve of this woman.* "Who are you exactly?"

"His sister."

* * * *

Once the mid-morning rush was over Amy was ready for a break so she headed outside for a breather. Across the street sat Hot Bods Gym and she decided to head over and visit Skylar. It has been awhile since she'd seen her roommate—who was never home anymore since getting engaged. She was actually in the process of moving her stuff out and in with her fiancé. Amy was thrilled for her friend but was full of envy. Every date she had been on lately had been bad. With her luck, Adam would be a bust too, if she ever got the courage for anything other than muffin talk.

Entering the gym, she saw Skylar up front chatting with Jane, the receptionist. Skylar waved to Amy, and then excused herself to come over and meet her.

"Hey, girl. What a surprise." Skylar hugged her.

"I just have a second, but I wanted to see you," Amy said.

"That damn bakery isn't going to burn down just because you're not there," Skylar retorted.

"You'd be surprised what some of those morons over there are capable of." She had stories she could tell for hours about different employees.

"So what's up?"

"Hot Combo Number Nine Guy came in like usual, but today a woman came in to eat with him."

"Oh no, I'm sorry." Skylar put on her sympathetic face.

"Wait, it isn't quite so bad. It was his sister. Oh, and he has a name now, Adam," Amy said, her voice full of excitement.

"Adam, I like that. So what's the problem then?"

"He has a sister."

"Lots of people have those, Ames."

"I think you might know who she is though."

"Who is she?"

"Does the name Francesca ring a bell?"

Skylar's face turned pale. "Bleach blonde hair and glitzy?"

"Uh-huh."

"Francesca is the one who was after Drew."

Amy said nothing. She didn't dare speak when she knew Skylar was about to explode. When Skylar and Drew reconnected, Francesca had her claws dug deep into Drew, hoping he was her ticket to someone rich.

"Shit, Amy, I sure as hell hope you're planning to stay as far away from him as possible. The last thing you or I need is that blonde bimbo in our lives. Geesh, small freaking world!"

Damn, Mr. Perfect had just become Mr. Untouchable. He never seemed more desirable. Biting her lip, Amy wondered if it was worth even trying to pursue it. Would she have Skylar in her ear the whole time, nagging her about it?

Chapter 2

Parking his patrol car in front of Sweet Muffins bakery, Adam took a deep breath. It was Wednesday, not his usual day to be here. Normally today he would be at some fast food place eating a stale biscuit and wishing he was here. There was something about Amy; she stirred unusual desires in him. He lusted over her, sure, but something about that sweet face of hers kept bringing him back.

A relationship was the last thing he wanted. He was too busy working his way up in his job. He didn't want to be a patrol officer forever. He liked it all right; he worked a lot of hours but not as many as those above him. The amount of time his co-workers spent on the job was one reason he hadn't pushed for a promotion.

He didn't think he was ready to settle down, but he was tired of the one-night stands. Being an officer, women fell at his feet. He yearned for something more, maybe a girlfriend. Even that thought scared him. Raking his hands through his hair, he wondered again what in the hell was he doing here. Amy was not the "play with" kind of girl. But he found himself drawn to her and was ready to ask her out.

Nervousness swept through him as he stepped out of the car. Slowly, he made his way to the bakery door. He took a deep breath and grabbed the handle, hearing the bell jingle as he entered. His eyes darted around the small place and took in everyone. Rooms always quieted when he walked in with his uniform on.

As he headed toward the counter to order, she stood there, her gaze focused on him. Today she wore a tight fitting bright yellow shirt. Her hazel colored eyes really stood out. Brushing her bangs to the side, she flashed him a flirty grin and he hoped it was only for him.

He cleared his throat and stepped up to the counter. "Hi."

"Well, hi." She beamed. "Same as usual?"

"Not today."

"Ooo, a change. I like that."

Laughing, he said, "I figured I might want to try something else."

"What can I get you then?"

She was beautiful. Once again, seeing her sweet and innocent face, he had to remind himself that getting involved with her was dangerous. She was likely to steal his heart and make him feel things. Yet, here he stood, ready to take this up a level.

"A date?"

"A date muffin?" She looked confused, and he liked that he had caught her off guard.

"No, a date with you."

He watched as her grin seemed to get even bigger. That was a good thing, he hoped. Maybe he had a chance of not getting turned down.

"I'd like that." She spoke in a quieter voice.

"I'm off duty Friday evening, does that work for you?" She nodded.

Happiness leapt through his body. She said yes and he didn't know why he was so giddy. He couldn't recall ever feeling this excited about a date before.

"Is there anything else I can get you?" she asked.

His gaze dropped to her lips a moment, and he imagined how soft they would feel against his. Wondered if they tasted as good as he thought they would.

"Uh, let me try a blueberry walnut muffin."

"Those are my special today." She turned to head to the container where all the bakery items were kept. She returned with a brown paper bag, rolled up tightly, and a cup of coffee. She handed it to him as he gave her the money. "I'll be looking forward to Friday."

"Me too."

He started to turn to leave when she called to him. "Um, should we exchange numbers or something? That way I can let you know where I live. Or do you want to meet somewhere?"

His face flushed, and embarrassment was all he felt. How could he have forgotten something as simple as a number?

Setting his order down on the counter, he pulled out his cellphone, trying to appear collected. "What's you number?"

She told him and he programmed it in.

"I think you've got everything now." She giggled.

While grabbing his order he said, "I think so. I can already tell you're going to be useful."

He gave her a slight nod and rushed back toward his patrol car to try and gather himself. Sitting down, he let out a long breath. He felt a little stupid and hoped he hadn't made a fool of himself.

Opening the bag, he reached in to take out his muffin. He took a bite without looking and he recognized the flavor. Pulling it away, he saw he was eating his usual banana nut. A quick glance in the bag and he saw another muffin, the blueberry walnut, and a small note.

Just in case you didn't like the
blueberry.
Amy, x o

A whole new emotion flooded through his body, and he couldn't quite pinpoint what it was. One thing he did know—it was nice, but it scared the hell out of him.

* * * *

By the time Amy was able to leave work Friday she was worried she was going to rip all her fingernails off and then start on her toenails. Her nerves were a wreck. She had two hours until Adam was going to pick her up.

Thinking back to when he came in the shop yesterday at his usual time, she wanted to scream; she had been a stuttering mess. Words had simply refused to form. All she had been able to think about was getting her hands all over him. He looked so sexy in his uniform that she couldn't imagine what he would look like out of it. Snickering to herself, she could only hope in the near future she just might get to see what was under it.

Amy started the car, quickly buckled her seat belt, and was ready to get the hell out of this place. A shower was in order and she still hadn't decided what to wear. She pulled out and hit the gas. The drive was short and she was about to make it even shorter.

She rolled down her window, then turned the music up and pressed on the gas pedal a little more. She began to sing with the radio when she saw something red and blue flashing in her rearview mirror. *Shit!* She stomped on the brakes. Was she going that fast? As she pulled off to the side of the road, tears began to build in the corner of her eyes. She knew it was silly to cry but this wasn't what she needed. She had already left work late and now she was going to waste another twenty minutes here as Bozo the Cop gave her a ticket and a speech about going too fast.

Looking in the driver side mirror, she suddenly wanted to die. It was just her luck; the officer approaching the car was Adam.

Chapter 3

Why in the hell did people have to speed when he had five minutes left of his shift? He had to get home and get ready for a date with a hot lady tonight. As he approached the car, the driver started to roll down their window. He planned to give this person quite the speech since they were interfering with his schedule.

"Excuse me, ma…" He started.

Holy shit, it was Amy.

"Amy!"

"Oh God, this is *embarrassing*." She covered her eyes in what to him was an attempt to hide herself. "I was late getting off and I was rushing to get home to get ready for our date. I'm so sorry."

"Looks like this puts the brakes on for both of us. I was just cursing the person who was going to make me stay over on my shift and force me to be late picking up a hot little lady."

Removing her face from her hands now, she smiled up at him. That smile went straight to his heart and he knew he was a goner for sure.

"So, officer, am I getting a ticket? I really need to get

home. I have a gorgeous man due at my place in less than two hours."

"I understand why you were speeding, but I'm still going to have to give you a ticket."

"I understand," she said.

He quickly scribbled on the ticket pad, smiling the whole time. Handing the ticket to her, he waited for her reaction.

A grin crossed her face and she giggled. "Do I pay this fine now or later?"

"It's up to you."

"I think now."

He couldn't have been happier that he'd written her a ticket stating that her current fine was a kiss. Leaning in toward her, he inhaled. The smell was heavenly, fruity, and sweet. He almost wanted to take a bite out of her to see if she tasted as sweet as she smelled.

Her lips lightly pressed against his and fireworks seemed to shoot out from behind his eyes. The kiss was nothing more than just a short peck but it was damn near the best kiss he had ever had in his life.

Taking a step back, he nodded at her. "See you in a little while."

"Bye," she said softly.

He turned and headed back to his patrol car. His dick pressed against his zipper, and he couldn't believe that one little peck had made him as hard as a teenage boy. This was going to be a long night to get through if he attempted to be on good behavior.

* * * *

In front of the mirror, Amy checked her white sundress. Something was missing. After a few moments of staring at herself, wondering, she decided to add a tan belt that matched her heeled cowboy boots almost perfectly. With her fingers she poofed her hair a little. Thankfully it had curled nicely and her bangs fell neatly to the side. It wasn't often her hair cooperated.

Leaving her bedroom, she went to the living room to wait. Unfortunately, as much as she thought she looked nice on the outside, she was a nervous wreck on the inside. It took everything in her not to chew on her nails. She was grateful Skylar had been home earlier to talk her through this, even though she was still skeptical about Amy getting involved with Adam.

She walked to the sliding glass door and peered out. An unfamiliar blue sports car pulled up. Biting her lip, she watched as it parked in front of her building. Out stepped Adam. Good God, he was hot, wearing dark jeans and a white button-down shirt. He walked with confidence radiating off his body as he approached her building. A knock sounded on her door and slowly she crossed the living room. Trying hard to gather the courage to answer, she wiped her palms together and counted to three.

As she opened the door and saw him standing there she was speechless. His eyes sparkled and as he smiled she noticed a dimple on his right cheek. An urge came over her to kiss him. It took everything in her not to yank him in by his shirt and throw him onto the couch.

"You look beautiful," he said.

"You look g-great too," she stuttered, wanting to kick herself. "Uh, you want to come in for a moment?"

"Sure." He stepped into the apartment.

"My roommate isn't here. Can I get you a drink?"

"You got any whisky?" He laughed.

"Uh." She wasn't sure what to say.

"Sorry, I'm just nervous. Thought it might take the edge off."

She smiled. "Me too, maybe we both should take a shot to get over our nerves."

She went into the kitchen, grabbed a stool, and climbed up. Opening the cabinet above the fridge, she pulled down a bottle of Jack and two shot glasses. A warmth crept up behind her. His hand was then on her waist.

"Don't want you to fall." He spoke in a raspy tone.

She said nothing, just tried to concentrate on not passing out. One small touch on her lower back sent tingles shooting through her whole body. She was already feeling moist between her legs.

Climbing down, she set the whisky on the counter. Amy unscrewed the top and then filled each glass halfway. Picking both shots up, she turned and handed one to him. He let his fingers linger against hers a moment. If she wasn't careful they wouldn't be leaving this apartment.

"Count of three?" he asked.

She nodded.

"One, two, three."

Each put their glass to their lips, eyes on one another, and tipped the glass up. The liquid was warm as it slid down Amy's throat. Hopefully this would calm her nerves and hormones.

"Can't say I've ever done a shot with my date before we went out," he said as he set the glass down.

"Yeah, this is new for me too."

Her head was already starting to get a little cloudy. Damn, she hadn't eaten since lunch. There was nothing to absorb the alcohol. She just might be feeling real good, real soon.

"This might be forward, but if I don't kiss you before we go out, it's all I'll think about." He looked longingly into her eyes and grabbed a hold of her waist, tugging her against his chest.

Without any hesitation she leaned forward, letting her lips press into his. Her eyes closed as his mouth took hers, lightly at first. She expected the kiss to be short and sweet but urgency took over her. She tangled her fingers into his hair and thrust her tongue into his warm mouth with a strong desire to taste the whiskey on his breath.

Her back hit the counter and then two strong hands gripped her ass, lifting her and setting her on the counter. She wrapped her legs around his waist, never breaking the kiss. Her pussy was wet and he hadn't even touched her erotic spots yet.

Pulling away, she gazed into his blue eyes. "I'm not sure going out is a good idea," she said, breathless.

She watched as his expression changed from passion to confusion.

"I guess I did just kind of take you," he said.

"No, this is fine. I like this," she said, letting one of her hands rub across his buff chest. "If we leave all we're going to be thinking about is getting back here. So why leave?"

A grin spread across his clean shaven face. "I guess you're right about that."

"You did say I was useful."

"Very useful. So, what do you have in mind?" His fingers lightly rubbed up and down her arms.

Flashing him a flirty smile she let her fingers dip down to rub just above his waistband. "Well, I could make us something to eat, and I think there might be a few beers in the fridge."

"You cook real food too?" His hands found her waist.

"I hear I'm pretty good at it."

"You are useful." Yanking her closer, he kissed her again.

Amy knew she was in trouble as she kissed him back. It was never like her to be this forward, but after they had flirted for months, to finally have him in her place was like a dream come true. She wanted to make the most of this evening and if he kept kissing her the way he was, she was going to end up flat on her back before dinner.

* * * *

Taking his seat at the dining room table, Adam knew he was a goner. In front of him sat a steak, baked potato, and a melody of grilled vegetables. A beer was already popped open and just waiting on his lips. Amy took her seat and set a basket of dinner rolls on the table, butter rolling off the tops.

"You have outdone yourself," he said.

"I love cooking."

"I love eating."

She giggled. "We might just get along then."

Adam nodded then picked up his beer and took a sip. As the cold liquid slid down his throat he had to remind himself that this was just fun. He wasn't ready for *this*. As much as he liked everything he saw in front of him—and he did like everything—this couldn't become any more.

"So the girl with you the other day—" she began.

"My sister," he interrupted.

"I know." She took a bite of her steak. He watched as a drop of clear juice slipped from her lips and ran down her chin. Her napkin then wiped it away and more than anything he wished it was his tongue there instead. "I thought I should tell you that my roommate knows your sister."

"Oh yeah?" He cut a piece of steak.

"Skylar, who is also my best friend, is engaged to a guy named Drew."

"Neither of those names sound familiar." He was a little confused.

"Drew and your sister Francesca used to be involved until Skylar came back into his life."

"Apparently he didn't mean that much to her. My sister is quite vocal, so if she'd been done wrong I would've had her up my butt to find out anything she could about the person."

"Good, I was worried this might have been awkward."

"How?"

"Francesca and Skylar don't like one another."

"Ahhh, gotcha. I don't think there will be a problem," he said.

Her face lit up. Taking a bite of his oh-so-delicious steak, he was glad that she was happy. In fact, she looked relieved. He could see what she was worried about might be a problem if they got serious, but this was just fun. At some point this evening he knew it would probably be a good idea to let her know that this was just fun. He wasn't looking for a wife.

For the rest of dinner they had light chit chat about growing up and all the background stuff people usually discuss while getting to know each other. For the first time though, he actually listened. She was fascinating and he wanted to know more.

"Want to help me with the dishes?" she asked.

"Uh, sure." He supposed he couldn't exactly tell her no. He rubbed his stomach, he was stuffed. Lounging on the couch seemed like a better idea.

"I promise I won't get you too wet," she flirted.

She strutted toward the kitchen, carrying her plate. Her ass was the perfect heart shape, and he could just imagine grabbing a hold of it as she rode him. Lifting his beer, he decided to finish it before helping her.

In the kitchen she was bent over, loading utensils in the dishwasher. Biting his lip, he fought the erection in his pants as his eyes did their best to see right up her dress.

He took his place at the sink and focused his attention on rinsing the plates. As he handed her the last plate, his eyes landed on her breasts. She turned slowly, placing the dishes in the dishwasher, and he let his gaze once again drop to her ass. He wasn't sure what came over him but as she spun back around he grabbed the sink hose and sprayed her with water right in the breasts.

"Adam!" she shouted.

Letting go of the sprayer, he focused on her wet skin. Her white dress had instantly become see-through and by luck, she had on a sheer bra. Her rosy nipples had puckered, and his jeans now tented below the belt.

He was so engrossed with her big breasts that it caught

him off guard when cold water sprayed him in the face. Before him stood Amy, holding the hose now. He laughed and yanked it out of her hand, shutting the water off. Her hand then dove in the sink letting soapy bubbles cover it. Before he knew it, her hands were in his hair, spreading the soap through it.

"You didn't just do that," he said.

"I did." She laughed. "Let's not forget you started it."

"That I did." His eyes dropped back to her breasts.

Her fingers daintily played with the straps on her dress letting them slid off her shoulders. Adam groaned then licked his lips, ready for a taste. Pulling her to him, he kissed her shoulders. He pulled the top of her dress down, along with the sheer bra, letting her breasts spring out. Licking the water drops on his way down, he greedily took her breasts. Pushing them together, he licked between and all around before taking a nipple into his mouth. Being gentle had never crossed his mind. His teeth lightly bit then sucked the nipple in deep, filling his mouth. He pinched the other, and considering how hard they were, he knew she was enjoying it.

He moved to the next breast, feeling an overwhelming need to taste it and a desire to get drunk off her skin. He twirled his tongue around her nipple and once again pulled it in as far as he could. Pressing her breasts together again, he rubbed his face between them. At this point, he knew he was lost and there was no turning back. He had to have her.

He stood up straight and yanked her to him, letting his erection press into her. His lips met hers, and in a force of passion his tongue thrust into her mouth. He tugged the dress in a downward motion but it wouldn't budge.

"Damn belt," he murmured against her lips.

She pushed him away and took a step back. He worried he might come just by looking at her. Her breasts were right there on display. She fumbled with the belt and let it fall to the floor. She then let her dress slide down and become a pile at her feet. All he saw now was her, naked except for her white g-string.

"You're a dream come true," he whispered.

Emotions ran through him as he just stared at her. His cock throbbed, and he needed release. As fast as he could, he released his belt buckle and unbuttoned his pants, sliding them down to a mound on the floor. He reached for the buttons on his shirt, but she stopped him.

"Let me."

She placed her mouth on his neck, gently sucking as her hands started to release his buttons. She appeared to be in control and he wasn't sure how. He hadn't felt this much desire to get inside a woman since he was a teenager. He ached to feel her pussy clenched around him, milking him. Her hands rubbed his chest as she pushed his shirt off him.

Taking a step back she said, "You look appetizing."

"I don't think I look damn near as good as you," he said.

Her hands met the top of his boxers. "I think you should lose these."

"I couldn't agree more."

She slowly pushed down his boxers. As her fingers grazed up his thighs, she wrapped her hands around his swollen erection.

"God, you're big."

"Lady, if we don't get this going soon I'm going to come before we even get started."

"What's the hurry?" she asked.

"Desire." He spun her around so her back was to him and pushed her against the counter. "I'm sorry, honey, but I just have to take you this time. I can't explain to you how I'm feeling. I just have to have you now."

He took hold of her g-sting, ripping it off. She spread her legs wide open and bent forward. Her pussy was wet. He wanted to taste her cream so badly, but he knew he wouldn't last through it. Quickly finding his wallet, he removed the condom, ripped open the package, and slid it on.

"I warned you." He grabbed her waist.

"Give it to me, officer," she said in a sexy voice. "I can take it."

"You got it."

He slammed his cock into her tight opening. Her body arched and she thrust back, giving as good as she got. She cried out in delight as he pumped into her. Gripping her waist and digging his fingers in, his eyes closed. Pleasure swept through him, and the pressure was building. He drove into her harder, pushing her against the counter. She chanted his name, and her walls tugged his cock tight. Her pussy milked him and he couldn't hold back any longer. He drove into her several more times before he cried out, saying her name as he let his release fill the condom.

Panting, he stepped away from her, wishing he had somewhere to fall back and sit, because it felt like his legs were ready to give out. As if reading his mind, Amy took his hand and led him to the couch in the living room.

"I don't know about you, but I've got to catch my breath." She grabbed a throw off the back of the couch and wrapped it around them, cuddling into his side.

She seemed to fit perfectly against him. Everything

about this girl was right.

"Next time we can go slower," he said.

"I rather enjoyed what we just did."

"Yeah, it was fun."

Sitting up, she faced him and said, "We could take this to my room, really explore each other, and afterward we will be in a bed and can just pass out."

"You mean, sleep together?"

Her hands rubbed along the back of his neck as she tried to pull him to her. "Yes, it would be the perfect way to end this. My roommate won't be home. Doesn't that sound good?"

Yeah, it sounded awesome, but it wasn't going to happen.

Pulling away, he wished his clothes were closer so he could make a clean getaway.

"I really should go." He stood, moving quickly toward the kitchen.

"Really?" she asked from the living room.

"I don't want to." He wasn't lying, but he knew if he stayed there he would never leave. Returning to the living room, fully dressed now, he saw she lay cuddled with her blanket. "I had a great time," he said,

"Me too. Why are you leaving?" she asked, with an

unsettling tone.

"I want to be truthful, I really like you."

"Okay, then what's the problem?"

That you're perfect. He didn't know what to tell her. If he stayed the night he would never want to leave, that he couldn't tell her. She erupted feelings in him he had never experienced and that scared the shit out of him.

"I'm not looking for anything serious. Just some fun."

"So a night of sex takes this from fun to what in your mind?" He could hear the slight irritation in her voice.

"It's just fun," he said, mainly for himself, "I'll call you."

Turning, he left, feeling guilty that he didn't even kiss her goodbye.

Chapter 4

Even though she was off today, Amy found herself sitting outside the bakery with a flavored coffee in hand. Being here always calmed her and left her relaxed. Sweet Muffins sat on the busiest corner of town. She enjoyed watching the hustle and bustle of everyone rushing to get to where they needed to go.

Thinking back to last night, she still wondered what had happened. She and Adam had flirted for months. Finally taking a step in the right direction, she thought the chemistry was mutual. In fact, she had worried things were so hot between them that they might set her kitchen on fire. Apparently suggesting that he stay the night put that flame out real quick. He couldn't get away fast enough, blubbering on about just having fun. Had she appeared clingy? She didn't think she had.

She pulled her phone out and contemplated sending him a message. She stopped herself though; it would be best to wait on him since he had the freak out. Skylar's words still echoed in her ears. "*Whatever you do, don't call him. He ditched you. I told you not to even get involved with him if he's anything like his sister.*" He seemed nothing like

Francesca though. If Amy didn't know better she would have thought they weren't even related.

Lifting her mug, she drained the last of the coffee. She pushed away from the table and placed the cup into the bin for customers by the front door. It was time to do one of her favorite activities, window shopping and imagine living the grand life.

As she turned the corner her phone started to sing. Digging through her purse she pulled it out and saw it was Adam. Speak of the devil.

"Hi, stranger. Are you looking for some more fun?" she answered, being a smartass.

He laughed. "I'm really sorry about running out last night."

"Don't be. I probably shouldn't have been so forward." *Be cool*, she reminded herself.

"Well, I want to make it up to you. Let's go bowling and get a bite to eat after. Can I pick you up later this afternoon?"

"How about I meet you?" Having him come to her place again would be a mistake. Adam was a bachelor treading on a thin line. She knew he had yet to figure out what he wanted.

"You sure?"

"I'm sure. If this is going to be just fun, then let's keep it light."

"Okay." He was quieter.

"Text me when you have it all figured out. I gotta go. Bye, Adam." She touched the *end* button and dropped the phone back into her purse.

Keeping it light wasn't as easy as she'd hoped. She really disliked being so short and acting like this was nothing more than it was. All she wanted was to talk to him for hours. It wasn't easy for her to act like this was just fun. Her mind wanted to wander into uncharted territories, and it was taking everything in her to keep the M word out of her thoughts. It probably didn't help that she had to see her best friend and fiancé in love and happy.

* * * *

Adam knew he should feel relieved. He was getting what he wanted—someone to just have fun with. Amy didn't even seem mad at him about last night. Yes, he should be thrilled, so why wasn't he? Shaking his head, he didn't even want to imagine why he wasn't. It was better to just keep telling himself that the fire was so strong between them simply because they had danced around for months. A few more times in the sack and the fire would be extinguished and she would become the past. With as cool as she was being, he wouldn't even have to find a new bakery.

Pulling up to the bowling alley he saw her standing out front waiting on him. She stood against the wall typing away on her phone. Her hair looked as it usually did, short and straight with her bangs falling in front of her hazel eyes. She had on blue jeans that were not too tight but still hugged her curves the right way. The white tube top she wore sent his mind to the gutter. All he had to do was pull it down and her breasts would be right there. Damn, and what a rack she had. She was perfect for a boob man like himself.

As he approached, she tossed her phone into her purse and gave him that smile he was so used to seeing twice a week.

"Hi!" she said.

"Hello. Ready?" He pointed toward the entrance.

"You betcha."

"You any good?" he asked as he opened the door for her.

"Maybe."

"This should be fun then. Go pick out a lane since it isn't too busy. I'll get the shoes."

"Size eight."

She strutted past him and he took a moment to enjoy

the view. Her ass was made for jeans. Damn, watching her bowl was going to be difficult.

At the counter he got their shoes and then headed to the lane she'd chosen. She stood studying the bowling balls at the rack right behind the seating area. Sneaking up behind her, he whispered, "Sometimes finding the right ball can be difficult."

She giggled. "Don't start."

He watched as her finger lightly stroked the yellow ball in front of her. She picked it up, rubbing her hands all the way around it.

"This one feels right. Not too heavy, so I should be able to cup it nicely in my hands."

He snickered. "You're just as bad."

Taking a quick glance, he decided on a blue ball. When he looked back at her a flirty smile had crossed her face.

"As long as you're with me you don't need to worry about blue balls."

Rolling his eyes, but thoroughly enjoying his time, he told her, "Let's get this game on. Ladies first." And a chance to see her bent forward in those curve hugging jeans.

As she stood in front of him and got in position to roll the ball, he grunted. His imagination did not do her tight little ass justice. Her ball shot down the lane and knocked over all the pins. Spinning around, she did a little victory dance. He hoped she would bounce a little more and that tube top would just happen to slip down.

"Take that," she said.

"Oh, I plan on taking something."

Stepping up, he eyed the lane. His mind was not on bowling. He wanted to get her out of here and have his way with her. Releasing the ball from his fingers, he cursed. He knew right where that blue ball was headed.

"Perhaps you should get your mind and balls out of the gutter." She laughed.

Groaning and somewhat embarrassed, he waited for his ball to come back. He needed to get his mind back and whoop this girl's butt.

* * * *

After two games and all the flirting, Amy was horny. There was no other word for it. She needed release. Her hands craved him. He had excused himself to use the restroom. Looking around and seeing the place was still not too busy, she strutted toward the restroom area. A locker room area sat between the two bathrooms. She walked into the side that was for women. Checking the restroom, she saw it was empty. Stepping out, she waited.

He walked out of the doorway, oblivious she was there.

She called out to him, and he walked toward her. She took hold of his shirt and tugged him into the ladies room and to the nearest stall.

"What are you doing?" he asked as the door latch locked.

Rubbing her hands along his chest, she leaned forward and let her tongue swirl around the back of his ear. "Having some fun."

"Here?"

"Uh-huh." Her lips trailed down his neck, sucking in slightly.

"You know we can get in trouble for this. I could get in a lot."

Amy snickered as her hands slid inside his pants and she found him hard as a rock. Her fingers danced around the tip of his erection.

"Oh God." He moaned.

A smile curved her lips as she realized what she was doing to him. Of course, if they got caught, it would be bad, but she had to have him. She rubbed his shaft up and down before she curled her fingers around his balls and lightly squeezed.

His body relaxed finally, and his hands found her breasts. Pulling her top down, he let his fingers slide inside her bra. She took a deep breath in to contain the moan as he pinched both nipples at the same time. If only she had some friction between her legs, she would be coming.

"You know we can't do this here." However he wasn't very convincing as he leaned forward, licking the tops of her breasts.

"It seems that we are."

"How about we head back to my place?"

"I don't know." She sighed, even though she knew going to his place was an excellent idea.

"We'll have a lot more room and not have to worry about being caught."

"Don't you get turned on more—" She gripped her fingers tightly around his cock. "—at the thought of someone finding us?"

She pumped her hand faster and forced him against the stall wall and kissed him. From the passion in his kiss she knew it turned him on that at any moment a woman's voice could echo through the room. His breathing was getting ragged and she knew he would come soon.

"We have to take this somewhere else," he pleaded. "I don't want to come in my pants."

Releasing his cock and leaning forward, she whispered into his ear, "I guess I lied. I'm leaving you with blue balls."

Unlatching the door, she pulled her top up and left the stall.

Chapter 5

The sexual tension was hot on the way to Adam's; Amy was almost surprised the windows weren't fogged. Adam gripped the steering wheel with both hands, keeping his eyes on the road. She knew it was taking everything in him to not pull over and do her right there. Then again, it probably didn't help that she let her top slide down just enough that the lace from her pink bra was barely peaking out.

Finally the ride was over and they arrived. He lived in a ranch style house, away from others. Tall, thick trees bordered each side of the property. The outside was taken care of. She couldn't wait to see the inside. Maybe he wasn't a slob like most men.

Inhaling deeply, tingles shot through her as he leaned over her to push her car door open. He lingered there a moment, and it was a moment too long. She pulled him to her and met his mouth with a yearning. Not even trying to be sweet and sensual, her tongue darted in.

He yanked her tube top down and she felt his hands sneak around back, undoing the clasp to her bra. "You don't need this."

Amy fiddled with the side of the seat until she found the handle to lean the chair back. As he climbed above her she pulled the lever and yelped as they crashed back from the weight of them. His hands tugged at her jeans and before she knew it, he had stripped her jeans, panties, and top off while he was still fully dressed. It turned her on even more knowing this.

Two thick fingers entered her before she even had the chance to get him undressed. He drew her nipple inside his mouth, sucking it in deep. Her right hand gripped the handle on the door as she tried to think about anything else other than what he was doing. She didn't want to come yet.

His thumb flicked her clit and she cried out. Her climax was building and fighting it off was almost not an option. Squirming a little, she tried to gather herself. As much as she wanted to get him naked, she knew that wasn't going to happen, so she concentrated on getting his pants off. She clumsily fumbled with his button and zipper until she finally freed them. Pushing his pants and boxers down slightly, she lifted her leg and her toes took hold and finished pulling them down. Her gaze dropped and she wished like hell there was more room so she could let that long, thick shaft fill her mouth.

"Do you have protection?" she asked.

He reached back toward his pants and when he sat up he had already torn open the package. With one hand, he gripped his cock and with the other he slid the condom on. She imagined him stroking it and got even more heated.

She opened her legs a little wider, propping them up on the dashboard so he could fit snuggly between her. He leaned over her, the tip of his cock teasing her opening. Arching up, she forced him to enter her. As his thick shaft squeezed into her narrow opening, she moaned.

This was going to be quick and it didn't matter to her. Picking up the pace, she grinded into him, bringing his dick all the way in.

"You're so tight," he said softly.

His rhythm matched hers. Breathing was rapid between them, and she knew he was ready and waiting on a cue from her. She was almost there but needed just a little more. Pushing hard into him so the force vibrated against her clit, she cried out as pleasure rippled through her. Her back arched as he gave the final strokes he needed to climax.

Taking in deep breaths, she watched as he tried to maneuver himself back to the driver's seat.

"This area wasn't as big as I thought." He laughed. "Perhaps we should try my bed out next."

"Maybe."

"Why don't you stay the night?" he asked

Confused, she squinted her eyes. "This is just fun, remember?"

"I'm not done playing with you. Besides, you rode with me, so you're my prisoner." He winked.

"Are you going to use your handcuffs on me later, officer?" she flirted.

"If it's the only way I can keep you here, then yes."

Her heart did a somersault. Staying the night was just what she wanted. It was surprising with the one-eighty he was doing, but she wasn't going to complain. To wake in his big strong arms was going to be heaven. Perhaps that thin line was melting away and he was ready for something more than just "fun".

"Okay, deal." She smiled.

* * * *

She was warm and snuggled against a hard body. A grin spread across Amy's face when she realized where she was. The sun shone through the window and let her know it was morning and that she had actually spent the night with Adam.

Lying there, her thoughts went back to last night. They finally took the time to properly inspect one another's bodies and had gotten use out of his bed at least once. And the couch and shower were also well used. When she had suggested he take her back to her car, he insisted she stay the night. Of course, that was what she had wanted all along, but she just needed to know he was on the same page.

Stretching, she heard Adam clear his throat. Propping herself up on her elbows, she gazed down at him.

"Morning," he said.

"And a good morning it is." Leaning forward, she gave a light kiss to his bare shoulder. She studied him and could almost see something was off. He had that panicked look on his face. That wasn't good. "You okay?"

"Yeah."

Letting out a slight sigh, she tried not to let it bother her that all she was getting was one word answers. If she played it cool and didn't cling to him, he would come around. She hoped.

She sat up and pulled the sheet around her. "How about we go grab some breakfast before you take me back to my car?"

He said nothing.

"It's just breakfast, Adam. We're both starved, I assume. Please tell me you have had breakfast with a woman before."

"Uh, I haven't," he said hesitantly.

"What? Seriously? Well, let's change that. Get your hot little ass out of bed and join me in the shower to freshen up."

Letting the sheet drop, she headed toward the shower stark naked, hoping it would tempt him. She smiled to herself when she heard him grunt and the bed squeak as he climbed out. In the bathroom she turned the water on and found the perfect temperature. Climbing in, the water sprayed across her body. She let the water hit her in the face.

The shower door opened and Adam stepped in. Spinning around, she faced him.

"Glad you're here, I need help scrubbing my back." She giggled. "Hope you weren't expecting anything else."

There it was, that grin of his that melted her heart.

"Get over here," he said, and pulled her into him.

His mouth took possession of hers. The kiss was slow and sensual, and as his tongue met hers, her pussy grew wet. Lightly, she sucked on his tongue, drawing it out of his mouth. One hand leisurely found its way to his hard cock. Wrapping her fingers around it, she stroked. Releasing his tongue, she kissed her way down his body, until she was before him on her knees. Right in front of her was his long and thick shaft, waiting for her mouth. Her lips met the head, and she kissed the tip softly, then swirled her tongue around, bringing only the tip in her mouth. As she sucked and licked, she imagined it was a Tootsie Pop and she wondered how many licks it would take to get to the creamy goodness.

One hand cupped his balls and applied light pressure. She moved her mouth away from the head and let her tongue skim along the bottom, concentrating on the vein. From the moan that he let out, she knew she was doing something right. Opening wide, she brought him into her as far as she could. Lightly, she let her bottom teeth graze as she stroked him with her mouth. His hands gripped her shoulders and began pulling her up.

With a force he picked her up and tossed her against the shower wall. She wrapped her legs around his waist and he thrust in. She screamed out and clutched his shoulders to steady herself. His mouth took hold of one of her nipples. Her head fell back and a climax rippled through her. She called his name repeatedly and he came with her.

His big muscular arms were still wrapped around her as she caught her breath. But as much as she was enjoying the closeness, her legs ached from holding herself up. She wasn't sure how much longer she could brace herself.

Inhaling deeply, she took in his musky scent.

She knew she was falling in love with this man. When they came together, it was as if they craved one another. It didn't hurt either that the sex between them was off the charts, and even though it never seemed to last long, the feelings that erupted inside of her were nothing she'd ever experienced. He had to be feeling the same way she did.

After the shower, Amy dressed in her same clothes. She wished her car was here now; she always kept a spare set in the trunk because she never knew what messes she would get into at the bakery.

She noted Adam was still quiet. He was affectionate but there was something else going on in his head. She couldn't quite pinpoint what it was. As much as she tried to keep this light fun, he always had a deer-in-the-headlight look. Patience, she reminded herself, and he would work this out.

* * * *

Adam felt like an asshole. Here he was at breakfast with an amazing woman. Things were so easy with her and he enjoyed every moment. Part of him wanted to get her to her car as fast as he could, and the other part wanted to take her back to his place.

He knew she sensed his mood. She wasn't her usual

talkative self that he liked. They ate almost silently.

His mind kept going back to them in the shower this morning. Something happened that shouldn't have. In fact, it scared him. He wondered if she realized what had happened and if she too was worried. Bringing it up was going to be hard. He would wait until they were alone, in his car. Looking around the busy diner, he knew this was definitely not the place.

"You ready?" she asked.

"Huh?" He was startled out of his thoughts.

"I said, are you ready? You've been off in space. Our plates are empty. Might as well get out of here so someone else can eat."

"Oh, yeah. Okay."

The bill was already on the table. When had that happened? Shrugging, he took out his wallet and laid out enough to cover the bill and tip. He stood and followed Amy outside.

At the car, he opened the door for her, then headed around to his side and climbed in. As he started the car he realized the flaw in his plan to talk—the bowling alley was across the street. Inhaling, he drove the short distance and parked next to her car.

"Well, I had a good time," she said. "But is this

weirding you out?"

Damn, she knew he wasn't himself. "No, us isn't weirding me out."

"So what is the deal? You wanted me to stay and now all morning you've looked scared shitless."

"It's just, well…"

"What?" He could hear the frustration in her voice.

"Geez, this is hard to say." Taking a deep breath, he blurted, "We had unprotected sex in the shower."

She laughed. He was shocked she was laughing about this. It wasn't a laughing matter.

"Adam, I'm on the pill. One slip up doesn't make you an instant daddy."

He found himself laughing, awkwardly.

"I'm glad you're concerned though. Is that what has you all worked up?"

He nodded.

"Well, there's no need to worry. How about taking this afternoon to think about what you want? You're sending a lot of mixed signals." She leaned forward and left only a light peck on his cheek.

He watched as she left his car and got into hers. With a slight wave, she drove off, leaving him there, dumbfounded.

Chapter 6

Amy's feet pounded on the treadmill. After leaving Adam's, she headed straight to Hot Bods to find Skylar, but she was in a staff meeting. Amy figured now was as good as ever to use the membership she'd paid for. So, here she was, running on this darn machine, and she was amazed that it felt good.

Adam was a puzzle. She thought back to his latest dilemma and in some ways it was sweet. The worry he had about being with her in the shower unprotected. Most guys probably wouldn't have thought twice about it, but here he was in complete panic. Perhaps before jumping into bed they should have had a discussion about birth control. Now he knew, so any slip ups wouldn't be such a worry, hopefully.

Finally Skylar emerged from the employee room. Waving, Amy watched as Skylar made her way over with Jane. Since the gym was slow, like usual on a Sunday, each hopped on a machine on either side of her.

"Nice to see you on one of these." Skylar snickered.

"I have to use it at least once a month, right?"

"I wish I could look like you and only work out when I

felt like it," Jane chimed in.

"So, what's up, Ames?" Skylar asked.

Taking in a deep breath, Amy said, "Adam is very wishy-washy. As soon as things get a little intense between us, he gets the deer-in-the-headlight look and panics. Withdrawing himself. In fact, just this morning all during breakfast—which might I add caused panic too—he was worried that I had gotten pregnant."

Both women laughed.

"Ya'll are using protection, right?" Jane asked.

"Yeah, but we slipped up in the shower. I'm on the pill, so it wasn't a concern to me. But still, it's getting annoying walking on egg shells around him. He begged me to spend the night yesterday and then this morning waking up with me scared the shit out of him."

"Has he been in relationships before?" Skylar asked.

"I don't know." Amy sighed.

"I get you like him but maybe you two need to get to know one another a little more. There is more to a relationship than sex."

"I know, but he was honest about not wanting anything serious."

"Sounds like you have to make a choice then. Keep it simple or tell him you want more," Jane said.

"I know you, and simple is not what you want," Skylar added.

The thought of not having fun with him sucked. Amy really liked the time she was spending with him. Being with him made her happy. But was it just because she was in a sort of relationship, or was it him? She'd had a crush on him for quite some time. *Ugh!*

"This sucks," she said.

"No one is saying you have to do anything now, but maybe cool it between the sheets and get to know him better. Go out to eat. Make a point to not be alone with him so you can really talk and learn all the basics about each other," Jane said.

"We have yet to make it to a restaurant before tearing each other's clothes off."

Jane let out a loud sigh. Amy wondered what it was all about, but didn't want to get too much into it. She wondered if there was a story behind Jane and the manager of the gym. She was never eyeing any other man but him, but Jane had never let on she was interested or involved with him.

Deciding she'd had enough of the treadmill, Amy turned the machine off and stepped onto the carpeted floor.

"How many times have I told you that it's important to cool down?" Skylar snapped.

"A million times, and I still don't care."

Jane and Skylar each stopped their machines and followed Amy toward the locker room. Apparently cooling down wasn't such a big deal.

"Don't you ladies need to get back to work?" Amy asked.

"Not I, no classes today. I'm only here in case someone needs one-on-one work," Skylar said.

"If the door jingles, I'll head out," Jane added.

Rolling her eyes, Amy went to change. As if on cue, the door did jingle and she heard Jane scuffle out to greet whomever was there. Amy wanted the support from them and the advice, but was slightly irritated. She really wasn't sure why. They hadn't said anything to upset her. Perhaps it was because she now had a lot think about, and all she wanted was for things to be simple.

Stepping out of the changing area, she stopped cold in her tracks. Skylar stood there with Francesca of all people. Leisurely, Amy walked over to them. She didn't think Francesca knew that the three of them were all somewhat connected, until now.

"Amy, right?" Francesca asked.

Amy nodded.

"That's right. You're the one crushing on my brother."

"I think he's crushing on her too," Skylar snapped.

"How would you know?" Francesca asked with her full attitude.

"Amy's my best friend."

Amy wanted to find somewhere to hide to get away from these two. She honestly couldn't understand why they disliked one another so much. It wasn't like Francesca and Skylar ever fought over Drew. Francesca willingly stepped back.

"What? You're kidding. My brother is involved with your best friend. That's just weird." She rolled her eyes. "I don't know about this."

"Small world." Amy smiled, trying to be nice in this awkward situation.

"Yeah, that's for sure. So how is my big brother? Haven't heard from him in a few days."

"Good, I guess." Amy shrugged.

"When I first meet you, I hoped you might be the one to get him to settle down. It'd been a long time since I saw my brother pay attention to anyone. But now that I know who you hang out with, I'm not so sure."

"Stay out of it," Skylar retorted.

"Do you think I want your best friend as a sister-in-law? I might be forced to see you more than I have to now."

"Give it up, Francesca. You were not all that into Drew to begin with. You just wanted him for the people he knew. Have you found that rich man yet to sweep you away?"

Crossing her arms, Francesca brushed by them. "I don't have time for this. If you will excuse me, I have a sauna appointment."

Amy watched as she strutted off. Skylar laughed, but Amy didn't find it much of a laughing matter. Giving her best friend the evil eye, she realized if there was a future with Adam, this was what she would have to deal with. Skylar had a mouth on her and there was no taming it. She assumed that Francesca was just as stubborn. Letting out a sigh, she left the locker room, Skylar still on her heels.

"That went well, I think," Skylar said.

Spinning around, Amy said, "If you say so. The way I see it, once she talks to Adam, this is over. What bachelor wants to bring unnecessary drama into his life?"

Chapter 7

Tossing the covers back, Adam grunted and wondered who in the world was pounding on his door. After dropping Amy off at her car, he'd returned home to nap. They'd had a full night of exploring one another and he was exhausted.

Making his way to the front door, he heard the familiar voice of his sister yelling his name. He loved his sister, but she was the most impatient person he'd ever known.

As he turned the knob to let her in, she forced her way through, stomping into his living room. "I hope you aren't planning on seeing Amy anymore," she barked.

He rubbed his hands through his hair. Where the hell had this come from? What had happened while he slept the afternoon away?

Sitting down on the couch, he glanced at her, standing arms crossed.

"Aren't you going to ask why?" she snapped.

"I'm sure you're going to tell me."

"Do you know who her best friend is?" she asked.

"Yeah." He shrugged his shoulders.

"So then you know how much I hate her?"

Drama followed his sister, and he was thankful Amy

had already mentioned this. Most likely at some point Francesca had said something, but usually he didn't really listen. Every week something new was happening with her.

"Adam, are you listening to me?"

"Yes, I am. But what does this have to do with Amy?" he said.

"Geez, don't you get it? If you and Amy marry, then I have to see Skylar at all kinds of events."

"You see her anyway at the gym." He paused. "And I'm not getting married. Also, what events are you talking about? You're confusing me."

"Housewarming parties, holiday events, baby showers. And don't play you're not marrying her. I've seen how you look at her. You're all ga-ga eyed from the mention of her name. But you just can't, okay?"

"Yes, master." He rolled his eyes. Any woman would be crazy to marry him anyway after meeting Francesca. In fact, as he thought about it, he wondered why Amy was even still talking to him. She knew his sister and yet, she stuck around. "Were you serious about this guy that Amy's friend supposedly took from you?"

"No. But that isn't the point."

"Let it go." He stood and headed toward the kitchen. Grabbing a beer from the fridge he went back to where his sister stood, her arms still crossed and a look of irritation on her face. "Everything doesn't have to be a big deal. These events you're worried about, if I were to marry Amy, which I'm not, would be in the far, far future. And I think you could be mature enough to be an adult."

Her arms dropped. "Whatever. And quit saying you're not marrying Amy. I know you, Adam."

"Just stay out of it. It has nothing to do with you."

"I'll try." She pouted.

Taking in a long sip of his beer, he added, "You know I love you."

"I know. I'm just looking out for you."

"No, you're scaring the shit out of me with all this marriage talk."

She smiled at him just as her phone started to ring. Opening her purse she said, "Oh, I gotta take this. Love you, bro. I'll catch up with you soon."

With that, she darted out the door as fast as she came in and left Adam scratching his head, wondering if any man would ever be able to handle her. He got a headache just thinking about it.

He finished his beer and headed for the shower. If Francesca had an encounter with Amy, he was going to have to see what damage she had done.

After his shower, he decided to take the safe route and send Amy a text message to get a feel for how she was doing.

Adam: Hey, beautiful. How is your afternoon?

His stomach rumbled. He groaned, then remembered that he needed to grocery shop.

Amy: Good. Yours?

Damn, he was hoping for a little more to get further insight.

Adam: Hungry?

Amy: A little

Adam: Let's meet. Little Italy's Pizza?

Amy: Okay. Give me twenty minutes.

Setting the phone down, he went to finish getting ready.

* * * *

Amy was later than she wanted to be. As she entered the pizzeria, her eyes darted around until she finally spotted Adam. He had chosen a booth near the back. She also glanced around for Skylar, since this was her and Drew's favorite spot to eat. Thankfully, she didn't see them.

As she made her way through the dimly lit restaurant, she noticed Adam's face light up when he saw her. Her heart raced at the sight of him in a light blue button-up shirt, with the sleeves rolled up to his elbows. He was so sexy, and each time she saw him, she had no idea why he was with her.

Taking a seat across from him, she smiled at him. "Sorry I'm late."

"It's fine. I was only slightly worried you were standing me up."

She giggled. "No, this is nice. I wouldn't miss getting to actually eat a meal with you. It's like a real date."

"I guess we have kind of skipped the dating parts of this."

"That's okay. I've been having fun." She winked.

The waitress came over to get their order. They choose to order a bottle of sweet red wine and a deep dish meat lover's pizza to share. The waitress excused herself and let them know their salad would be out shortly. While waiting for their food, they shared small talk as they took sips of the flavorful wine which seemed to be going straight to her head.

She'd spent most of the afternoon with Skylar. Her and her fiancé Drew had a weekend trip planned and the two of them shopped for new outfits for it. She was exhausted after keeping up with her friend. Right now, she wished she had found the time to stop and eat.

The salad arrived and Amy noticed they had each requested ranch dressing. She wasn't sure why it excited her, but it did.

"Crap, I always forget," he said.

She looked at him, confused.

"I usually request no croutons. They hurt my teeth."

He scooped the crunchy squares onto the plate that held a half eaten breadstick.

"Would it be weird for me to take them? I love their croutons. The seasoning they add is to die for."

"Go ahead. Once again, you're useful. You can eat my croutons when I forget to not order them," he said with a big grin across his face.

She laughed. "Geesh, I just get more and more useful to you, huh?"

She studied his face, waiting for the deer-in-the-headlight look again, but instead she received the most adorable smirk she had ever seen.

The pizza came next. Adam put a slice on a plate and handed it to her. She thanked him, and as she took the pizza, she let her fingers linger next to his for a moment. They sat there, looking at one another, with the plate held up. Just feeling his rough hands against hers had her ready to get the hell out of there and back to her place.

He was the first to move his hand and release the shared gaze.

"This looks good," he said as he put two slices on a plate for himself.

She took a bite, and the pizza met all her taste buds. It was delicious.

"So, I'm curious. Have you ever had a serious girlfriend?" she blurted out. After saying it, she regretted it. But this kind of stuff needed to be talked about and that was why she was here. She wanted more than just fun, and knew she had to begin to feel Adam out a little more.

His face was blank. She could tell he was shocked and she had crossed the line from light and casual to a little more personal conversation.

"Not in a long time," he responded.

"Why?" she pushed on.

"It isn't what I'm looking for right now."

Once again, it was loud and clear that this was going to go nowhere. She either had to accept this for what it was, or end it. She returned to eating her pizza.

Chapter 8

Adam signed the slip for their dinner, that for some reason he had to insist on paying. He wasn't sure why Amy had put up a fight about it. All he wanted was to take her in his arms and tell her to give him time. Each time he was almost ready to say the words, it was like his tongue just wouldn't move.

As they walked out to the parking lot, he placed his hand on her lower back, guiding her toward her car. Touching her seemed so right. His index finger made small circles.

By the time they arrived at her car, the urge for more of her was too much. Both hands gripped her waist as he shoved her against the vehicle. His lips devoured hers and his tongue darted into her mouth, needing her. Her hands curled around his neck and she tilted her head slightly. The kiss deepened. His erection grew. He pressed into her, wanting her to feel what she did to him.

One hand slid down, grabbing her firm ass. She wrapped one leg around him, bringing his erection closer to her core. Good God, he was going to explode in his pants if this kept up. As much as he didn't want this to end, he knew it had to.

Placing his hands on either side of her, he pulled himself away from her. Her eyes stayed closed for a moment before she slowly opened them and looked directly into his.

"Your place or mine?" she whispered.

"Mine. I want you in *my* bed."

"I'll follow you there." She lightly pushed him away and opened her car door.

He turned and headed toward his car at a fast pace.

* * * *

Amy was nervous the entire way to Adam's place. This man heated her up in ways she didn't know were possible. She couldn't wait to touch him again. To rub her hands along his firm body, to let her tongue taste him anywhere she pleased.

If she was smart, she should probably turn her car around and not go with him. She was getting in deep. When he decided the fun was over, she knew where that was going to leave her—a train-wreck. She had never had the feelings she was having for Adam. She wished there was some magic trick to get him to feel the same way.

Her thoughts then reminded her of dinner, when he once again said he wasn't looking for a relationship. But that kiss... it seemed like it had a deeper meaning. When he kissed her in the parking lot, it was as though he was trying to tell her differently. She rolled her eyes and knew she was putting too much into it. She needed to stop thinking.

When she parked her car, Adam was there at her car door, waiting. He pulled her from her seat and into his arms. He grabbed a hold of her waist, lifting her. She wrapped her legs around his broad hips as best she could. His erection was hard and was firmly pressed into her ass.

Adam fumbled with the keys as he opened the door to the house. He said nothing. As soon as they were in, he kicked the door shut and headed straight down the hall toward his bedroom. He dropped her right on the bed and then edged his way on top of her, forcing her legs wide open.

His mouth began to kiss her neck, his hands lifting her shirt. She sat up slightly so he could take it off.

"You're so beautiful, Amy," he whispered against her skin as he kissed his way down her belly.

His tongue swirled around her belly button. He then slightly bit into her hips as he fumbled with her pants. Amy smiled to herself, remembering these were the jeans that only buttoned up, no zipper.

He grunted as he undid each button. With a force he

jerked her pants, along with her panties off. Gripping her thighs, he shoved them open and positioned himself in between. A warm tongue met her sex, and she bit her lip to keep from crying out. It felt like his whole mouth was open and sucking on her core. His tongue circled the folds and then around her clitoris. Her nails dug into the comforter.

He lightly blew where his mouth had been. "You taste so good."

The words vibrated against her and she gasped. A finger entered her. His mouth sucked her on her clit, and she screamed as the pleasure built. "I'm going to come!"

He increased the drive of his finger and let his tongue flick her sensitive bud in a fast rhythm.

"Adam!" she cried out.

She pulled at the bedspread, her back arched, and let the climax take over. When she finally relaxed against the mattress, his tongue was still licking, lapping up all her juices. Her breathing was ragged, and typically she would be completely spent after an orgasm that intense, but she found herself growing with an insatiable desire, with a need for more from him.

He kissed his way up, then rolled off and propped himself up beside her. He lay silently, looking at her. She could smell herself on his breath and she knew she had to have a taste. Leaning in, she kissed him. She found a sweetness as she let her tongue explore.

Pushing him firmly across the mattress, she climbed on top, straddling him.

"I'm still turned on." She let her hands rub against her breasts. She squeezed gently and pinched her nipples.

"Amy, you are something else." His eyes focused on her hands.

"I think you're just a bit over dressed for this occasion. Let me help you with that."

She tugged his shirt over his head. Tossing it across the room, she started on his pants. In a swift move, she had his pants and boxers removed and his long, thick erection filling her hand. She stroked his length up and down in a slow rhythm. His mouth opened, breathing in deeply.

"You're so thick. Your cock feels amazing when it enters me," she said.

Her hand moved faster. As a drop of pre-cum seeped from the tip, she let her index finger swirl around it, spreading it over the head.

"Do you want inside me?" she asked.

"Yes," he said.

She wrapped her hand around his neck and pulled him into a sitting position. Still straddling him, she lifted herself up slightly. She positioned his tip right at her opening, and let his cock play with her.

"I can't wait to have you fill me," she whispered. "Are you ready for my pussy to grip you?"

His hands gripped her waist, trying to force her down onto him.

She resisted. Kissing his neck right behind his ear, she said, "You feel so good."

"If you don't quit teasing me, this isn't going to go well."

Releasing his cock, she clutched his shoulders and slowly lowered, letting him fill her.

Adam grunted.

"You're so big," she moaned.

His fingers dug into her hips and he began to guide her. Wrapping her arms around his neck, she pulled into him and began to ride him with intensity.

She rose to where his tip almost came out and then drove back down his long shaft. Her climax was building slowly. She enjoyed the sensations that sent pleasure through her body. This was one of those times when she understood wanting to feel this for hours. From the sound of Adam's breathing she could tell he too was enjoying it.

Adam wrapped his arms tightly around her waist.

"Let's come together," he said.

The rhythm increased. She cried out as the climax built in her. Biting her lip, she tried to quiet herself so she could listen for him, to know when he was ready. Through her closed lips, grunts escaped and she knew she couldn't force this orgasm away much longer.

"Now," she yelled out.

He lifted her off him slightly and let just his tip enter her.

"Go," he said with urgency.

Tossing her head back, she called out his name as the climax took over. He groaned loudly. He stopped moving and she moved down his shaft slowly, making sure she fully milked him.

Breathing heavily, she pushed him back down toward the pillows. They lay across the bedspread naked and exposed. This man was an amazing lover. Rolling off of him, she then curled up next to him, resting her head in the crook of his neck. She waited for his arm to wrap around her and hold her close, but it didn't. A feeling of coldness swept though her. Reaching behind her, she pulled the comforter up to wrap it around her.

Just as she started to snuggle in for what she hoped was a night spent with Adam, she heard him clear his throat.

"Don't get too comfortable. I have to be up early in the morning for work. You probably don't want to stay the night."

Biting her lip, she kept her head rested where it was a moment before speaking. "Okay," she said softly.

He pulled away from her, sitting up. She watched as he reached down and found his boxers and slipped them on. Sitting back on the bed, he turned and looked at her. "I had a great time."

She took his cue. Getting up, she quickly dressed. She could feel the tears wanting to build behind her eyes, but she wouldn't let them through. This was just fun, she reminded herself. A sleep over wasn't a necessity.

Adam walked her to the front door. He pulled her to him and gave her a light, sensual kiss before opening the door.

"I'll talk to you soon. Be safe."

"Good night." She still spoke softly, trying to hide the hurt in her voice. She really wasn't sure what the hell was happening, but she didn't know if she had it in her to argue right now.

As she walked to her car, she let the first tear fall. Climbing in, she saw Adam watching her from the doorway. She gave a slight wave before starting her car and backing out the driveway. Once on the road, away from his view, she let the tears flow freely.

* * * *

As Adam headed back to his bedroom, he knew she was upset. More than anything he wanted to keep her in his bed all night and make love to her until they could no longer move, then fall asleep with his arms tightly around her. He didn't fully know why he'd sent her away. He was used to it with other women, but Amy was different. He had to put distance between them. If he let her stay the night again, then he might as well let her move in. He had to break the attachment he was feeling and keep this as fun as possible. Or even worse, end it altogether.

Chapter 9

Monday came and went. Amy didn't hear from Adam. In some ways she wasn't surprised, but then she was. The man was confusing, that was one thing she was sure of. He expressed not wanting anything more than what they currently had, but when he kissed her, it was like he wanted so much more. Sending her away last night was something she actually hadn't expected. Maybe her pushing him to open a little more at dinner had been too much for him.

Staring into the mirror, she was happy with her appearance today. It was Tuesday, which was his usual day to visit the bakery. She had no idea if she would see him or not. Either way, her makeup was applied perfectly, and she wore a nice cream v-neck top that let her cleavage just barely play peek-a-boo, making it appropriate for work.

When leaving the bathroom, she stopped in front of her roommate's room. Skylar was almost never there. The room was bear and unused. The lease was coming to an end soon, and that was when she was officially going to move in with Drew and Amy would be downgrading to a one bedroom. It saddened her. It seemed like everyone's life was moving forward but hers. She had hoped that this thing with Adam would have turned into so much more.

Enough of this pity party. She had the ability to change things and find happiness. She put herself out there, and Adam made it clear what his intentions were. They weren't good enough for her. Period. If she heard from him again, which she highly doubted, she knew the fun was over. She deserved better.

In the kitchen she grabbed her to-go tea cup and headed for the bakery. She was ready to get her frustration out and bake. Maybe she would bake something new today and run a special to promote it. That thought quickly put her in a better mood. She was now ready to tackle the day.

* * * *

Adam pulled into his usual parking spot in front of Sweet Muffins bakery. As much as he was ready to bite into the best muffins he had ever had, he was even more excited to see Amy. He had been a dick Sunday. Then yesterday he didn't even bother to call her or text her, making him even more of a jerk. He was embarrassed that he had just sent her away like she was nothing special. He was realizing now that she *was* special. She meant something to him. When he caused her the pain he did, his heart ached.

He was experiencing something he had never felt. He was falling in love with her, and it scared him. One moment he wanted to run and scream, and the next he wanted to find her and shower her with kisses.

Right now, he had to get out of his police cruiser and hope she would accept his apology.

The door jangled its usual jingle as it opened. As he stepped inside, he inhaled the sweet aroma of coffee and baked goods. His senses lit up and his stomach rumbled in approval. As he approached the front, he didn't see Amy. A different girl stood there, waiting to take his order. In all this time, he had never had anyone but Amy take his order.

"Hi. What can I get you today, sir?" the girl asked with a huge smile across her face.

"Where is Amy?" he asked, uncaring about being rude.

The girl pointed to a chalk board next to the register and said, "She's been swamped. She decided to try a new recipe today for her muffins and it's been very popular. So, she's been baking up a storm."

He glanced at the sign. *Chocolate strawberry pecan muffins.* It sounded interesting, though he wasn't sure it was anything he wanted to try.

"Would you be interested in trying one? The special today is 'try the new muffin and get any other muffin free'. It's been a hit. In fact, she's been getting special orders just for the chocolate strawberry pecan."

"Sure, why not." He shrugged, his eyes darting around, hoping Amy would just appear.

"Okay, and what free muffin can I get for you?"

"A banana nut and a black coffee, please."

"For here or to go?"

He wasn't used to so many questions. Amy just knew what he wanted, always. "Here."

"Okay. It'll be just a moment." The girl started to turn to walk away before he stopped her.

"Can I see Amy?" he called after her.

"Is everything okay?" She looked confused.

"Yes, yes. We're friends and I just wanted to see her."

"Oh, okay. Let me see if she can come out. Your name?"

"Adam."

The girl went through the swinging door that led to where he presumed the kitchen was. When the girl returned she told him to find a seat and Amy would be out as soon as she could to see him. Paying for his food, he then looked for a table away from others. He spotted a small bistro table next to the bathrooms. Sitting near a restroom was not ideal, but it would do.

He took a bite of the new muffin. It was good. Really good. He could see why she was so busy. Hell, he thought about ordering a whole box for himself to snack on all day.

"Hi, Adam," Amy said as she took a seat in the chair directly in front of him.

The first thing he noticed was she looked tired. The second was, she didn't seem all too thrilled to see him. Which he deserved.

"This is really good," he told her, pointing at the new muffin.

"So I've heard. I'm surprised you decided to try something different." She paused and then added, "When I get frustrated I love to bake. So, I decided today I would be in charge of all the baking and try something new."

She was frustrated. He knew it was from him. He was the story behind this new muffin that was quickly becoming a huge success.

"You wanted to see me?" she asked.

"I know you're super busy so I won't keep you. How about dinner tonight? I was thinking maybe get some take-out and go back to my place so we can relax."

"I don't know. I'll probably just want to crash when I get off today. My feet are already killing me."

"Your place then." He knew there was desperation in his voice, but he didn't care.

The look on her face caused his gut to flip and his

appetite to disappear.

"It's not working, Adam," she said softly.

"It can."

"I want more than this so-called 'fun'. I really like you and the time we have together. I thought I could just have something casual with you, but I can't."

"I want that too."

"Really?" He saw a glimmer of hope in her eyes.

"Yes. I really like you too, Amy. I feel horrible about Sunday night. I was a dick. I treated you like a booty call and nothing special. But you are so much more than that to me."

She bit her lip and he could see she was contemplating what he'd said. More than anything he wished he was in her head right now. What in the world was she thinking and what was taking so long? She wasn't even looking at him. Instead, she was focused on whatever the hell was on the corner of the table.

"Amy…" he started.

"You hurt me Sunday. You're sending me so many different signals that I don't think you know what the hell you want. One minute you tell me you don't want a relationship. I can barely get to know you. You won't let me get below the surface. Then you kiss me, and it's a kiss with so much passion behind it, that it feels like you're trying to tell me how you feel about me. Then you treated me, as you said, like a booty call. I just don't know, Adam." She paused. "I don't think it would be a good idea to continue this any further."

"I just need a little time. That's all. Yes, I do freak out, but I'm getting better."

She rolled her eyes. "I'm at a different place than you. I'm ready now, I don't want to wait for someone to be ready for me. I'm sorry, Adam. I really like you and I wanted to see this work. But you just admitted you weren't ready, again. You still need time, and I don't have that time to give you."

He reached out, taking her hand. Their eyes locked. He pulled her to him and let his lips softly touch hers. It was a slow kiss, one that got his heart beating so hard he could hear it in his head. The kiss was over much sooner than he wanted and he was left with Amy standing, tears in her eyes, looking at him.

"Please," he said. "You're who I want to be with."

She smiled and said, "Come see me when you're actually ready. Maybe I won't have found Mr. Right by then."

She turned and walked away and Adam sat there

knowing he'd just lost the best thing that had ever happened to him. No longer hungry, he stood and tossed the muffins in the trash. With coffee in hand, he left Sweet Muffins. The pain he was feeling was the reason he never let anyone in. He finally decided to let Amy in and no one else mattered and now he was left broken hearted.

In the police cruiser, he took one last look at the bakery. He wouldn't be back.

Chapter 10

Going home to her empty apartment wasn't an option. Amy didn't want to have to think about what had happened, yet here she sat alone in the employee break room at Hot Bods waiting on Skylar. She missed the days of going home and finding her scatterbrained roommate telling her about the latest drama. She would cook her some comfort meal and like always Skylar told her she was going to make some man very happy one day. At this point, she didn't think that was going to happen, ever.

Seeing Adam sitting there, pleading for her, and then she just walked away, had been hard. It was the right thing though. He still wasn't ready and she just didn't have the time. It wasn't fair to her or him. Ugh, life sucked sometimes.

The door opened and Skylar came in, a sympathetic look on her face. With her she carried two take-out boxes. From the aroma, Amy could tell they were from the little Italian eatery that she loved.

"Sorry for making you wait, but if I know you, you need some spaghetti and meatballs and a big ol' piece of ooey gooey garlic bread." Skylar set the black take-out box in front of Amy and took a seat next to her.

Flipping the lid open, Amy stared at the large meatballs, already feeling better.

"I might eat all of this," she said.

"Go right ahead!" Skylar laughed as she opened her box, which was filled with a salad.

"A salad, really?" Amy gave her a cross look.

"What?" She shrugged. "Drew and I haven't been eating healthy, and I thought veggies might be a good idea."

Amy watched as Skylar chomped down on a crouton and her thoughts went back to Adam as she remembered he didn't like them. This was the sucky part about break-ups. Everything reminded you of that person.

Quietly, Amy began biting into her food. It was heavenly, and it really did hit the spot.

"I'm sorry you had to end things. Maybe it'll still work out. Sometimes they just have to lose you to know what they had," Skylar said.

"Wishful thinking. Knowing him, he's done and ready to go back to one-night stands or whatever he was up to before me."

"You never know. Give it time."

"Time. Ha, that's what he asked for." She rolled her eyes.

Skylar grinned and shook her head. "It's nice not having to do this anymore. Amy, you're a great catch. If he doesn't see that, someone else will."

"But I want someone now."

"Yeah, well, you don't get to choose when. It just happens."

For the rest of her visit with Skylar, she tried to not talk or think about him. But that wasn't happening. She couldn't help but wonder what he was doing. Did he miss her? Did he just say *fuck it all* after she left? Would he show up Thursday at his usual time?

After they finished eating, Skylar suggested they go to a movie or something. Amy declined. Every movie had some sort of romance in it. She just wanted to head back to the apartment and sleep. She was exhausted from the business at the bakery, and she was emotionally drained too. Hugging Skylar bye, she thanked her again for dinner and then headed home. Tomorrow was a new day.

* * * *

As the week went on, Amy found herself deeply missing Adam. It didn't seem right for him to suddenly be completely out of her life. Just like she figured, he didn't show up on Thursday. Mr. Combo Number Nine was no longer a regular. She hated herself for it, but she watched all day for him and hoped that he just might show. Again on Friday, she wished he might come in, even though it wasn't his day. But he was a no-show on that day too.

Sighing, she finished up her duties before leaving. The week had been busy, and today being Saturday was no exception. She grabbed her purse from the office, told everyone goodbye, and headed for the front. As she opened the door, she collided into Francesca.

"Sorry," Amy said, and tried to brush past her. She had no time for that woman right now.

Luck wasn't with her; Francesca followed her out the door. "Amy! Hi."

Amy turned to her, smiling. "Oh, hi. I didn't recognize you."

Francesca looked herself over, apparently assessing why someone wouldn't recognize her. She shrugged then asked, "How's my brother? Ever since you two hooked up I haven't seen him. You must be keeping him pretty busy."

"We broke up."

Her mouth dropped open. "What?"

Amy didn't say anything. It wasn't her place.

"He's crazy about you. Goodness, he's been staring at you for months at that darn bakery. The way he looks at you..." She paused. "I'm surprised. Did he end things? God,

I could kill him."

"Actually, I did."

Francesca froze. "No way? Why?"

"This is something you should really be discussing with your brother."

"Hell no. Come on, let's sit." She grabbed Amy's arm and led her to a small black table.

This was crazy and Amy knew it. She should not be sitting here with Adam's sister. Heck, if Skylar even knew she would have a fit.

"I really thought you would be the one to be patient with him," Francesca said.

"I tried. Really I did. But it's not fair to me. I'm ready now. I want the whole package deal and your brother is just starting to get to that point. My problem is what happens if I wait for him. He is most likely the kind of man that once we get engaged it'll be ten years before we marry. I want kids, dogs, cats, all of it. And I want to do it while I'm young." Wow, it felt so good to actually get it out.

"I see your dilemma. So glad I'm not ready for all of that. Kids…now that's scary."

Amy rolled her eyes. It was going to take a very special man to tame this woman.

"I hope my dear brother comes to his senses soon

before some other man snatches you away. Even though I'm not fond of your so-called best friend, I like you with my brother. You seem right for him."

"Thanks, I think that was a compliment."

"As best as you're gonna get. Now tell me, do you have a non-fat version of that new muffin of yours?"

Amy laughed. "You're the first to ask."

"Just something to think about." Francesca stood and said, "Well, it was nice chatting with you. Perhaps I'll see you around sometime."

Then without so much as a wave bye, Francesca went on her way. Amy sat there a few more minutes trying to collect herself before going home to an empty apartment.

Chapter 11

It had been almost two weeks now and Adam had never felt so lost in his life. All last week he'd tried out different bakeries for a new banana nut muffin. None of them were anywhere as good as Amy's. He missed her. Each night he wanted her in his bed. He desired her each time he pulled his crisp, cool sheets up. He wanted her warm body next to his.

One evening last week, he and a few other officers went to eat at Little Italy's, and once again he forgot to ask for no croutons. Staring at the pile on his bread plate, he wished she was there so he could watch her snatch them up and devour them with her full lips.

His sister had also been calling non-stop, and he'd had to resort to ignoring her calls. She was adamant about letting him know he was a moron for letting Amy get away. He already knew that, it wasn't like he needed her to tell him.

Life just wasn't the same without Amy. He had to get her back, but he was too scared that if he tried she would turn him down. He supposed, however, he was going to have to try if he wanted her here with him where she belonged.

* * * *

It was another Tuesday. Amy hated herself for looking at the clock. He wasn't coming and by now, she knew it. The fact that she still hoped at 10:30 he would strut in made her want to bang her head into the wall.

"Mary," she called.

The tiny blonde turned toward Amy and said, "Yes?"

"Run the front. I need to compose myself."

"Are you okay? You've been baking a lot."

Amy closed her eyes and inhaled deeply. "I'm getting there, Mary." She pushed her way through the door and decided to get started on the next round of baked goods before the brunch rush.

She checked the inventory sheet Mary had just made to see what she needed to make. The morning had been slow, which was not good. The rushes kept her mind on a topic she preferred, not on the person she was trying to not think about.

Opening a new bag of flour, she began to measure what she was going to need. She then gathered the rest of the supplies and laid them out for easy access. She double checked to make sure the oven was set to the correct temperature. It was now time to get busy.

"Amy!" Mary shrieked and appeared with a huge smile across her face.

"Yeah," she said as she measured out walnuts.

"You're needed out front."

Amy groaned. "Are you kidding?" Wiping her hands on a white towel, she tossed it on the counter. "Is it a customer? Why do they always have to talk to me?"

Mary said nothing, but kept grinning. Amy rolled her eyes and pushed her way back through the swinging door.

The first thing to catch her attention was a big silver balloon with red words written in cursive that said *I love you* sitting on the counter. Her gaze followed the string down to a vase that held an arrangement of many different exotic looking flowers of all colors.

"Amy," a deep voice said just behind her.

She jumped and slowly turned around to face Adam. Her heart sped up to the point she was worried it was about to beat right out of her chest.

"What's going on?" she asked.

"I love you." Adam looked deep into her eyes and said it without even blinking. "I can't live without you. It took you walking away to show me what a fool I was."

"Are you sure it's not just because you missed my baking and you find me so useful?" She blinked rapidly.

She wasn't going to cry.

"You're more than useful to me, Amy. You're everything to me. I want you to be my wife."

Her mouth dropped open.

His hands wrapped around her waist, bringing her to him. His grip was tight and jolts of desire were already shooting through her body.

"What are you saying?" she managed to get out.

"Amy, will you marry me?"

She shook her head slightly. "I don't know. I don't want to be engaged for years before you're ready to walk down the aisle."

"If I have to call a priest here now to marry us just to prove I want to, then I will."

She giggled. "This is what you want?"

"God, Amy, yes. Do I need to get down on bended knee?"

Leaning forward, she wrapped her arms around his neck and pulled him to her. She pressed her lips to his and passion stirred more. He was obviously feeling the same as his erection grew and pressed into her belly. She deepened the kiss and let her fantasies take her back to where they always did when he entered the bakery—him lifting her up onto the counter and taking her right there. If only they

More Than Useful / Lacey Wolfe

didn't have an audience.

Breaking the kiss, she stared into his sparkling blue eyes and said, "Yes, Mr. Combo Number Nine, I will marry you."

A grin crossed his face. "What did you call me?"

She whispered in his ear, "Let's find somewhere we can be alone and if you're lucky I might explain." She lingered a moment, sucking his earlobe. She turned, looked at Mary, and said, "It's all yours. We have some celebrating to do."

She took note of where Adam stood, then she smiled and shoved him through the swinging door. He took control and pushed her against the wall next to it.

He leaned in close. "You know I can't show you how sorry I am back here."

"You have a lifetime for that. Right now I just want you to kiss me. Let me savor this moment."

He cupped her face and she got lost in the kiss of her future husband.

Accidental Love

Has Jane accidentally fallen for the decoy?

Sometimes there is only one thing to do when you get dumped—make the ex jealous with someone new. Which is exactly what Jane plans to do with Ben, an older, handsome man who has agreed to act as her new love interest.

When Ben meets Toby, Jane's unruly dog, he offers to help her train him. But as Ben helps Jane gain control of her dog, he realizes he's lost control of his feelings, and he's beginning to fall for the much younger woman.

Suddenly, Jane can't seem to remember what she ever saw in her ex. All she can focus on is the way Ben makes her feel each time he kisses her. But now the ex has decided he wants her back, and he's willing to play dirty to make it happen.

Content Warning: Explicit sex

Chapter 1

Jane's lips trailed down Matt's neck and stopped at his collarbone. Lightly, she blew where her mouth had been. She wrapped her hands around his neck and gazed up into his eyes.

"I don't think I can keep this a secret much longer," she whispered.

Matt pulled her hands from his neck and held them tightly in his. "You have no other choice. When we got involved you knew no one could ever know." He kissed her knuckles. "Besides, that's the thrill of it."

"But I really like you. And I'm tired of this secret."

Matt put his hand up to stop her. "I'm your boss."

"I'll quit."

He shook his head. "I think we might need to end things. You're too involved. This was never supposed to be a relationship. But now you're calling and texting me as though I'm your boyfriend. And I'm not."

Jane yanked her hands from his and spun around. She couldn't look at him, and she certainly didn't want to hear what he was saying. They'd been sleeping together for a while now. He'd call and she always came. Every now and then he'd pull her into the office, like he did today, and they'd fool around. Somewhere along the way, she assumed they were more. Apparently she was wrong.

"I don't want this to be over," she pleaded, trying to be firm.

"It isn't like you're leaving me any choice. You're getting clingy."

"I'll do better."

A warmth came up behind her and his breath blew across the back of her neck. She closed her eyes and waited for his lips to touch the spot that drove her over the edge.

"It's too late. There's no going back." He pressed a small kiss behind her ear. After that, all she heard was his office door opening, then closing.

Jane's shoulders slumped, and she counted to ten. She wasn't going to cry. No way. Matt just needed time, and then he'd realize how wrong he was. In the meantime, she would wait patiently for him.

Straightening her posture, she left the office, walking with a confidence she wished she actually had. She plastered the biggest smile she could across her face and entered the reception area of Hot Bods Gym. The front door jingled and a couple walked in.

"Welcome to Hot Bods," Jane chimed.

The woman waved and they headed to the workout area. Maybe one day that would be her and Matt. She just had to come up with some sort of plan to get him back. Who could she ask for advice that was not connected to him? Currently Skylar was her closest friend, but she was away on her honeymoon.

At least the day was almost over and Jane could stop being the happy, perky receptionist everyone knew. She could escape to her home with her fat cat and slobbery dog. They always made her feel better.

"I'm heading out, Jane. Can you handle the lock-up alone tonight?" Matt asked as he walked up behind her.

Jane spun around, looking at the handsome man. "Uh, yeah."

"Great. See ya." Flipping his keys in his hand, he headed for the front door without even glancing back.

She stared after him longingly. It was suddenly like she was just another employee. And she wasn't...was she? Hell, she'd been in his bed last night.

"Why the long face?"

Jane looked over and saw one of the regular gym patrons approaching the desk. "Hey, Francesca. It's been a long day."

"I don't buy it. I know that face. You have the hots for

that hunk that just left, don't you?"

Jane shook her head. She'd never admitted it to anyone, and now wasn't the time to start.

"Please." Francesca rolled her eyes. "I'm not blind. Does he know?"

Jane nodded. Shit, why did she just do that?

"And he doesn't feel the same way?"

She shook her head.

"Well, perhaps the problem is you don't speak."

"I can't talk about it here," Jane whispered.

Francesca looked around the gym. "It's kinda empty, minus a few people."

"I just can't here."

"Whatever. I'm going to shower. I'm here if you want to chat."

Jane's gaze followed Francesca as she strutted toward the locker rooms. Her blonde ponytail swayed, and her stride was full of determination, as always. No one could knock that woman down.

Over the loud speaker Jane announced that Hot Bods would be closing in thirty minutes. She got busy with her few closing tasks. Once the last member left, she checked all the rooms for any belongings that might have been left, turned off lights, and made sure all the equipment was off.

In the employee break room, she went to her locker and grabbed her purse. She did a double check that the coffee maker wasn't on. Her last stop was the locker rooms to make sure everyone was gone. The men's was empty. Next was the women's.

Francesca was applying makeup in the vanity area.

"Hey. We're closed," Jane said.

"I know. I was hanging around so we could talk." Francesca closed her cosmetic bag.

"Oh. Well, thanks, but…" Was Francesca really someone she could trust? Skylar strongly disliked the girl. Amy said she was okay, but Amy was partial since Francesca was her future sister-in-law.

"I don't want to hear it. Your buddy is away getting her head banged against some headboard as we speak. Who else are you going to talk to?"

"I guess you're right."

"Come on, let's go over to Sweet Muffins and get a coffee."

Jane agreed. After she locked up they walked across the street. It was a nice evening. Jane always liked Sundays. She closed each Sunday and loved that when she got off, it was still daylight. Francesca told her to take a seat at an outside table, the coffee was on her.

Amy owned Sweet Muffins and Jane wondered if Francesca got a discount since Amy was marrying her brother. If so, it was no wonder she'd offered to pay.

Behind her, Jane heard the bell on the door. A woman giggled. "You're so funny, Matt."

Jane froze. Her heart rate sped up. It couldn't be. It absolutely could *not* be. Feeling as though she was moving in slow motion, she turned to look.

It was.

"Matt," Jane said, surprised she was able to get the word out.

Matt grinned, not even looking one bit ashamed. "Hi, Jane."

She stood and stared as her eyes danced back and forth between the two, trying to wrap her mind around what she was seeing.

"Matt, who's this?" the other woman asked. She was no longer smiling, obviously getting a feel for what was going on. She tugged on Matt's shirt and whispered something then tried to walk away. Jane expected him to just let the lady leave, but instead he took her hand.

"She's just the receptionist over at Hot Bods," he told the woman.

Jane's mouth dropped open, and her heart felt like it

had been ripped out. He'd completely dismissed her as though she'd been nothing to him.

Chapter 2

"Here." Francesca shoved a coffee into Jane's hand. "Sit. Now."

Jane did as she was told. She was too stunned not to. Taking her seat, she took a long sip of her drink. It was good. But at the moment she had no idea what the flavor was.

"You're sleeping with him, aren't you?" Francesca asked. "Perhaps *was* is a better way of putting it."

Jane couldn't hold back any longer. She had to tell someone. "For a few months. It started one evening when he and I were closing. We'd been flirting like crazy. He called me into his office, and the next thing I knew his desk was cleared and we were having sex on it. We agreed to keep it hush-hush. But I thought it would only be for a little while. Today we were fooling around and I told him I wanted more. To go public. I'd quit if I had to. He ended things. But I didn't think he really meant it. And I definitely wasn't expecting to see him with someone else already."

"No one knows?"

"Nope. I've been keeping this to myself. Wow, it does feel good to be getting it out though."

"So, what's your plan?" Francesca took a long sip of her drink.

"Plan?"

Shaking her head and rolling her eyes, Francesca said, "Do you want him back or do you want him to see what he no longer has?"

What did she want? That was a good question. Before seeing him with that woman she was sure she wanted him back, but that really hurt. He'd discarded her like she was an empty water bottle. She'd hoped that after a few days of not being with her, he'd crawl back and let her know she'd been right and they should start telling people. But he had moved on very fast. Had he already been seeing this other person? Could he have been cheating on her? Then again, they would've had to be in a relationship for her to be cheated on. Wow, this was way more complicated than she'd expected it to be.

"I don't really know," Jane finally said.

"How about you show him what he's lost?"

"How?"

"A make-over and a fake new boyfriend."

"Fake boyfriend? Where am I going to get one of those?"

"Leave that to me." Francesca pulled out her

smartphone and tapped away at the screen. "Call in sick tomorrow. We have a full day ahead of us."

"I can't do that," Jane objected.

"Sure you can. Heck, he probably expects it. The man dumped you today and already found a new lady. Seriously, he'll be relieved if you don't come in tomorrow. Plus, it'll give him time to see if he misses you. Aren't you always there?"

She nodded. It was sad, but yes, she was always there, rain or shine. She was dependable Jane.

"Great. Meet me at the mall about ten tomorrow." Francesca stood and picked up her cup. "I better go get my beauty sleep. Bye."

Jane waved. What had she gotten herself into? Deciding to go home, she picked up her coffee. Tomorrow would be here before she knew it, and she was going to need all the rest she could get.

* * * *

Wow, just wow. That was all Jane could think as she stared at herself in the mirror. When Francesca did a make-over, she went all out. They'd gone shopping today, and Jane now wore a pair of designer jeans that looked so good on her she feared she would never take them off. She had on a simple white blouse, but with the jewelry Francesca insisted she buy, she admitted she looked hot. Her normal brown hair that she'd never colored had several sets of lowlights and highlights. It was shiny, and when she ran her fingers through it, it felt amazingly soft. It was slightly curled under, but still rested below her shoulders. Then there was her makeup. Francesca had done that herself. And wowzers, she'd taught Jane a few new things.

Now she was meeting this fake boyfriend who was going to be coming by the gym a lot. The plan was just to make Matt jealous. Jane didn't know if she wanted him back but making him see what he'd lost sounded like a great idea.

"I think I'm ready." Jane could have stared at herself for hours.

"Good, because we don't want to hold Ben up," Francesca said.

As Francesca drove them across town, she talked about the delicious shrimp and steak that was served at the restaurant. Jane's mouth watered at the thought of eating a juicy steak, but once Francesca said the name of the restaurant, Jane lost her appetite. It was one of the more expensive ones in town. Jane had never eaten there. Her wallet was hurting from today's purchases, and it was really going to be in trouble after this dinner.

This is crazy. Why am I doing this?

Francesca pulled up to the exquisite looking steak house. Taking a deep breath, Jane unbuckled and climbed out. As she followed her friend to the entrance, all she wanted to do was run in the opposite direction. She should be embarrassed that she was sinking this low. A fake boyfriend to make an ex-lover jealous.

She started to say something, but right away, the hostess greeted Francesca as if they were long lost friends and showed them to their table. Ben wasn't there yet, but had already reserved the table so they wouldn't have to wait. That was very considerate of him.

Francesca took a sip of the water already on the dark hardwood table. It was one of those places where you drank water out of a fancy glass that somewhat resembled a wine glass.

"This is crazy. I'm way out of my element here," Jane said.

Francesca rolled her eyes. "You're fine. Every lady deserves to be treated like one. It's about time you were."

Well, she had a point. Just as Jane was about to say something else, her eyes locked on the most magnificent man she'd ever seen. He was tall and lean, but not skinny. There was muscle on that firm body for sure. He was older.

His hair was dark with a few speckles of gray that made him look distinguished. He wore jeans and a sports jacket over a button-down shirt. The guy was hot, and he was walking their way.

"Hi," he said with a big smile. He had dimples too. Jane thought she was going to burst.

"Ben, so good to see you." Francesca stood and greeted him with a kiss on the cheek. Already Jane felt a twinge of jealousy that she had just laid her lips on the guy who was going to be her fake boyfriend.

"You too," he said.

Jane was the only one sitting and wondered if she should stand up and greet him the same way. But then they both took a seat. He was directly in front of her.

"You must be Jane," he said.

"Hi," she managed to say.

This man was drop dead sexy. How he was single, she had no idea. She was definitely happy to be able to call him hers, even though he wasn't.

"You look beautiful," he complimented.

"Thank you."

How was she supposed to have a conversation with him? She could barely form any words. In fact, she wondered if she was drooling.

"Jane isn't a big talker," Francesca said. "We're working on that."

"It's quite all right." Ben smiled at her.

The waitress came to the table, a bottle in hand.

"I hope you don't mind, I took the liberty of ordering some wine."

A man who took charge. Jane liked it, and strangely it turned her on. She wondered where else he would take charge.

She was still out of her element. This seemed like Francesca's scene. She was completely comfortable, while Jane was curious if this was the type of place she should be concerned about which fork to use.

A glass of wine was placed in front of her. Francesca raised her hand to the waitress. "I'm not staying."

Jane's head spun toward her. She was *not* ditching her.

"I'm sorry, but I have a previous engagement. You two enjoy." Francesca kissed Jane's cheek then Ben's. Before Jane could even argue, Francesca was gone.

She gazed across the table at the gentleman. Lifting her glass, she took a big sip. It then occurred to her that Francesca had driven her there, and now she either had to call a cab or ask Ben to drive her home. She needed another drink of wine.

Chapter 3

Ben thought it was adorable that Jane was so nervous. He couldn't recall the last time a woman had been nervous around him. He'd always dated women like Francesca. They were only looking for a man with money and power. But Jane here, she was out of her element. He'd just poured her a second glass of wine, and he could see the wheels turning in her head, debating if she should devour that one too. He could already tell he was going to like her.

When Francesca first called and begged for the favor, he was skeptical. He was sure that somehow it would benefit her, especially since she reminded him repeatedly that he "owed" her after setting her up with one of his colleagues who turned out to be a complete nut job. Francesca explained that they needed him to be Jane's "fake boyfriend". Something about making the guy who hurt this beautiful woman jealous.

Letting his eyes drift over Jane and take her in, he could tell she was a natural beauty. Tonight was probably the most dolled up she'd ever been. She was likely a jeans and t-shirt sort of girl who spent most of her time with her feet bare and chipped nail polish. With Jane, he knew he could be comfortable. But she wasn't on an actual date with him. Most likely she had taken one look at him and saw a man in his mid-forties and wondered what the hell she had gotten herself into.

"Tell me a little about you," he asked.

"Uh, well…" She fidgeted in her seat. The last thing he wanted was for her to be uncomfortable.

"What do you do for fun?"

"When I'm not working I enjoy reading."

"Romance?"

"Horror."

His eyes widened. He could imagine her in jeans and a t-shirt sprawled out on a couch reading, but the horror part surprised him.

"Do you like scary movies too?"

"Oh yes. I love them. Especially the true ones. Makes them that much scarier knowing it happened to someone."

He would have to remember to pick up something scary if they ever had a real date. Which he hoped they would.

Dinner arrived and as they ate, they shared small talk. He enjoyed learning about her. She talked about her pets as if they were children. He was a dog lover himself. At his house he had two great danes. They even had their own room with two twin-sized beds.

"I feel like all we've done is talk about me. What is it you do for a living, Ben?"

"I flip houses."

"You what?"

"I buy houses for cheap, fix them up, then sell them."

"That's how you have all this money." She paused. "That was rude. I'm sorry."

"Don't be. I did very well before the economy tanked. I'm still doing good, but I'm a saver too. I try not to spend too much."

They finished dinner and she declined dessert. As she reached for her phone to call a cab he insisted on giving her a ride home. She was easy to persuade, which was good. He didn't want too much of a fight and she seemed eager to please. The more he got to know her, the more he liked her. Playing the part of her boyfriend was going to be easy.

* * * *

It was almost lunchtime on Tuesday, and Ben would be arriving any minute to pick Jane up. She was grateful to be getting out of there. Matt had given her the cold shoulder all morning, except for the one time he'd pulled her into his office. She had slight hope that he was going to apologize for Sunday night, but that wasn't how it went.

"*I can't believe how you embarrassed me in front of Tabitha,*" *Matt said.*

"*How do you think I felt? We were together in your office just that afternoon. Then I see you with her. You sure move fast.*"

"*I told you many times, it wasn't a relationship. I could see whoever I wanted.*"

"*Well, that's fine.*" *Jane crossed her arms.* "*It just so happens I'm seeing someone else too.*"

Matt laughed a full-out laugh. "*You're shitting me. I don't believe that for a second.*"

For a moment she wanted to punch his pretty face, but she didn't. She knew he would get what was coming to him. Somehow, someway, he'd get his payback.

"*I guess you'll find out.*" *Jane turned and left his office without looking back, beaming that she had finally stood up to him.*

For the rest of the morning, he'd avoided her. Which was fine. At this point she didn't have any idea what she ever saw in him. If it wasn't for him laughing at her, she would've called off the farce with Ben, but after that she wanted to prove to Matt that someone could want her.

The door to Hot Bods opened and she plastered her smile on, ready to welcome whoever was there. It was Ben. Once again, he was dressed to fully impress. And he did it well. Her nipples puckered just at the sight of him and a jolt went straight through her and right to the core between her legs.

"Jane," he said with a warm smile.

Jane left the front desk and came around the corner to greet him. She expected a kiss on the cheek, but instead his lips pressed against hers and her breath left. The moment he kissed her, lights were shooting off behind her eyelids. She slid her hand around the back of his neck and slightly opened her mouth to meet his tongue. Her sex grew wet.

When the kiss ended, she gazed up into his blue eyes, completely speechless. She'd never been so turned on by just a kiss. She could only imagine what he could do to her in bed.

Matt cleared his throat behind her. Her eyes widened in shock and she slowly slid her hands from Ben's neck, down his firm chest. She turned to face her ex-lover, and Ben's arm tightened around her waist, holding her close.

"Hi, I'm Ben." He extended his hand toward Matt.

Matt kept his arms crossed. He looked pissed, which was good, she hoped.

"Well, I'm off on my lunch break," she said.

"Don't be late, Jane. We have a staff meeting, so you'll need to be back to handle any gym members." Matt walked away, heavy footed.

Ben took her hand and led her outside to his car. As they reached the vehicle she expected him to drop the act, but instead he opened her door for her and then closed it once she was seated.

He climbed in and asked, "How long do you have?"

"An hour. Fast food is fine if you want to drop me off and then pick me up."

He chuckled. "I know a place where we can share a meal in under an hour."

"You don't have to eat with me."

"Jane, I want to."

The hour went much faster than Jane would have liked. Ben was a lot of fun and took his boyfriend duties seriously. He had opened her car door and held her hand. This was something she could easily get used to. She was going to tell him he didn't have to pretend when they were away from the gym but each time he touched her she was at peace. Was it wrong to have a crush on the decoy? Perhaps it was the George Clooney look he had going on. It was every girl's fantasy.

Ben parked in front of Hot Bods and quickly came around the side of the car and helped her out. Taking her hand in his again, he walked her back. She started to object and it was like he sensed it. Releasing her hand, he tugged her closer and wrapped his arm around her waist, cradling her to him.

They stopped in front of the door.

"I had a lovely lunch," he said.

"Thank you. Me too."

He stepped closer. She sensed what was coming next, and she was more than ready. He rubbed her cheek with the back of his fingers then tilted her face toward his. Leaning down, he gently brushed his lips across hers. She moaned and was almost embarrassed to be reacting this way. He kissed a small line to her neck and her mouth opened, still whimpering. She was lost in the sensation of his light kisses and forgot they were out in the open. She was so turned on that if they had been alone she would have let this man explore her entire body.

Ben released her face, and she was slightly disappointed it was over.

"Have a good day." He kissed her once more on the lips.

He'd kissed her speechless. She didn't say a word.

Instead, she simply watched as the most amazing man she'd ever met headed across the parking lot to his car.

He was good. Very good. Maybe that was why Francesca was always after older men. They really knew what they were doing.

Shaking her head, Jane knew she had to get back to work. As she walked inside, for the first time in her life she felt as though she was floating on air. This was a new feeling for her and she had no idea what it was, but she knew that Ben had everything to do with it.

After locking her purse up in the employee room, she dashed for the front. The gym always closed for an hour and a half so all the employees had time for their lunch break. In about fifteen minutes it would be open again, and with the meeting she needed to make sure everything was ready.

"Jane," Matt called from his office. "I need to see you a minute."

Usually this would have excited her, but not now. However, he was the boss and she had to see what he wanted. Once she was in the office, he shut the door and locked it. Jane backed away from him but he was fast. Before she could even get a word out he'd slammed her back against the wall and forcefully thrust his tongue into her mouth. His hands were all over her. She kept hers at her side, not sure what to do. This was not what she wanted.

Finally gathering the courage, she pushed him off her. "Stop."

"I want you so bad, Jane." Matt leaned in again, trying to kiss her.

Jane jerked her head away. "No, Matt."

He released her and started to pace the room. "Do you think I'm stupid? You brought that man here to make me jealous, and it worked. Seeing him kiss you…" He clenched his fists. "You're mine."

"You ended it, remember?"

"Well, I want to *un*end it. Send that man away."

"Will we go public with our relationship?"

Matt laughed. "Is that what it will take?"

"I don't want to just be a plaything. I want someone who will take me out and be proud to have me."

"I just don't see why we have to tell anyone. I like the thrill of the secrecy. No one knowing and the fact that we can get caught at any time." He stepped closer and leaned in for another kiss.

She gazed into his eyes, looking for any sign that he meant what he said. But she didn't see anything. Right as his lips were about to brush against hers, there was a knock on the office door.

Matt stepped back and smirked. "That is what I'm talking about. God, I'm hard as a rock now."

Wishing she didn't, but she did, she glanced at his crotch. He was hard all right. His cock looked as though it was going to burst through his zipper.

"You know the drill." He walked to the door. "Wait a few minutes before coming out."

Jane didn't know what had just happened. Had she somehow agreed to start things back up with him? Was that even what she wanted? She then thought about Ben and how he made her feel. Even though what she had with him was fake, she would rather have that than what she had with Matt.

She left the office and went to her place up front. Matt was not who she wanted. And she was going to do her best not to go down that path again.

Chapter 4

"Slow dooooown!" Jane's voice echoed as her gigantic yellow lab pulled her down the street.

Taking the dog for a walk originally seemed like a good idea, but the dog was forcing her to run, and if she wasn't careful, she'd soon be dragged. Finally Toby stopped to smell something and Jane was able to catch her breath. Wiping the sweat from her forehead, she decided not to do this again anytime soon. She really should have signed up for those training classes everyone told her about.

Toby lifted his leg and peed on something then was ready to explore again. She'd watched the show *The Dog Whisperer* many times and knew she was supposed to show the dog who was in charge, but Toby wasn't buying it.

"Let's go home," she commanded in the firmest tone she could.

As she expected, the dog ignored her and dragged her in the direction he wanted to go. She tugged, trying to get him to stop. Then a squirrel ran by and the dog took off running full force. Jane's legs were moving so fast now she really was worried she was going to fall. She decided she had no other choice. She released the leash and watched

Toby chase the four-legged creature.

Now what was she going to do? Well, what else was there to do but follow him? At least now she could walk at a pace that she liked. She crossed the street and headed toward the woods it looked like Toby might have ventured into. Just great.

Her back pocket vibrated. She pulled out her cellphone and answered without checking the ID. "Hello."

"Jane, you sound breathless. Did I catch you at a bad time?" Ben asked.

"Kinda. I was attempting to walk my dog, but it didn't work out and now I'm not sure where he is. He chased a squirrel into the woods. I really should get off here and find him."

"Would you like some help?"

"Are you good with dogs?"

"I like to think so."

"I need help. I'm on Carter street. Know where that is?"

"I do, and I'm not too far. I'll see you in a few." He hung up.

Sliding the phone back into her pocket she called to the dog. She really did not want to go in after him. So she hollered all kinds of things, promised Toby if he came out she'd buy him a pizza and such. Of course, none of it worked. She was just getting ready to go after the dog when a familiar blue BMW pulled up. Ben stepped out and she took in one of the hottest and most distinguished men she'd ever seen. Each time she saw him, he got even more attractive. She never imagined herself liking an older man. But Ben, she liked—a lot.

"What's your dog's name?" he asked.

"Toby. He's a yellow lab."

Ben walked up close to her. "Well, let's go in. I brought some chicken liver treats. My danes love these."

"I forgot you had dogs."

"Love them." He reached out and took her hand, which surprised her. They weren't pretending here, and yet he still showed her affection.

Jane hated the woods. There was something about being engulfed with trees all around you that she didn't like. One wrong turn and you could easily get lost. Not to mention what happened if you ran into someone in the woods. Shivers swept through her. She didn't even want to think about that.

Thankfully, they didn't have to go far before they found Toby sitting under a big pine tree, staring straight up. The squirrel had escaped and the lab was waiting patiently for it to come back down.

Jane called Toby, and he glanced her way but ignored her. Ben released her hand and crouched down. With a treat in his palm he called the dog over. Go figure, Toby came right to him. Once Ben grabbed ahold of the leash, he gave Toby the treat, praised him, and led him in her direction.

"You made that look so easy. I'm not so sure I like you anymore," she joked.

"Will you like me again if I get you and Toby home safely?" he asked.

"I'll think about it."

Ben took her hand, still holding the leash in his other one. The darn dog walked right beside him as if he'd been trained to. Ben did walk with a confidence that he was in charge. It must have made the dog feel safe. It sure made her.

Once they were at his car, he opened the back door, letting the dog in, and then held the passenger door open for her. She thanked him as she climbed inside. She directed him to her place. As they pulled in her driveway, she hoped he might stick around. She found she really liked his company.

"Would you like to come in?" she asked.

"I'd love to."

She grinned. She couldn't help it. "I'll let you get Toby."

Ben handled the dog like a champ—again. Maybe he had some pointers for her.

Inside her fat cat Patty greeted them. Jane scooped her up and introduced her to Ben. He looked a little clueless when it came to the cat, which was good. It meant he wasn't perfect.

"Can I get you a drink?" she asked.

"What do you have?"

"Tea, Coke, water."

"Tea sounds good."

Jane left him in the living room and went to get the drinks. She was thirsty after that walk. Of course the cat followed her, nipping at her heels and meowing loudly. The darn cat was most likely complaining because she could see the bottom of her food bowl. Jane swirled her finger around it, making an even layer. That seemed to satisfy Patty and she quieted down.

After getting the drinks Jane headed back to the living room and found Ben sitting on the love seat. She had options at the moment. She could sit on the couch next to the love seat or she could take the spot beside him. What the hell, you only live once. She sat next to him, handing him his drink.

"Thanks for your help today."

"You don't have to thank me."

"Yes, I do. You didn't have to help." She stopped a moment. "Wow, I'm so rude. I've been so caught up in myself I haven't even asked why you called. There must have been a reason. Was there something you needed?"

"Actually..." He set his glass down on the coffee table. "I called because I didn't want to have to wait until Thursday to see you."

He didn't? She was off work today and tomorrow. So, she hadn't expected to see him again until sometime on Thursday.

"I like you," he said, taking her hand in his.

She set her glass down now.

"I wanted to see if you might be interested in going on a real date with me."

"You like me?" she repeated.

"Is that so hard to believe?"

"I didn't think I was your type. Don't you usually date women like Francesca?"

He chuckled. "Usually, yes."

"Well, as you can see, I'm nothing like her." She motioned toward her clothes. She wore a baggy t-shirt and a pair of jeans from the local superstore.

He pulled her toward him. "I like what I see."

"Are you okay with me being only twenty-seven?"

"Age is just a number, and when I'm with you, I feel as though I'm in my twenties again."

Her heart did a somersault and right as she was about to speak, he kissed her. She wrapped her hands around his neck and scooted closer to him. His body was rock hard, and her hands ached to explore it.

His tongue thrust into her mouth, and once again it was as if fireworks were going off behind her eyelids. She was ready to burst with desire. She had to have him. It was crazy and forward, and maybe in some way it was some fantasy she had to play out. She'd never been with an older man, and she wondered just how much more he knew than the men her age.

"You taste like heaven," he murmured.

How he was able to speak, she didn't know.

His hands teased the bottom of her shirt. "Are you okay with this?"

She nodded. Please, she thought.

He yanked her shirt off and tossed it across the back of the chair. His eyes devoured her breasts. She realized then she was wearing a plain, white bra. Why hadn't she opted for the lacey black one that morning? Though Ben didn't seem like he cared. He planted light kisses to her cleavage and let his tongue dance around the top of the bra. Her eyes closed and she decided to just feel what he was doing. To enjoy the pleasure he was willing to give.

A finger dipped inside and swirled around her nipple, then he lightly pinched it.

"Does this feel good?" he asked.

The way his hot breath felt on her skin was about to have her come right there.

"Talk to me, Jane."

Did she have to? "Yes, it does," was all she was able to get out.

His mouth claimed hers again, and he pushed her back against the couch. He wasn't gentle about it, and that turned her on even more. He was a take charge kind of man, and Jane was realizing more and more that she got a kick out of that.

Her legs spread open so he could easily position himself between them. She tugged at his shirt and let her hands slide underneath it. Rubbing her palms across his chest, she moaned. He was so hard and built. This was a man who took care of himself. Damn, she couldn't wait to see him out of his clothes.

"Uh, Jane," he said.

Realizing he was no longer feasting on her, her eyes opened and she stared up at him.

"By any chance, your feet aren't wet, are they?"

"Huh?" What was he talking about?

"I didn't think so." Ben pulled away from her and Jane looked around him. Toby had joined them at some point and was licking Ben's back.

"Oh my God!" She jumped up off the couch. "Toby, no! Bad dog! Oh my God, I'm so sorry," she shrieked.

Could this get any more humiliating? She glanced at Ben and saw he was laughing.

"It's okay," he said.

She shook her head.

"He just got overexcited. It's fine, really."

She sat back down beside him and buried her face in her hands. "I don't know how you're laughing. I'm so embarrassed."

"Don't worry about it. Really."

Looking at him, she saw he actually was amused and not at all mortified by her dog. Where had this man come from? Ben handed her shirt to her and she slipped it back on.

"It was probably a good thing we stopped anyway," he

said. "I think we should get to know one another better before we go where we were most likely headed."

Yes, she was a goner. Was this man sent from heaven? What man ever wanted to get to know a woman better before getting her into bed?

"How about I pick you and Toby up tomorrow and we work on a little training?" he asked.

"Oh, you don't have to do that."

"I'd like to. Maybe a picnic at my place and while we eat he can play with my danes. Does that sound good?"

She nodded.

Ben laughed. "Francesca was right. You really are a woman of few words." He cupped her face and kissed her. "I like it though. It keeps me on my toes. I never know what you're thinking."

He stood and pulled her up with him. Taking her hand he led her to the front door.

"I'll pick you up around five tomorrow. Sound good?"

"Perfect," she said.

He cupped her face and kissed her again. A light and sensual kiss that restarted her engine and told her a cold shower was in order.

"Sorry, I had to have one more taste." He kissed her hand and then left.

Once again, she stood in awe as he went to his car. He was amazing.

Turning toward her dog, she pointed a finger at him. "You. I don't even know what to say. You licked his back? Geesh." Jane scratched the dog behind his ears. Perhaps the dog did do her a favor. She didn't need to sleep with Ben. At least not yet.

Chapter 5

Ben was ecstatic to be picking Jane up. She was a mystery and a woman of few words, which surprised him. She came across as a bubbly type person and he had expected her to talk his ear off—which was what he was used to. Most of the women he'd dated were stuck on themselves. Everything revolved around them and what they liked to talk about.

He wasn't getting any younger, and since he was almost over the hump in the forties, he was ready to settle down. He'd had his fun. Jane seemed like someone who didn't want to play the field. Someone that was ready for what he wanted too.

The only thing he had to figure out now was did she actually like him? Or was this all about her ex? Francesca had made it seem as though Jane wanted the guy back, but that wasn't what he was getting from her. In fact, as he got to know her more, he was clueless about how she'd gotten caught up in a scheme like this. She seemed so levelheaded, there was no way she came up with this idea. He was sure Francesca had dragged her into it.

He'd known Francesca for years. He'd debated a few

times about asking her out, but he knew she wasn't the marrying type, at least for him. She cruised from man to man, let them spoil her rotten, and then moved to the next guy with money. Maybe one day she would finally settle down, but until then, there were plenty of men who would gladly hold their arms out for her to hang on to.

Ben pulled up to Jane's house. He liked her little place. It was charming and cozy. He wondered what she would think of his. Usually it impressed women, and while he wanted to do just that with Jane, he didn't want it to be the same way. He really wanted her to just like him.

Before he even made it to the door, Jane was on her way out, being tugged by Toby. Ben laughed and took the leash from her. This dog definitely needed some training and so did the owner. He hoped he could be some use to her.

He was about to lean in for a kiss, but she turned her back to him and locked the door. She put her key in her purse then smiled brightly and asked if he was ready to go. Without a glance back she trotted toward the car. He followed with Toby, wondering if she'd purposely brushed him off.

As she climbed in, he took a moment to look her over. She was dressed in khakis and a light pink blouse. Before she shut the car door, he caught a glimpse of a light brown heel on her foot. He chuckled, she was dressed up more than he was. He'd actually dressed down for today. A feeling of concern came over him now as he wondered if she was doing it because she felt she had to.

Toby hopped into the backseat and then Ben sat down in the driver's side. Jane looked serious, but she was still breathtakingly beautiful. Once again her long brown hair had a slight curl to it. Even though he thought she looked nice, she had looked downright sexy yesterday in her torn jeans and baggy t-shirt. Her hair had been in a messy bun and he still imagined himself grabbing her by it and possessing her mouth.

He had to brace himself. He'd always been a take control kind of guy, especially in the bedroom. Each time he was with Jane, he just knew she was perfect. She wouldn't mind letting him take the lead. Blinking his eyes, he warned himself yet again to get away from this thinking.

"How are you today?" he finally asked.

"Fine."

Ben couldn't help but feel a bit frustrated. And he didn't play games. "Are you upset about yesterday?"

She shook her head.

Normally he found it cute the way she didn't speak a

lot. But at the moment, it was irritating. "You don't seem like yourself."

"It's nothing."

"It's obviously something. I'm not driving until you tell me what's wrong. If you don't want to go to my place, just say so. I'm not going to force you to do anything you don't want."

"I want to go. I guess I'm still a little embarrassed about yesterday. It was awfully forward of me to have been doing what you and I were doing on the couch. I don't normally move so fast. There's just something about the way you make me feel...I don't always feel like I'm in control," she rambled.

"You have no reason to be embarrassed about anything. We were both there. Like I said before, don't do anything you don't want to." He grinned and leaned closer to her. "Though I must admit, it does this old man's pride good to know you have a hard time controlling yourself around me."

She averted her eyes, and he dropped his gaze and stared at her lips. They parted slightly and he knew that if he wanted to, he could take them. Suck them, lick them, treasure them. But not yet. He settled back in his seat and started the car. When he glanced back at her, he could see the slight disappointment on her face. He would make up for that later.

The drive to the house was mostly quiet. The dog panted the whole time and he could tell Toby didn't go on many car rides. Maybe that would change if he and Jane started to see one another. The dog needed some interaction with his kind and his girls would be perfect.

As they pulled up to his driveway and he came to his gate that required a code to punch in, he was actually nervous. Never before had he wanted a woman to *not* be impressed by his place. He worried it would be too much for her and she wouldn't want to see him again.

He looked at his house with new eyes as they pulled up to the almost mansion looking place. There were four white columns that went from the ground floor up to the second. The house was mainly brick with white siding at the top. Windows were all over. He liked light. The yard was well cared for by a weekly landscaping crew.

He looked over at Jane. She appeared to be in awe. Her eyes were wide as she took it all in.

"Wow, this is your house?" she asked.

"It is."

"And only you live here?"

"Me, Olive, and Pepper."

She smiled over at him.

He parked the car outside the garage. He didn't dare open the door for her to see that he had three other vehicles.

He got out of the car and got Toby first. As he jogged around to get her door, she opened it herself and stepped out. He let his eyes take her in again. She looked sexy. Her blouse was unbuttoned low enough that he caught a glimpse of a white camisole playing peek-a-boo. There wasn't any way he couldn't explore today. If she was willing, he was definitely taking. He wasn't turning her down.

He took her hand and like always it fit perfectly in his. With Toby's leash in the other, he took her inside his house. Right as they entered and before he got the door shut Olive and Pepper came running to greet them. Jane's eyes lit up as she saw his giant girls sitting in front of them, doing their best to control themselves as they waited for him to pet them.

"I get knocked over by Toby each time I come in."

"I had to train them not to do that. Could you imagine two one-hundred-and-fifty pound dogs knocking me over every day?"

She shook her head.

He pet both his girls and then led them all through the house to the door in the kitchen where it took them to his fenced in back yard.

"Let's go out here a moment and let them get acquainted."

He kept Toby on the leash, but left it slack so the three dogs could freely sniff one another. It only took a few minutes before the dogs all had wagging tails and he decided to let Toby off the leash. The dogs ran around the yard and seemed to be instant buddies.

"I need to make a quick phone call. Want to come inside for a bit?" he asked.

"Sure."

Inside he offered her a drink but she declined. He wished he could get into her head and know what she was thinking. Maybe after a few minutes to herself she would be more open.

* * * *

As soon as Ben left the kitchen, Jane worried she just might faint. She had only seen houses as big and as gorgeous as this one on TV. This place was magnificent. The countertops were a dark marble and all the appliances were chrome. The kitchen had one of those islands with pans hanging above it. You could probably fit an entire army inside of the kitchen. She was completely out of her element.

A glance out the window showed the dogs having a fun time. If she had driven here she most likely would've grabbed Toby and ran while Ben was busy with his phone call. This house probably impressed many women right into his bed, but all it did for her was make her feel embarrassed that he had seen her tiny house.

As she watched the dogs she started to think about the future—if they had one. Her parents weren't too much older than him. What would they think? Plus, he had never been married, which was a bit unusual for a man his age, and she wondered if maybe he had a commitment phobia. After the games Matt had played with her, was she willing to be with someone who might not want a long-term commitment? This was all a lot to think about, but if she didn't clear her mind soon, she was going to have a panic attack.

She moved away from the window and peeked her head out of one of the kitchen doorways and saw a grand dining room. It had a huge table that sat eight people on each side. Good God, who had that many people over at once? Stepping back into the kitchen she decided that maybe she needed that drink. Her mouth was feeling dry.

As she was about to open the fridge Ben returned.

"Miss me?" he asked.

She smiled at him, knowing it was one of those

awkward smiles that would leave him asking questions to himself.

"Just thirsty, actually."

"What can I get you?" he asked.

"Water would be fine." Jane stepped back as he moved toward the fridge and opened it for her.

He pulled out a bottle and she saw it was no store brand water. It came in a glass bottle with a name she couldn't even pronounce. The man even bought expensive water. Didn't he know water was water? Geesh, rich people.

Ben removed the cap and handed it to her.

"Thanks," she said.

"Want a tour?"

She hesitated, taking a long sip of water before setting the bottle down. The more she saw of the house, the more out of place she felt. But then she remembered her manners. "I'd love one."

Thankfully, he skipped the dining room and led her to the living room then to his study. Each room was spotless and looked as though it had been professionally decorated. She couldn't find anything out of place. He took her up the spiral staircase where she saw a row of doors closed, except the one at the end. He took her straight to the open one. When they went inside her eyes widened and she burst out laughing. The room was a wreck. Clothes were strewn everywhere, the bed was unmade. Books and DVDs were in piles all over.

"I think the maid forgot this room." She crossed her arms with a smirk on her face.

"This is my room, and I take care of it. I keep it the way I like it."

"Messy?"

"Damn right. Did you see the rest of the house?"

She nodded.

"Then you see why this place is a wreck."

"I wasn't expecting to see your room like this. It makes you seem a little more human." She felt a lot more comfortable in here than anywhere else.

"Believe me, I'm not clean. You'll either find me in my study or up here. I never use the dining room or the living room. I'm too afraid I might get a fingerprint on something."

"But it's your house. You don't have to keep it that way."

"You're right, but I don't really need all those rooms anyway."

"Why the big house then?"

"To be honest, I thought once I had the house I'd find

my wife and we'd fill this giant thing with kids."

"You might still find her."

"I might." He smiled.

He took her hand and walked toward the double doors. When opened they led out to a deck that overlooked the back yard. Toby ran around with Olive and Pepper, having a grand time it looked like. Hopefully he would be good and worn-out and not be too much of a pest later when they got home.

As she looked over the yard, two strong arms wrapped around her waist. Ben's warm breath tickled her neck, and she braced herself for his lips to meet her skin. It didn't take him long. He kissed a line from the back of her neck to her chin. Spinning her around, he slammed his lips against hers and she gasped from the force.

"I can't control myself around you." He groaned. "I just have to touch you."

"Then touch me," she panted.

His hands yanked at her waist and his erection pressed into her. Just the feel of him hard made her squeeze her legs together to contain the wetness. He kissed her from her mouth, down her jaw, and to the spot right at her collarbone that made her moan. His kisses were light and fluttery and sent shivers through her. At this point she didn't care how far they went, just as long as his mouth was on her.

Jane rubbed her hands across his chest and then up around his neck and into his hair. It was softer than she expected and long enough that she could curl her fingers into it. One leg came up out of instinct and wrapped around his waist, pushing his erection right into her core.

He leaned her back against the railing, and she silently prayed it was strong enough to hold them both, otherwise it was going to be a long, hard fall to the ground. But as one of his hands snuck under her shirt and into her bra she no longer cared about that fall.

Jane was greedy and she needed his lips back on hers. She tilted his head up and took them. There was nothing gentle about this kiss. It was raw and full of desire.

He fiddled with the top of her pants and when she thought about what was to come her pussy grew more moist. She couldn't wait to see how his fingers would feel. Would he be rough and just drive into her, or would he take his time, getting his fingers fully coated with her juices before he thrust up into her?

His hand slid in and right before he met her sex his lips left hers and returned to the spot on her collarbone that drove her insane. His finger dipped into her pussy and she groaned. He circled her clit several times before she got her answer. Two fingers at a time he entered her.

"Oh my…" she called out.

"Do you like that?" he asked.

She couldn't answer. Not only was he entering her, but with his thumb he flicked her clitoris and she saw stars and fireworks.

"You're so wet." He kissed her neck again.

Jane couldn't hold back anymore. She thrust her hips into his hand and rode out the orgasm. His speed picked up and she cried out, waves of pleasure rolling through her body with the force of a hurricane.

When it was over, she clung to him and laid her head on his shoulder. She had never been fingered so damn good in her life. She could only imagine how good he could fuck.

After she finally caught her breath, she realized how selfish she had been and that she should return the favor. Licking her lips, she knew just what she wanted to do to him.

She kissed his neck and started to move down his body when he caught her and pulled her back up. Jane looked at him confused. He was still hard, she knew since he was still pressing against her.

"We have plenty of time for that later." He pressed his lips to hers.

Enjoying the kiss, she was sad when he stopped.

"I'm starved. How about that picnic I promised? Then we'll work with Toby some."

"Sounds great."

Ben took her hand and led her off the balcony and back inside. As they made their way through the house, Jane straightened her clothes and she couldn't help but feel a little raunchy. She let him have his way with her right out in the open, and she enjoyed every second of it and fully lost herself in the pleasure. And he seemed absolutely okay with not receiving anything back. She supposed she could have been more persistent about pleasuring him, but she'd never been one to take control in the sex department.

Chapter 6

It had taken every ounce of Ben's self-control not to let Jane drop to her knees and let that pretty little mouth wrap itself around his swollen cock. As much as he wanted things to go forward, he knew how out of place she felt and realized it was best to go slow with her. From now on they would only share a few kisses, even though whenever he kissed her, something ignited in him and he had to have her.

Groaning, he remembered her pussy had been so wet and so ready for him. As he'd slid his fingers in and out, he'd imagined what it would feel like on his dick. She was tight, and when her muscles spasmed and milked his fingers, his manhood had been very jealous.

Now he had to get through lunch somehow without bending her over the table and having his way with her. He shook his head in an attempt to clear his thoughts.

He opened the fridge and reached for two Cokes. Originally he had planned on a chilled bottle of wine, but he didn't need any alcohol in the mix. Things would definitely get out of hand then.

Jane was already outside taking out all the contents from the picnic basket he'd packed and setting them on the patio table. He kissed her on the cheek before he took a seat. She blushed and it warmed his heart to know he had that effect on her. She was so different from other women. She was real and kind, and he knew she wasn't concerned with what he could do for her. Jane seemed like she genuinely enjoyed her time with him the way he did with her.

He was falling for her, that was for sure. He'd been waiting his entire adult life for someone like Jane. There was no way he could let her go. All he could do now was hope she felt the same way, and if she didn't then he could persuade her to. Jane wasn't someone who he could buy things for to make her fall for him. No, that would be too easy. He was going to have to show her. But it didn't seem too hard. With Jane it just seemed to fall into place.

Jane took her seat after setting everything out.

"Thank you so much. I got lost in thought and I must look so rude."

She giggled. "You're fine. What was going through that head of yours anyway? You looked miles away."

"I was just thinking about you."

"Good, I hope."

"Always."

Jane opened her Coke and he watched her press it to her lips and tilt her head back, letting the liquid flow from the can to her mouth. Good God, what was wrong with him? There was absolutely nothing sexy about a person drinking, but somehow his mind was turning something so simple into something erotic. His mind was being clouded with thoughts he hadn't experienced since he was in his twenties.

"Thanks for all the trouble you went through on the picnic," she said as she placed the drink down.

"I wasn't sure what you liked, so I went the safe route with sandwiches, fruit, and good ol' fattening potato chips."

"You did awesome. And I love chips."

As Ben was about to take a bite of his sandwich, Toby came bounding toward them at full force.

"Stop, Toby!" Jane yelled.

Ben dropped his sandwich onto his plate and stood quickly. "No, Toby."

The dog halted and he let out a sigh of relief. That could've been bad. As he was about to take a seat, Toby plopped his paws onto the table and laid his head on it, giving them a sad puppy face. Jane ooed and awed over the dog and then handed him a chip. No wonder the dog did whatever he wanted. Even though he was being disobedient, he still got rewarded.

"You know that isn't helping if you want to train him."

"I know." She shrugged. "But look at that sweet face. Are you going to tell me you could resist it?"

"Yes, I could."

"I guess I just love this boy too much." She proceeded to scratch him behind the ears.

A bit of jealousy swept through Ben. Perhaps he should lay his head on the table and see what would happen. Would he get rewarded the same way?

"Okay, Toby, that's enough," she said to the dog.

He wasn't the least bit surprised that the dog didn't listen and even whined a bit when Jane was no longer paying attention to him. He was beginning to think Jane needed more training than the dog did.

"Toby, off," Ben commanded.

The dog ignored him too. He couldn't help then but laugh about this.

Jane looked at him quizzically. "What are you laughing about?"

"I love this. This moment, our time together, and your dog. He brings so much to the mix."

"He is something all right." She petted the dog on the head again.

"I spent so much time training Olive and Pepper that I don't often enjoy moments like this. And seeing Toby in all his glory just reminds me that dogs can bring an abundance of joy into your life."

Toby barked in response. Ben had hoped for a romantic picnic with Jane, but instead it turned into something fun.

By the time they finished lunch, he had laughed more than he could remember. Jane was so much fun and she erupted all these feelings in him that he hadn't had in so long. He really hoped she felt the same way.

* * * *

Jane did her absolute best to pay attention as Ben went over the basics with her. But each time he bent over to help put Toby in a sit, her eyes went straight to his backside. She could probably stare at that round, firm ass all day. He obviously worked out and she bet that if she got the chance to squeeze it, she would find it rock hard.

"You try," Ben said, snapping her out of her thoughts. "Put Toby on your left side. Only tell him to sit one time. If you repeat it, your dog will learn to ignore you until you reach a certain number. If he doesn't listen, place your hand gently on his back, put him in a sit, then hand him his treat."

She placed herself next to Toby. The dog looked up at her as if waiting for her to tell him something. So she told him to sit. Fully expecting the dog to ignore her, she was surprised when he just sat and looked up at her. Jane jumped up and down and praised the dog over and over then handed him his biscuit.

"Great job. Now pick a word such as okay and use that when you want him to be released from the sit."

"Okay, Toby," she said animatedly.

The dog stood.

"Do it again," Ben said.

She gave the dog the command once again and was impressed when Toby sat. "He really picked that up fast just from you working with him." She handed the dog his treat.

"Labs are smart and fairly easy to train. Just be sure to have a quiet environment while you teach him so he concentrates on you. Once he sees you as the alpha, things should get a little better. I have an awesome book inside you can take home and read. And of course, I'll keep working with both of you."

Jane stepped forward and wrapped her arms around Ben's waist and placed a kiss on his cheek. "You're a miracle."

He smiled down at her. She felt so comfortable and at home in his arms. Several times he'd told her that he liked her and she wondered if things would actually work out. Would a relationship really work between them when they came from such different worlds? He was used to women who went to the spa, got their hair and nails done, and probably oohed and ahhed over his house. Maybe she was just a fling for now until he realized she was nothing like them.

"I guess I should probably get you home," he said as he released her and stepped away.

She couldn't help but feel a little sad. She enjoyed his touch. Ben seemed to keep finding ways to distance themselves from one another. Maybe he thought she was easy after she fooled around with him upstairs. Or worse, maybe she looked selfish. Perhaps at her house she could persuade him to come in.

"I guess so. I've had a great time today."

"Me too." Ben called Toby over and hooked the leash onto him. "I bet he sleeps well for you tonight after training and playing with my girls."

"I can't wait."

The drive home was fairly quiet. They chatted a little more about training and he assured her if she stuck with it both she and Toby would be happier, which made her chuckle. Did a dog really care? She spoiled her pets rotten and was pretty sure they were already loving life. She figured she'd give it a go, but wasn't making any promises.

She really just cared about getting control on the leash.

Once back at her tiny little house that looked like a shack compared to his, she let Toby into the house and then came back onto the front porch where Ben waited.

"Would you like to come in for a bit?" she asked.

"Normally I would love to, but I don't think I should today."

"I promise not to bite."

He smirked. "I'm not worried about being bitten."

She took his hand and held it in hers.

"You're making it hard for me to resist you," he said.

"Then don't."

Ben pulled her to him and took her lips. Reaching up, she gripped the back of his neck, pressing her body into him as much as she could. She loved the way he made her feel every time his lips touched her. She didn't know if she could ever tire of it. It was as though he lit her insides on fire, and every nerve ending stood and sent shivers through her body. Her heart would race and all she wanted was more.

What if she was coming off as a clingy woman and that's why he was resisting? As much as she was enjoying this kiss and the way his hands rubbed circles on her lower back, it was best to end it.

It took a few more moments before she was able to will her lips away from his. Ben started to kiss her cheek and down her jawbone, then over to her ear. Dear God, this man was going to do her in. As his tongue came out and he lightly left little licks with his kisses she thought her knees just might give out.

"No more," she finally said, pushing him away. "If we don't stop now we're likely to give the neighbors a free show. And since you don't want to come in, it's probably best to say goodbye."

"You're probably right."

Her eyes drifted down and she saw the bulge in his pants. Hopefully this was as difficult for him as it was her. She would love to have him in her bed right now.

"Thank you for today. I had a great time," she said.

"Me too. I hope we can do it again soon." He paused a moment and she could tell there was something he was wanting to say. "Before we take this any further, I need to know where I stand when it comes to Matt."

Matt, damn she'd forgotten about him. "I'm not with Matt."

"I hope not. But do you still want to be putting on this show that I'm your fake boyfriend?"

Shit, he used the word fake. Was he already tired of

her? "No, I suppose not. You're released from you duties."

He leaned in and planted a kiss on her cheek. "I'll call you soon, and we'll plan something. How does that sound?"

"Good." She hoped he meant it and this wasn't his way of saying goodbye. "You're welcome to come by anytime and take me to lunch."

"Maybe I'll come tomorrow."

"I'd really like it if you did."

"I'll text you in the morning to let you know for sure. Is that okay?"

She nodded.

"You are a woman of few words." He laughed then turned and headed toward his car.

Jane stood on the porch and watched as he pulled away. She couldn't figure out yet if he really liked her and they would continue seeing each other, or if this was the end. He'd finished what he'd agreed to and he could return to his usual life.

Letting out a loud sigh, she headed inside. She'd wait for the text message in the morning and maybe then she would have her answer.

* * * *

As Ben drove home he couldn't help but feel giddy. It was those damn teenage feelings again. Now that he knew that jackass Matt was out of the picture, he could fully move forward with Jane. He'd hated having it in the back of his mind that she might have still wanted him. When he had mentioned Matt's name, Jane had actually looked confused for a moment, as if she had totally forgotten the man existed. That was a good thing.

Now he hoped he could get his schedule changed around tomorrow so he could meet her for lunch. If he had his way, he'd meet her for lunch every day for the rest of his life.

Ben entered his house and was immediately greeted by Olive and Pepper. He petted both dogs and then headed up the stairs to the only room he was comfortable in. Maybe one day Jane would help him fill this house with love and children.

Chapter 7

"Morning, Jane!" Francesca bounded up to the front desk.

"Hey. You're here early." Jane glanced at the clock. Francesca usually came later in the day.

"I have a date tonight."

"Cool."

"So, how's it going with Ben?"

"Good."

"Has he been making Matt sweat and realize just what he could've had?"

Jane shrugged. Matt was just around the corner and she worried he could walk up at any time.

"Don't you have anything to dish?" Francesca asked.

Jane had always kept her life to herself. She supposed she had Francesca to thank for setting her up with Ben, but until she knew for sure what Ben wanted from her, she didn't want to talk about it.

"No news, sorry."

"Guess I'm going to workout since you don't want to chat. Maybe once you wake up a bit." Francesca did her usual Ms. America wave and jogged toward the cardio area.

Jane grabbed the window cleaner and paper towels and decided to wipe off any prints that had gotten on the door already today. Once all the streaks were gone she turned to head back to her station. But as she turned, she walked right into a chest she was familiar with.

"Excuse me, sor-ry," she stuttered.

"It's nice to see I can still make you stutter." Matt arrogantly laughed.

"I just wasn't expecting to bump into anyone. It had nothing to do with you."

He crossed his arms. "Can I see you in my office?"

"What is it about?"

"Last I checked I was your boss, so what does it matter?"

"It matters if it's professional or not," she snapped.

"I like you being feisty." He leaned by her ear. "It makes me hard."

Her eyes widened. What had she ever seen in this man?

"I need you in my office in ten minutes." He walked away.

Jane stomped back toward the reception area and threw the paper towels away. She tossed the window cleaner back into the cabinet. Could she continue working here if she wasn't with Matt? He was going to make her life a living hell. He was the one who ended their relationship and now the jealousy over Ben was causing him to be a jackass. Why did she ever take Francesca's advice? What good was coming from this?

If there was one thing she knew though, she wasn't going to his office. Whatever he needed to discuss could be talked about out here. Even if things didn't work out with Ben, she wasn't going down that road again. It was over with Matt, and all she could do was hope he got the message soon. Maybe once the next bombshell paid him attention.

Matt poked his head around the corner and said, "Jane, I'm waiting."

"I'm sorry, but whatever you need to tell me can be told here."

"Are you sure?"

"Yes." Thank God the gym wasn't booming like usual or this would have been extremely inappropriate.

"Fine, have it your way. I'm cutting your hours to get our labor under control."

"You're what?" Was he kidding her?

"You'll now work the morning shift, no lunch break, and will leave each day by two."

Oh, he was a jealous asshole all right. Cutting out her

lunch break.

"When will I eat lunch?"

"After two. Or during your thirty minute break at ten. Oh, and this is effective immediately."

"I have lunch plans today."

"Sorry, guess you'll have to tell Grandpa you can't meet him today."

Jane rubbed her hands through her hair. This was a disaster. Why the hell did she ever like that jerk?

Matt left with a smirk on his face, and if she could have, she would have loved to slap it right off. *Ugh!* She picked up her cellphone and sent a text message to Ben letting him know her hours had changed and lunch would have to be canceled. As she started to slide the phone back into her purse it beeped. He asked if she had a break and said he needed to talk to her. She replied that she had one at ten. Was this day about to get even worse?

* * * *

At ten Jane grabbed her purse and went out front to wait on Ben. She was surprised to see he was already there. Since they only had a little time they decided to head across the street to Sweet Muffins for coffee and a snack.

Amy greeted them as they entered. Adam, her fiancé, was behind the counter with her. Those two were inseparable these days as they prepared for their wedding. Amy wanted a big, grand wedding and all Adam wanted was to make it official so they could start popping babies out. It was ironic since only a few months ago Adam was running from the idea of just a commitment.

After they had their order they took a seat at a small bistro table near the front.

"Sorry you're having a bad day," Ben said.

"Is it going to get better or do you have bad news for me?"

Ben took a deep breath and she knew it wasn't going to be good news.

"It depends on how you look at it. A buddy of mine out of state has told me about a property that I would be crazy if I didn't try to get it. It's a steal. I have to catch a flight later today to go out there to place my bid. And if I get the house, I'll need to spend some time there getting it ready to turn around. So, there could be a lot of travel in my future or I'll be back in a few days and wait for the next deal."

That wasn't too bad she supposed. He hadn't told her he didn't want to see her anymore.

"I really hate giving you that news on a day like today."

"Well, it's not like you can control it."

Ben reached over and took her hand. His fingers rubbed the inside of her palm. "When I get back I want to take you out."

"I'd like that."

"Jane, I like you. A lot."

"I like you too."

His other hand rubbed her thigh under the table. "I wish we had more than thirty minutes."

"Me too." She leaned forward a little. "I'd like to do a little more than kissing."

Ben groaned. "You make me feel so young again."

She laughed. "It's not like you're old."

"Compared to you I am."

"You and I are very opposite in more than one way. But I think that's why I like you."

His hand crept up her thigh a little more. As she gazed back at him, she heard a ringing in her purse. Reaching in she took her phone out, seeing it was the gym. As she hit the *answer* button she pulled away from Ben.

"Hello," she said.

"We don't need you back today. We're over budget for the week so take the rest of the day off," Matt said.

"Are you kidding me?'

"Nope. See you tomorrow. Enjoy your time with

Grandpa." He disconnected.

Jane let out a frustrated sigh. Then she remembered the hunk of a man in front of her and an idea crossed her mind. "What time's your flight?"

"Later this afternoon. Why?"

"Well, it's only ten thirty and I'm not needed back at work today."

"He can't do that," Ben argued.

Jane reached under the table and squeezed his knee. "How about we go back to my place and do a little more than kiss?"

Ben's eyes lit up. "Are you sure it isn't too soon?"

"Every time you kiss me you set me on fire. And I know exactly how you can hose me down."

"Then let's go. You don't have to tell me twice."

Ben grabbed her hand and they rushed out of Sweet Muffins without a glance back.

They drove separately and Jane arrived first. She raced toward her door and once inside, she debated stripping down right there. But then the thought of him taking her clothes off layer by layer as his lips kissed all over her body sounded even better.

She let Toby out for a quick potty break and hoped like hell the dog would *not* bother them this time. Just as Toby finished his business, Ben pulled up. The dog greeted him and came right in with him.

An awkwardness set in for a moment but then Jane remembered what they were there for, and it wasn't to stand in her living room as the dog sniffed Ben up and down.

"I believe you're needed in the bedroom," she told him, then looked at the dog. "And you are not."

Ben followed her to her room and she shut the door behind him. Now she wished she'd taken the time to clean the place up. Then again, she'd seen his room and they weren't all too different.

Her gaze followed Ben's hands as he rubbed them up the tall columns on her bed. "I'm getting a few ideas."

"Oh really, and what are they?"

"Maybe I'll restrain you as I explore each and every inch of you."

Her pussy immediately grew damp at that thought. She would be giving him full control of her pleasure, and she really liked that idea.

Jane pulled her shirt over her head, revealing a simple white bra. At least she had on a matching thong, even though this wasn't her pretty underwear. She then slithered out of her slacks. Climbing on the bed, she sat back and said, "I'm ready."

"Good God, Jane, you're going to be the death of me."

"There are scarves hanging in the closet."

"You're really okay with this?"

She nodded. It didn't take him long to go to the closet, yank out two scarves, and return to the bed. As he tied her loosely to the bed, his cock was near her face. She couldn't wait to get a taste of it.

"Is it too tight?" he asked.

"No, it's perfect."

"You have no idea how turned on I am right now."

"I think I do." Her eyes were on his zipper that looked as though it might bust open any second.

Ben groaned and she licked her lips, hoping he would take the sign. The thought of his cock in her mouth while he had full control of when she would stop sucking turned her on immensely.

He took the hint and at the speed of light he wiggled out of his pants and boxers. He gave her an extra treat when he removed his shirt too and she was left with the sexiest man she'd ever seen. He was better looking naked than she had imagined. His chest was firm and his muscles were outlined like those men in magazine ads. His cock stood long, hard, and thick. Her mouth watered as he straddled her and brought that piece of perfection to her mouth. She opened right away and let him slid in. He was so thick she had to open her mouth wider to accommodate him.

"I don't know how long I can do this. I'm so turned on." His eyes glared down, watching as he pulled out and then entered her again.

She moaned against him as he pumped in a slow motion. As he got deeper into her throat, she swallowed, letting her muscle squeeze him. Based on the grunt that came from him, she was pretty sure he liked that. Her tongue massaged the vein on the underside.

His breathing quickened and just as she thought she was going to get a taste, he slipped out, leaving her mouth open and empty.

"Your mouth is wicked. But I don't want this over yet."

"I'm looking forward to what your mouth can do."

"Don't worry, I'm going to have my way with you." He eyed her restraints. "And there is nothing you can do to stop me as I send you over the top repeatedly."

Shivers swept through her as she braced herself for what was to come. She couldn't believe they were doing this, but she was glad and couldn't wait to do it again and again.

Ben started to kiss her. As always, it was magical and

got her engines roaring to life. Each time he pressed his lips to hers, it was as though a magnet was pulling them together. If he only kissed her for the rest of her life, she'd die happy. But as his lips moved off hers and started a trail down her neck to her breasts, she was about to find out how much more pleasure those lips could give.

She gripped the pole as he unbuckled her strapless bra. Tossing it across the room, he drew in a nipple and pinched the other one. His tongue swirled around and then he changed breasts, teasing the next.

Not only were his lips amazing, but his tongue sent a whole new set of waves through her. As he started to move lower she wanted to squeeze her thighs together. She was going to come just thinking about it. His fingers gripped her thong and tugged it down, and she gasped as the cool air met her pussy.

"Lift your legs and spread them," he commanded.

Not sure what he was wanting exactly, she opened wide and then lifted up onto her toes.

"Perfect." He slipped between her thighs. "Wrap your legs around me now, tightly, and hold on."

Doing as he said, she really had to brace herself now. His hands held her up by her ass and her pussy was in his face, and as she glanced down at him, he looked ready to feast. She wasn't sure how long she could stay in the position, but she was pretty sure she was going to enjoy what was next.

His mouth covered her core and as he sucked the whole area. His tongue poked at her opening. "You taste like honey," he said into her.

He then started to lick her from back to front. Her eyes closed as she focused on the pleasure he was giving her. One of his fingers dipped to the opening of her ass and lightly swirled around it as his tongue flicked her clit.

"Have you ever had your ass fingered?" he asked.

She shook her head. Anal play had never been something she was interested in, but the way he was making her feel at this moment, she had full trust he wouldn't do it unless it was going to intensify her pleasure.

Holding her up with one hand now, he started to finger her pussy, getting his hand all coated in her juices. Between how incredibly good he was making her feel and the slight pain from her body protesting the position, she didn't know how much more she could take.

His mouth reclaimed her entire sex and his digit, which was fully lubricated by her juices, once again played with the opening between her cheeks. He entered slowly and a whole new wave of pleasure shot through her and she screamed out. Her body felt the need to move, but it was impossible to do with the way he held her.

"I need more, and I need it fast," she called out. "Please, I need it."

His tongue dove into her pussy opening and his finger pumped into her ass, and all she could do was scream from the pleasure. Her orgasm hit her with such force that she thought she might die as it tore through her.

Ben released her body down to the bed and kissed his way up to her breasts. "Are you ready for more?"

"I think so."

"Good, because it isn't over yet."

He got off her a moment and reached into his pants and pulled out his wallet. He found a condom and then climbed back onto the bed. She watched as he rolled the condom over his erection, and she was amazed how wet she was again with anticipation that it was going to fill her. Ben untied her arms before nestling his way between her thighs.

She wrapped her arms around his neck and brought his mouth to hers. She thrust her tongue in right as he entered her. He pumped into her fast. The kiss was sloppy, but she didn't care. She needed his mouth on hers.

Grinding her hips up, moving into him the way she needed to, she couldn't believe an orgasm was already building. This man was incredible.

He broke the kiss and held himself up by his arms. He brought his dick out until it was only tip deep and shallowly thrust into her.

"That feels amazing." She panted.

"You feel amazing wrapped around me. You're so damn tight, I can't hold out much longer."

"Don't."

He smirked a little and then drove back into her. Arching her body, she moaned as a ripple of pleasure started to move through her. Ben pinched her nipples and he slammed into her harder. She found her release right as he did. Gripping his shoulders as he flicked her nipples, they each rode it out.

Ben collapsed on top of her. His body on hers felt incredible. Being with him was even better than she thought possible. He had pleasured her fully. She'd only known him a short while, but she was beginning to think she just might be falling in love with him. He certainly wasn't who she thought she would find herself with, but as she got to know him more and more, she wasn't sure she could live without him. It seemed as though she had accidentally fallen in love with him along the way.

Chapter 8

It had been a week since Jane had seen Ben. Luck was in his favor and he got the house he had bid on. So he was fast at work getting the house all set up. Each night he called her and she enjoyed hearing the excitement in his tone. She could see he really loved what he did. He would be traveling a little more for now, but promised when he was home he would spend all his free time with her. It was the thing keeping her going at the moment

Work was hell. Matt was making her life as horrible as possible. At this point she was actually worried she was going to lose her job. He hired a new receptionist, which made no sense. He claimed they needed to save money, but was able to find a way to hire a young girl who didn't look much older than twenty. She giggled and texted all day. The men at the gym loved her, including Matt. As much as Jane hated to admit it, she was jealous. And not for the reason that Matt obviously wanted the girl, it was that she was taking her job.

Jane was lucky if she got to work until two. There was always an excuse as to why she had to leave early. Jane hated the idea of leaving Hot Bods. Her co-workers were what made the place so enjoyable, and she couldn't imagine not seeing them every day like she had over the past five years. But with the situation with Matt, she might have to start looking for another job.

Letting out a loud sigh, she stood up from the table in the employee break room. It was time to return to the front and quit having a pity party. Jane put on her happy face and made her way through the gym, saying "hi" to different members. She wished Skylar was back from her honeymoon. Right about now she could really use a friend.

At the computer up front, she logged on to clock-in but was interrupted by Matt.

"Casey will be here in about ten minutes. We probably don't need you."

That was it, she'd had enough. "I need the hours. I was hired full-time and I'm not even getting twenty hours a week right now. You need to call her and tell her to wait until two."

He laughed. "Who made you boss?" He stepped up behind her and leaned in to whisper, "Maybe if you start fucking me again we can work something out. I always liked the way your mouth wrapped around my cock felt."

Her eyes opened wide. "Enough. This isn't appropriate. If you keep it up I'm going to report you."

"To who? I'm the boss."

She spun around and looked at him. "You don't own the gym. And I'd like to think the owners wouldn't want the man running it to be harassing their employees."

"Don't mess with me, Jane. And now that I think about, you need a change in attitude. Perhaps you should take a few days off to decide if Hot Bods is the right place for you."

"I need the money or I won't have rent."

"Not my problem. You brought this on yourself."

Jane huffed. "Like I said, you're not going to get away with this."

"That's what you think." With a smirk he turned and walked through the gym.

Now she needed to decide what to do. Did she want to just say 'screw it' and get a new job or go after him with everything that she had? She had a few days to figure it out.

"I heard what happened," Francesca said as she came around the corner. She must have been leaving the locker rooms. "And I think I just might be your new best friend."

Jane raised an eyebrow and said, "Why?"

Francesca held up her cellphone. "I recorded it."

"You what?"

"I recorded it. Are you deaf now?"

"All of it?"

"I don't know what he whispered in your ear, but the rest of it is right here. Got an email? I'll send it to you in a file."

Jane scribbled her email on a paper and handed it to Francesca. She tapped away on her phone.

"All sent. Go get your stuff. We can hang out for a bit."

As Jane gathered her things, she was beginning to wonder if Francesca was lonely. She was always hanging around the gym. She'd even made an effort recently to get to know Jane. It wasn't all about her. In fact, the woman never talked about herself, which seemed strangely odd. She came across as self-centered, but in reality Jane knew nothing about her. The most she shared was that she had a date recently. Maybe Francesca wasn't the person she portrayed.

"Ready?" Jane asked as she made her way back up front.

"Yup."

"What did you have in mind?"

"We can go shopping." Francesca opened the door that led outside.

"I wish. With no hours, I'm broke."

"Don't worry, we'll get him together. That jerk won't know what hit him."

Jane smiled. Maybe with Francesca on her side, they really could give Matt what he deserved.

"You can ride with me. We'll start with an early lunch and then go from there. Sound good?"

"As long as it's cheap." Which was something she worried Francesca knew nothing about.

"We can do one of those places that does the meals and appetizer for twenty bucks."

"That works."

"Yay!" Francesca started the car and they were off.

* * * *

Glancing at his watch, Ben saw it was after two. Jane should be off work and he was dying to hear her voice. He still had at least another day here. But he didn't know if he could stand much longer without feeling her in his arms.

"Hey Stan, I'm gonna take a break. You got it?" Ben called.

"Yeah, man. Take your time."

He decided to head to his hotel room for a bit. As he entered his room, he pulled out his phone. Taking a seat on the bed, he realized how worn-out he was and he sprawled out on the bed. He unlocked the screen and was greeted by a picture of Jane as his background. Maybe if he was lucky she'd be home and alone. He could ask her to go to her room and close the door, and then remove her clothes. He'd tell her everything he wanted to do to her. He'd start out with kissing her, then feast on those luscious breasts as he entered her soaking wet pussy two fingers at a time. She'd be so tight around his fingers that his cock would be jealous.

His mind then jumped to her naked and on all fours. He really wanted to take her that way. While he would pump into her, he'd grip her firm ass, maybe even give it a spanking. His cock throbbed as he imagined seeing his handprint on her as he drove into her.

He couldn't take it any longer. Ben unbuttoned his pants and wrapped his hand around his erection. The chance of her being home was slim and he needed relief now. Turning his thoughts back to Jane, he decided to take his fantasy one step farther. He would take her in the ass. That opening would be so tight. As he pumped into her, with his free hand he would tweak her clit. She'd pant and call his name out, letting him know how well he was fucking her and that only *his* dick could pleasure her like this. She'd beg him not to stop.

He jerked his hand fast, up and down the whole length of his cock. As he imagined her screaming, he let out his own moan and shot cum into his hand. Lying there a moment he set the phone down. He needed to gather himself before calling her. Ben sat up and headed to the bathroom for a quick shower.

* * * *

Jane was worn-out and so happy they'd taken a break to get coffee and a snack at Sweet Muffins. They'd shopped all afternoon and neither of them bought anything. Francesca had dragged her up and down the strip, going to this store and that one. She wanted every detail about Ben and was thrilled about how things were working out. Jane was amazed that she actually had a wonderful time with her. There was definitely more to Francesca than people knew. And she was glad she gave her a shot.

Now they were seated outside the bakery, enjoying the cool breeze as they sipped their drinks. Francesca chatted a bit about her brother Adam and his upcoming wedding to Amy. Francesca and Skylar were both going to be in the wedding party. Jane couldn't help but wonder how that was going to go since Francesca and Skylar had a history of not liking one another. To this day they still barely spoke.

"You know Skylar better than I do. Is there a way you think we can get through this in one piece?" Francesca asked.

"You just have to put the past behind you. Skylar is stubborn. Maybe invite her to lunch and talk. I'm sure you two can be friends."

"I was never all that into Drew to begin with. We never even...you know."

Jane smiled as she remembered when Drew first came back into Skylar's life. He had been seeing Francesca at the time, but it wasn't serious. But Skylar held a grudge, and it was hard for her to forgive. "You're going to have to make the first move," Jane said.

"Of course."

Taking a bite of one of Amy's latest creations, Jane was startled by her phone ringing. She picked it up and glanced at the screen. "It's Ben."

"I'll just run inside for a refill."

As Francesca went back into the bakery, Jane answered the phone. "Hey, sexy."

"People are going to think you're a little weird talking to yourself," he said.

Jane giggled. "Whatever. When are you coming back? I miss you, and work really sucks."

"Soon, I promise. I don't think I can stand another day without you."

"I'm glad to hear that."

"Things still aren't better at Hot Bods?"

"Nope. In fact, I stood up to Matt today and then he told me to take a few days off to fix my attitude problem."

"Are you going to report him? He can't get away with that."

"I know, and yes, I am. Actually, Francesca was there and she got it on tape," she told him.

"Do you have the file?"

"Yup."

"Email it to me. I'll get this taken care of real fast."

"I can do it. I'm not helpless."

"I know you're not, I just hate what he's doing to you."

"Me too."

"Since you're off work anyway, how about I fly you out here?" he suggested.

"Really? Who would watch Toby? I've never left him."

"Drop him off at my place. My dog sitter can watch him."

She supposed she could. All she had to do for Patty was make sure the litter box was clean and there was plenty of food and water. The cat couldn't care less.

"Oh, but I don't really have the money though."

"I want you out here, I'll pay for it," he said.

"I can't let you do that."

"Jane, I'm getting you a ticket. Check your email later for the information. You're going to love this small town, and you deserve to relax a little."

Who was she to argue? It sounded wonderful. A few days with Ben and no Hot Bods. She was definitely game.

She chatted with him for a few more minutes before hanging up. Francesca must have waited for her to end the call because as soon as she dropped the phone into her purse, Francesca appeared.

"How is Ben?" she asked.

"Great. He's flying me out to see him. I'm so excited. I need to go home and pack."

Jane could see the slight disappointment on Francesca's face. She wished she had more time, but she had no idea what time the flight would be and she had a ton of things she had to get done before she left.

"I'll drive you back to the gym," Francesca said.

"It's right there. I'll walk, no biggie."

"I'll walk with you. I need to burn the calories I've already consumed today."

"Deal." Jane smiled.

She and Francesca jogged across the street. When they got to the gym's parking lot, Jane looked around for her car.

But it wasn't there. Where the hell was it?

Anger flooded her veins as she went inside. She expected to be greeted by the new receptionist, but no one was up front. Jane stomped past the desk and down the hall to Matt's office, where she wasn't at all surprised to see the door closed. She didn't even bother to knock, she just pushed the door open.

Thankfully, she didn't catch the two in the act like she thought she would. Instead, the girl looked grateful that Jane had busted in and interrupted them. With as arrogant as Matt was he'd mostly likely assumed that the girl would jump at the chance to be with him.

"What the hell are you doing, Jane?" Matt barked.

"Where's my car?" Jane demanded

"Casey, we'll continue this talk later," Matt said. The young girl left the room without even looking back. Matt turned and glared at Jane. "You should've knocked first."

"Like it would have mattered. She can't be more than twenty and she isn't interested in you, Grandpa."

"Oh, ha ha." He rolled his eyes.

"Where's my car?"

His expression changed to amusement. "I had it towed."

"You what?"

"You weren't working out or on the clock so you know the policy. The gym's parking lot isn't a public place to just leave your car. All violators will be towed."

"I work here and I'm a member."

"Technically, you aren't a member. You workout only because you're employed here. And you weren't working, were you?"

"You've gone too far. Way too far," Jane snapped. Her hands were in tight fists as she did her best not to walk over and hit him. She wanted to—badly. "You're going to get what's coming to you."

"I'm just counting down the days until you're gone or you change your mind and come back to me."

"I will *never* be with you again." Jane left before things got even more heated. There was no point in arguing any further. She knew he would get what he deserved. She had the proof of what a scum bucket he was.

In the lobby Jane found Francesca with Casey. She asked if Francesca could give her a ride home. Francesca agreed. On the way she sent a message to Ben about what happened. She hated asking for help, but she didn't think at this point she had a choice. Hopefully he could get her car back so she could still fly out and visit him.

Chapter 9

Jane was feeling very spoiled. Ben had gotten her a first class ticket. She never knew that it was so much nicer and the seats were so much bigger than the ones in coach. The flight attendants were kind and gave her practically anything she wanted. Could she ever go back to coach?

So far the plane ride had been very calm, with little turbulence. However, she was still anxious for the flight to be over. But at least she had some quiet time, and she had a lot of thinking to do. Unfortunately, she hadn't been able to get her car back before she left, but Ben gave her the code to his garage and told her where the spare key was. She was now driving one of the many cars he owned—a silver Mercedes. Wow, was the car luxurious. She didn't want to give it back.

He had taken care of everything. The fact that he hadn't been married before shocked her. How was it possible that some woman hadn't snatched him up yet? She had every intention of keeping him.

As Jane gazed out the window, she knew she needed a distraction. She didn't fly often. The thought of being high up in the air scared her. If the plane fell she was screwed.

Shaking her head, she decided it was best to have those thoughts after the next flight. She still had to go home. For now, she decided to put on headphones and watch the romantic comedy that played on the screen ahead of her.

The flight wasn't too long. As she grabbed her bag from the overhead compartment, she was able to breathe a sigh of relief. She had made it here, and the ride had been fairly smooth.

Once the attendant announced they were able to get off the plane, Jane got into the forming line and made her way to the exit door. As she walked into the airport, she immediately searched for Ben. Her eyes met his and a grin spread across her face. She quickly made her way to Ben. He looked even better than she remembered, and it sent flutters through her knowing that he belonged to her.

Ben leaned in and let his lips meet hers and all felt right again. Her everyday stresses were forgotten, and the only thought she had was that she never wanted the kiss to end. But one thing might make the moment better—if they were in his hotel room where they could let the kiss go as far as they wanted.

"I missed you," she said.

"I missed you too."

"How crazy is this?" Jane giggled.

"What do you mean?"

"Us. That's what I mean."

"There's nothing crazy about us." Ben took her hand. "Any more bags?"

She shook her head.

"You only brought one bag?" He genuinely seemed shocked.

"Yeah, it's just a night. What would I need that doesn't fit in one bag?"

"You're perfect, you know that?"

"I wish."

"Let's get the hell out of here."

"You don't have to tell me twice." She couldn't wait to get to the hotel. She was starving, and not for food.

* * * *

Ben was happy the hotel wasn't far from the airport. The last thing he wanted was a long drive. He had plans to get Jane naked and quickly. He wanted to explore each and every part of her body over and over until she was begging him to stop. And even then he just might keep going. There was something about Jane that he knew he would never tire of. He hoped that while she was here he could find out once and for all what she thought of him and what kind of a future they would be having.

In the hotel room he watched as Jane laid her bag down and looked around the room. "It's no different than your room at home. Clothes everywhere."

"Did you think it wouldn't be?"

Leisurely she made her way to him. "It's one of the reasons why I like you. I hate cleaning."

"Is that the only reason why you like me?"

"I like the way you kiss me and how it makes me feel."

"I'd like to see you out of these clothes and in that bed over there." He nodded toward the unmade bed.

She grinned and then went toward a chair. Her hands rubbed across the back of it. "Have a seat."

He chuckled as he sat.

"Got an iPod?"

He pointed to the nightstand. She smiled and then put on some music.

"I guess this'll do. Too bad we don't have any speakers to plug in."

He didn't really care about the music, speakers, or whatever. Right now he was just hoping that what he thought was about to happen was going to happen.

Jane stood before him. "There is only one rule—no touching."

"That's a sucky rule."

She leaned in and whispered, "You won't regret it."

He was sure she was right. Laying his arms across the sides of the chair he focused his attention on the sexy woman in front of him.

She bit her lip and he could see she was slightly nervous and that made it all the more hot. Her hips started to sway a bit to the music. As much as he liked the way she moved he was very happy about her hands lingering at the end of her shirt. She toyed with it a moment before lifting it over her head and tossing it across the room.

"You're beautiful," he said.

She wiggled out of her jeans, and he thought he might die from the sight of her in a purple lace bra and thong. The little vixen must have planned this, because she had on matching garters and stockings.

His cock was hard and pressing against his zipper. It begged to be touched the same way his hands and lips pleaded to touch her.

Jane set one foot next to his leg on the chair and then leaned forward so he could take a peek at her full breasts. Her brown hair fell over her shoulders, and the scent of lavender filled his senses.

"I'm going to burst out of my pants," he said.

"We don't want that." Jane unbuttoned his pants and

lowered his zipper. His aching cock sprang out. Now all he needed was for her to touch it.

But she didn't. Instead she walked around the chair and bent down, kissing his neck. Her palms rubbed the length of his chest, stopping right above his waistline.

"I'm so wet right now," she whispered.

"I want to taste."

She moved from behind him and presented herself in front of him again. His dick felt like it grew another inch. She'd removed her bra and her fingers circled her nipples. Sucking his bottom lip in, it was taking everything in him not to touch her.

"Want a taste?" she asked.

He couldn't speak, he just opened his mouth. She leaned forward and placed a nipple in his mouth. He drew it in deep and moaned as he sucked it. On instinct, he reached up and kneaded the other breast.

"I said no touching." She removed her breasts from him.

"You little tease."

"You agreed on our one rule. And if I'm a little tease I guess you wouldn't mind if I touched myself in front of you and let you watch."

His eyes widened. She was going to kill him and he

was going to die in pure ecstasy.

Jane set one long, slender leg on the chair again. Wasting no time, she slid a hand into her panties and all he could see was the movement of her hand as it dipped in and out of her entrance.

"I want to see," he finally said.

"What do you want to see?"

"I want to see your damn finger going in and out of your pussy."

With her other hand she pulled her thong to the side and there it was, her finger pumping in and out, and the liquid on her hand made his mouth salivate.

"I don't know how much longer I can take this."

"Touch yourself then." She eyed his dick.

"You want me to touch myself?"

"I want to see your hand wrapped around your cock, stroking it as you watch my finger enter my pussy."

"I like this side of you, Jane." He did as asked, and it felt so damn good to be touching himself. "But I want to come in you."

She didn't say anything. Her mouth opened a bit and her breathing picked up. He jerked harder on his dick, feeling the pleasure build as her finger thrust faster into herself. That was it, he couldn't take it anymore.

Ben stood, kicking his shoes off. He removed his clothes in record speed. He picked Jane up and tossed her on the bed, then roughly yanked her panties down. God damn she looked hot lying there spread-eagle. As much as he wanted to taste and feast on her he had to bury himself in her. On the dresser behind him was a box of condoms he'd picked up once he knew she was coming. He opened it quickly and rolled one on. Climbing on the bed beside her he pulled her so she was on top of him and straddling him.

"No more playing. Fuck me," he demanded.

She lowered herself onto his cock, and he immediately let out a moan at how good her tight, little pussy hugged him.

"I don't think I can go slow." She panted.

"Go with it. Do what feels right."

She bounced up and down his shaft, and her hands squeezed her breasts. Pleasure was building at a rapid speed through his body, and he was doing his best to hold off. Ben gripped her hips and dug his fingers into her ass. He held her still a moment and thrust up into her.

"Oh my…" she screamed.

Jane released her breasts and leaned forward, taking a hold of his shoulders as he kept her steady and drove into her. She cried out and her walls tightened around him. As she rode out her climax he finally exploded, and it was one of the best damn orgasms he'd had in a long time. They moved in a slow speed now, enjoying the pleasure and just feeling. Jane was the first to stop and relax on top of him.

He was completely spent and was one hundred percent relaxed. He rolled her off of him and wrapped his arms around her. She yawned and he whispered for her to take a nap. Having Jane in his arms just seemed right, and he fell asleep not long after her.

* * * *

This was heaven. Jane lay in bed with one of Ben's button-down shirts on. He'd run out to get them something to eat. All afternoon they'd made love and napped. After he left she'd taken a quick shower to freshen up. She was sore and tender all over but wouldn't have it any other way. Ben was an incredible lover. Hopefully, tonight they would get a chance to talk and maybe figure this thing out.

While she waited she flipped mindlessly through the channels, but nothing was catching her attention. Late tomorrow morning she would have to catch a flight back home and return to a mess. It was time to do something about Matt, but she knew she wouldn't come out of this on top. She'd been fooling around with him on company time, so she was probably going to have to find a new job either way.

She finally gave up trying to find something on the TV that would get her mind to quit wandering. Picking up her phone, she decided to see what was going on in the world of social networks. She posted a status that she was having a great trip with Ben. She knew that would throw a lot of people off since no one knew she was seeing anyone. It dawned on her that she'd never really posted anything about a man. She never could about Matt. It felt wonderful to be able to freely talk about Ben and it didn't matter who knew.

But now that she was putting it out there, letting her friends and family know, they would soon learn of their age difference. It wouldn't be long before her mother called wanting all the details. Could she bring herself to tell her parents they were only ten years older than the man she was seeing? The man who clouded all her thoughts and kissed her until her mind went blank. Certainly she wouldn't tell them that. Being with Ben wasn't going to be a walk in the park. However, Jane thought it just might be worth it.

After she set her phone down the hotel room door opened and Ben came in holding a brown paper bag.

"I picked up Mexican, hope that's okay."

"You could have brought back ostrich eggs and I would have eaten them. I'm starved."

"Sorry it took me so long. I had a few calls to make." He set the bag down on the table. "I rearranged my schedule, and I'm flying back with you tomorrow."

Excitement flooded her and she jumped up.

"You look so damn sexy in my shirt." He tugged Jane to him. Right away she felt his hard-on pressed into her thigh.

"Settle down. As happy as I am you're flying home with me, that food over there is priority number one."

"You sure? I can make it quick."

She laughed. "Tempting, but no."

After they finished eating they climbed back into bed together. Jane sat cuddled into Ben's side as he flipped through the channels and finally stopped on a movie station. It was a romantic comedy, one she was sure she'd seen a dozen times.

Ben reached over and took her hand. "Can we talk for a little?"

"Is there something in particular you wanted to talk about?"

"Yes."

She looked up at him.

"I really like you, and I know we started seeing each other on the craziest of terms but from the moment I met you, I knew you were the one."

"The one?" Her heart sped up.

"I know it's a little forward, but I've waited years to find the right woman. And now I have."

"Me? I'm what you've been looking for?"

"Yes. You're so honest and kind. You're beautiful and sexy. You're smart. And when I'm with you nothing else matters. I want to wake up every day with you and your crazy dog and cat. I want to fill my unused house with children and have you as their mother."

Jane's eyes watered, and she tried her best to hold the tears back. "I really like you too. Is it safe to say that somewhere along the way we accidentally fell in love?"

"It was no accident." He pressed his lips against hers. "Do you want to spend your life with me, Jane?"

She nodded. "Do you think our age difference is going to matter?"

"To who?"

"Won't people talk? How are my parents going to react? You're closer to their age than you are to mine."

"Jane, look at me."

She looked into his eyes, and it calmed her immediately.

"We'll cross that bridge when we get to it. The only

thing I know for sure is that I've finally found the woman I want to be with, and I don't want to give that up just because of what others might think."

Ben pushed her onto her back and climbed on top of her. His kiss was deep with passion. The whole world melted away and all that mattered was him. It didn't take long before they were both naked and Ben climbed between her legs to make love to her. He was tender and thorough, making sure she got everything she needed.

As they made love they looked into each other's eyes. A connection was felt so deep in her she would have thought they had actually attached to one another.

When she fell asleep in his arms that night she knew everything was going to work out and as long as she had Ben she didn't have to worry.

Chapter 10

After another successful plane ride, Jane hoped she didn't have to do that for quite some time. They made their way to the parking garage where they would part ways. Ben had promised to come to her place later with Toby and he would stay the evening with her. She had a feeling he liked her house better than his own.

Jane leaned against the vehicle as Ben held her in his arms. Never had she been so connected to someone that she actually hated the idea of parting ways.

"I really had a wonderful trip," she told him.

"It was much more enjoyable having you there."

"Well, I might be out of a job soon and have plenty of time to travel with you." Damn, maybe there were more plane trips in her future than she wanted.

"You're not going to lose your job. From what I heard on that tape, you made it clear you wanted him to leave you alone, and he made it clear he was a pompous ass."

Jane laughed. "I guess I'll see you later. I'm going to hate giving you back this shiny Mercedes."

"You can drive it as long as you want."

"You're just saying that since we're sleeping together."

Ben shook his head and grinned. "You might be right."

She punched his arm playfully. "Careful now."

He yanked her to him and let his mouth devour hers. Her engine roared to life. Good God, she was like the Energizer Bunny. If they were alone she'd likely do him again. But then she remembered they had the rest of their lives together. Settle engine.

"Okay, I've got to go." Ben left a light kiss on her cheek.

He turned to walk away and she called to him. "Wait, Ben." He turned back to look at her. "I love you."

"I love you too." He blew her a kiss before walking toward his vehicle, pulling a rolling suitcase behind him.

Climbing into the car, Jane started it up. It was time to return to her everyday life. Hopefully with Ben in it now, it would be getting a lot better.

* * * *

As Ben headed toward his house to take care of a few things, he couldn't wait until the day they lived together. Excitement swept through him and stayed there like he was sixteen and in love for the first time. Jane loved him.

Their time together had been amazing. He was going to have to thank Francesca soon. If she hadn't thought of him and the favor he owed her, he'd be driving home right now with the same loneliness he'd been feeling for years. He'd had his fun when he was younger, but it had never been his intention to be a bachelor for life.

He understood Jane's concerns about their age difference, but to him it didn't seem like such a big deal. He was almost positive that once her parents saw how much they loved each other, they would be happy for their daughter.

The first thing he needed to do was go ring shopping. At first he thought Jane needed the biggest and most expensive one he could find. But this was Jane. He'd better tone it down just a bit.

He hoped she'd want to start a family right away. He wanted a little girl who would look just like Jane with dark hair and blue eyes. That giddy feeling came back just thinking about being a father.

Once home he went directly to his office. He made a call to the dog sitter, informing her that he was home but to just bring Toby back for now. He would be out all evening and would pick up Olive and Pepper in the morning. Next he started his computer up. He had a few things to take care of before he could go see Jane. He just hoped he could concentrate long enough to get it done.

* * * *

A few hours later Jane woke from a nap. She hadn't realized how exhausted she was until Patty climbed into her lap and as she pet the cat she dozed off. The cat, of course, was gone now.

She wasn't sure what time she would be seeing Ben, so she decided to go online and look through the help wanted just in case she did end up jobless. It was best to be prepared. There happened to be a new gym opening in the next town over. Perhaps tomorrow after work she would head over and see the place.

As she closed her laptop she heard a car door shut outside. A big smile spread at the thought that Ben was back. Jumping up, she went to the door to greet him. She flung the door open and froze. Matt was on the other side.

"What are you doing here?" she asked.

"I can't believe what you did to me." The smell of alcohol on his breath was strong.

"What are you talking about?"

"You recorded me and sent it to the owner of the gym. And they fired me today." He narrowed his eyes and glared at her. "And now you're going to play stupid."

"I didn't send them any tape. I've been out of town." She knew she needed to stay calm. This didn't need to escalate.

"Oh, please. No one knew about us but you and me. And I sure as hell didn't tape myself and give it to them. They even have a tape from when you came in my office after I had your car towed."

She didn't know about that one. Francesca must have followed her back. Now that she thought about it, Francesca must have been the one who turned him in. Who else could it have been?

"Well, it wasn't from me. Now will you please leave?"

"No, I'm not going to fucking leave."

"Do I have to call the cops?" Shit, where was her cellphone at?

"That's not going to happen either."

"Get the hell out of here and quit acting like you're some tough guy when you're not. I wish I was the one who turned you in, but I'm not."

She started to close the door but Matt pushed his way in and stumbled into the living room. She wished Ben and Toby were there. It wasn't good having Matt inside in his condition. Her mind ran a mile a minute as she wondered what to do. Was he dangerous? She really didn't know. He'd done a lot of things lately she hadn't expected.

She stepped back slowly until she was on her front porch.

"Get in here. We need to talk about how you're going to get me my job back."

Like hell. Very thankful that she had neighbors on each side, she started to run across her yard. Jane jogged up the steps to her neighbor's house. After knocking, she glanced back toward her place and saw that Ben had pulled into her driveway. Before going to him she asked her neighbor to call the police.

By the time she made it back to her yard, Matt was outside trying to start a fight with Ben. Ben told her to stay where she was. She watched as Ben held his cool and Matt went off about everything he could. It didn't take long before a cruiser pulled up, and Matt got even more hysterical because she'd called the authorities. This was *so* embarrassing. And she was sure Ben was second-guessing why he'd even gotten involved in this mess to begin with.

An officer motioned to her. As she walked over to him, she knew her face was flushed. Of course the officer who had to show up was Adam—who was Francesca's brother and Amy's fiancé. Could this situation get any worse?

"Hi, Adam," she said.

"I thought I recognized you. We have a couple of questions for you."

She nodded and followed him to his car. It only took a

few minutes to answer their questions. Adam asked if she wanted to press charges. She thought about it a moment then decided *hell yeah*. Matt was going to get what he had coming to him. He'd put her through hell, and she was sure she wasn't the first girl but hopefully she would be the last.

She couldn't help but grin as Matt was handcuffed and put into the back of a police car. Once they left Ben wrapped his arm around her and said, "I'm sorry this happened."

"It's over. And no one got hurt." Jane glanced up at him, giving him a smile.

Ben took her hand and led her back into her house. Toby padded his way through the living room and plopped onto the couch. Jane sat down by the dog and was happy when Ben took a seat next to her, wrapping his arm around her shoulders.

"I'm sorry I wasn't here."

"It isn't like you knew he was going to pull this stunt."

"Do you know who gave the owners a copy of the recordings?"

"I'm pretty sure it was Francesca. We are the only ones who had copies and it wasn't me. And she must have followed me without me knowing in order to get the second recording."

Ben pulled her closer. "We owe her a big thank you."

"In more than one way."

"I really am glad that this wasn't as bad as it could've been. I meant what I said before, Jane. I want to spend the rest of my life with you."

Jane moved into Ben's lap, straddling him. Looking into his eyes she said, "I just have one request."

"Lay it on me."

"Can we get a smaller house?"

Ben laughed. "You don't like my house?"

"It's just so big, and it's sorta intimidating. I think we should find one together."

"If that's what it takes to get you to be with me, I'm all for it."

Jane kissed Ben and just as she thought things might start to get hot and heavy Toby barked. Breaking the kiss she turned and looked at the dog then back to Ben.

"We'd better take this to my room. I think Toby is a little jealous."

Ben scooped her up and they headed for her room. She couldn't wait until he devoured her body once again. Then when she remembered it would be just his lips on her for the rest of her life, she wished they would live forever. She would never tire of this man.

Chapter 11

"Seriously, where are we going?" Francesca asked for the tenth time since getting into Jane's car.

"I'm treating you to dinner for your birthday. Now sit back and relax."

"I don't like surprises."

Jane rolled her eyes. She didn't believe that for a second. Francesca loved to be pampered. And she probably already sensed that Jane was driving her to a surprise party.

"I just want to thank you once again for what you did for me with Matt," Jane said.

"I just did what any friend would do. And hey, it worked out great for you, didn't it?"

Jane smiled. It sure had. She got to keep her job at Hot Bods, but she was no longer the receptionist. The owners felt like Jane knew all the ins and outs of the gym and had promoted her into management. It was a wonderful feeling too. Matt had already passed a lot of work to her, so it was pretty simple once she got going. Plus, there was more pay and she had the perfect hours. Life really was going well.

They pulled up to the steak house where Jane had first met Ben.

"I love this place," Francesca said. "Ben must be paying."

"Hey, I'm not so bad off that I couldn't afford to treat us to dinner here."

"Yeah, but it doesn't hurt having a rich man cither, does it?"

"You know, Francesca, once you stop looking for a rich man who can pay for everything, you just might find love."

"Keep dreaming."

Jane laughed and got out of the car. She walked behind Francesca and had a grin across her face the whole time. As she followed her in she laughed as an echo of "surprise" filled the room.

"What in the…" Francesca covered her mouth in shock. "Jane, I didn't see a party being here."

Jane hugged Francesca, very glad that she'd given her a shot at friendship. She hoped tonight went well since she'd invited Skylar in an attempt to get them to at least be civil with one another.

As the crowd of Francesca's friends welcomed her, Jane found the most handsome man she'd ever laid eyes on standing to the side. Greeting her with a kiss, he slid his hands around her waist and rubbed her lower back.

"How is my future bride and the mother of my child doing?" Ben asked.

"Shh, we aren't telling anyone yet. It's bad luck. We have to wait until I hit the twelve week mark."

He groaned. "It's killing me not being able to tell everyone. I've waited forty-five years for this."

"Well, it's only a few more weeks."

Ben rubbed her belly. "Maybe if we're lucky it'll be twins."

"I don't care if it's one, two, three, boy, or girl. I'm just so glad to be spending the rest of my life with you. I love you, Ben."

"I love you, Jane."

Opposites Attract

Francesca thought she knew what she wanted in life until one stormy night when she got a blast from the past.

When Randy receives a call at his auto shop one night from a woman whose car has broken down and needs a tow, he never imagined he'd be coming face-to-face with his high school sweetheart. Randy has never loved a woman the way he loved Francesca, but she broke his heart, claiming he could never provide the life she was determined to have. That was years ago, but he's still bitter about the way she tossed him aside.

Seeing Randy again, Francesca realizes what a mistake it was to breakup with him. She'd like to try to rekindle the old flame, and she can tell he's still attracted to her too, but every time they're together, all they do is argue. Can she convince Randy she isn't the girl he remembers and that she can settle for love even if it comes without money?

Content Warning: explicit sex

Chapter 1

The hot water sprayed against Francesca's body, easing her aches. She'd just put in an intense workout with weights. As the warmth engulfed her, she wasn't sure she ever wanted to get out of the shower.

It was Friday evening, and she had absolutely no plans. Once again she would be going home alone to her apartment. But that was how things had been recently. Sure, there was probably someone she could call up to take her out for the evening, but it was all so meaningless. Everyone she knew was getting married and starting lives with babies and all that mushy stuff. And all she did was bounce from one rich guy to the next, hoping that maybe one would fall in love with her and not just want her for arm candy.

Turning off the shower, Francesca stepped onto the cool tile floor. She wrapped a big, white, fluffy towel around her and made her way through the Hot Bods locker room. After opening her locker, she dug through her bag. Of course she had designer clothes packed, but today she just didn't feel like it. Why get glammed up just to go home alone? As she dug deeper in her bag, she saw an extra set of gym clothes. And they were her loose ones for when it was that time of the month. Could she do it? Wear these clothes out of the gym?

Letting the soft cotton fabric skim across her fingers, she decided, hell yeah she could. People left the gym all the time without even showering and no one seemed to care. So surely she could do this. Taking the bag, she slammed her locker shut and went toward the dressing stalls.

After getting dressed she went to the vanity area where she usually spent much of her time doing her hair and makeup until it looked perfect. As she stared at herself, she decided to just pull her hair up into a high ponytail. She then applied a light layer of makeup. There was no way in hell she was going to leave this place without that.

After she was finished, Francesca made her way to the front of the gym. Maybe she could get out of there before anyone she knew saw her.

"Francesca," a familiar voice called.

Damn. Francesca turned to see Skylar. These days they were sort of getting along. Skylar was a gym instructor at Hot Bods, and at one point they had been involved with the same guy. And to make matters worse, Francesca's brother was getting married in a few weeks to Amy, who just happened to be Skylar's best friend. So they were having to put the harsh feelings behind them and find a way to get along.

"Hi, Skylar. I was just leaving."

"I'm glad I caught you then. The gym is putting together an event next week to show our customers our appreciation. I wanted to make sure you knew, and I hope you stop in. Here's a flyer with all the details." Skylar shoved a neon orange paper in Francesca's hand.

"Thanks, I'll be sure to come by."

"Is everything okay? You don't look like yourself." Skylar looked Francesca up and down.

"I'm fine."

"Are you sick?" Skylar asked.

"No, I'm not sick." Geesh, did she look *that* bad?

"Okay. Well, I'm here if you need to chat."

Sure she was. She could be her new best friend. Yeah, right. "Thanks, but I'm just going to go home. Have a good evening."

Francesca didn't even give her time to speak again, she headed out the door as quickly as possible. A glance up at the sky showed the clouds looked as though they were ready to open up with a nasty storm. She hoped she made it home before it happened. She hated driving in the rain.

Climbing into her white Lexus, she started it up and left in a hurry. As she drove, her car wasn't handling the way it usually did. She pressed her foot on the gas a little more and gazed up at the sky again. She really wanted to get home. The sky was getting awfully dark, and she knew the storm was going to hit at any moment and this stupid car just wouldn't go as she accelerated.

Francesca took a left at the stop sign and was now on the homestretch to her apartment. Pushing the pedal even more, the car began making some weird noise and then smoke started coming from underneath the hood. What the hell? She pulled over to the side of the road. This wasn't good. Was the car going to blow up? Did she need to get out?

Panic set in and the tears started. She knew nothing about cars or what she should be doing right now. Grabbing her purse, she searched through it until she found her cellphone. She opened an app to try and find someone who could help her.

A rumble shook her car and then the rain pounded the windshield. Shit, she was going to be sitting in this stupid car as the storm hit. Maybe she should just call 911. This was an emergency.

Adam! Yes, she could call her brother, he was a policeman.

No, he would laugh at her.

Scrolling through the results on her phone, she called the mechanic that was closest to her. The sooner they could get there, the better. A man answered on the second ring and after she explained what happened he said he would be out there quickly with his tow truck. Francesca let out a sigh as she hung up.

Lightening lit the sky, and she prayed like hell there wasn't a tornado watch going on. In the south, it was always a possibility. And this road was all flat land—no ditch anywhere to take cover. But she wasn't going to think that way. There wasn't going to be a tornado.

The wind picked up and the rain got messy, whipping this way and that. It wasn't looking good at all. Had she done something horrible that she was being punished for?

From the rearview mirror she saw a set of bright lights pulling up behind her. Finally, help had arrived. The tow truck drove around her and then backed up slowly in front of her vehicle. Francesca opened the door and went out into the pouring rain, ready to get into the tow truck.

The driver got out of the truck and Francesca froze. She couldn't believe who had come to help.

"Randall."

Chapter 2

Cupping his hands over his eyes so he could see through the downpour, Randy gazed at the beautiful woman. He couldn't believe that Francesca stood before him. It had been years since he'd seen her. He wasn't sure this was going to be a happy reunion. They'd been high school sweethearts, and after graduation they went their separate ways—not by his choice.

He'd moved back to town a year ago, after his father's death, and had kept up with her from afar. The only thing he really knew about her now was what he heard through the rumor mill, some would call her a 'gold digger'.

"Francesca," he called. "Get out of the rain. Go climb into the truck."

But she just stood there, letting the rain drench her. She was a sight to see in the rain. Her clothes hugged her body and he could see all her curves.

A flash of lightening shot through the sky and the ground shook. Francesca yelped and ran toward his truck and climbed in through the driver side. Walking over to her car, he wished he'd brought help. This storm looked like it was going to get nasty, and quick.

Page 302

Another bolt shot through the sky and once again the thunder was loud. There was no way he was getting killed just to load her car up. He could come back for it after the storm. Without a second thought, he jogged to the truck and climbed inside.

"What are you doing?" she asked.

"I'm not looking to get killed tonight in this storm. Once it clears, I'll come back for your car."

Francesca bit her bottom lip and then nodded. Good, she wasn't as cold-hearted as he'd heard. Pulling onto the road, he glanced at her and asked, "Where to?"

"I'm not too far from here. Just about four miles, and my apartment complex is on the right."

"You live in Meadow Creek Apartments?" That apartment complex was the only gated place around and had its own rent-a-cop on duty twenty-four seven. Of course she lived there.

Francesca rubbed her arms up and down. It dawned on him that she might be chilly in her wet clothes. Leaning forward, he flipped on the heat and then stole a glance at her breasts, catching a glimpse of her hard nipples.

"Thanks," she said in a soft tone that sent shivers through him.

Sitting next to Francesca was like sitting next to a

stranger. They had a past together, one that still stirred in his thoughts from time to time. But the way they sat silently, doing their best not to look at one another, you never would have known that they'd been each other's first. That together they'd learned all about the opposite sex's body. And now, it was like he'd never even known her.

Meadow Creek Apartments came into view, and he turned his blinker on as he pulled up to where you would usually punch a code in. But the gates opened right away. Glancing over, he saw that she had what looked like a remote on her key chain. Once through the gates she directed him to where she lived. His truck was too big to park in a spot, so he pulled up in front of the building and wondered what the hell to say now.

"Thank you." She ran her hand through her long blonde hair. "What do I owe you?"

Owe? Oh yes, she needed her car towed. This woman still made his mind mush. "It depends. I can either tow your car to the shop of your choice, or if I bring it to my place, the tow is free. You just pay the charges of whatever it takes to fix it."

"Did you take over your dad's place?"

He nodded.

"I was sorry to hear about him."

"Well, we all gotta go up to the big pearly gates one day."

She didn't say anything. Death was always one of those topics where no one ever knew what to say. His dad had been a great man, always going out of his way to help people. Randy hoped to one day follow in his father's footsteps.

"Here's my card. How about I take your car back to my place to fix? I promise I'll give you a good deal."

"Sounds great." Francesca's hand lingered on the door handle as she gazed into his eyes. "I guess I should get inside. I just wish the rain would let up."

"Yeah, this is a nasty one all right."

"Thank you again. I'll call you in the morning. Will that be okay?"

"Sure. Stay safe."

She nodded and then climbed out. After slamming the door shut, she ran through the rain toward the breezeway. He watched until she was out of sight. Hopefully safely in her home. Now he had to figure out how the hell to turn this truck around without hitting someone's overpriced car.

* * * *

Francesca stood in the middle of her living room. She was drenched from the rain, but she didn't care. She was still getting over the shock of seeing Randall. She had loved him with everything in her, and then she'd just dumped him. Told him she wanted a better life than anything he could have given her. She was certain if she'd married him, he'd never be able to give her all the things she dreamed of. At that time, she thought money would buy her happiness. But now that she was in her early thirties, and had been nowhere close to marriage, she was beginning to wonder just how smart her life plan had been. Maybe if she had made different choices, she'd be somewhere else right now.

Almost everyone she knew was married or getting married. Their lives were full of love, and they all floated on air. They weren't worried about what the other could buy. All she had ever wanted was the most expensive of everything. Growing up, her parents always joked she needed to marry a rich man to be able to afford her tastes. She took their advice to heart and for years searched for that wealthy guy. Sure, she'd found plenty, but she hadn't kissed one yet that caused her to lose her breath. Not like Randall did.

Francesca groaned. She needed to stop thinking about him and get out of these clothes. In her bedroom, she stripped her wet clothes off and suddenly realized what she was wearing. Embarrassment flooded her. But as she slipped into her light blue silk pajamas, she realized he probably couldn't have cared less what she was wearing. It had been pouring rain and anything she had on would be clinging to her. Maybe it was good she had gym clothes on. Her suede boots she had packed to wear home would have been ruined, and they had cost seven hundred dollars. Talk about heartbreak.

Francesca ordered take-out and decided to spend the evening watching movies. Not her ideal Friday night. But at least now if someone asked, she could tell them she was without a car, so what other choice did she have?

Chapter 3

It was eight o'clock in the morning and Francesca was wide awake. She was *never* up this early on a Saturday. If she was up by ten, that was early. Of course it probably had something to do with the fact that she had fallen asleep around nine the night before.

She wished she felt more energized, but Randall had haunted her dreams. All night she had replayed the way she had broken not only his heart, but hers as well.

"Well, baby, we did it. We're high school graduates. We have our whole lives ahead of us. Just you and me. Let's take off before college and travel all around the country together." Randall kissed her neck.

Normally, whenever his lips touched her, she lost the ability to think. But today was different. She was done with high school, and it was time to start her life. And she hadn't yet told Randall that she had been accepted to a college out of state and she wasn't going to be attending the community college with him in the fall. She'd been putting off telling him only because she wasn't sure she was making the right choice. But her parents fully supported it and thought that going to college without Randall was the best decision she was making.

"What do you say?" he asked again.

"I don't know," she whispered.

He pulled away and looked up at her. "What's the matter?"

Taking a deep breath, she blurted out, "I think we should breakup."

He jerked away from her and started to pace her bedroom. "Why?" he finally asked.

"I don't think we want the same things in life. I don't want to just settle for a normal life. I want to have it all."

"And you don't think I can give that to you? We can have anything, as long as we're together."

"You're going to school to be an automotive technician and following in your father's footsteps. We will always struggle and live paycheck to paycheck. That isn't what I want."

He looked stunned. "I plan to open my own shop."

"And that takes money. And face it, the chances of that actually happening aren't looking good. You'll probably be just like your dad and have a heart of gold, always doing jobs for free. I'm sorry, but I want more. I want to see the world and eat at fancy restaurants."

"Didn't I just ask you if you wanted to travel before college in the fall?"

"I got accepted to Berkeley, and I'm leaving in a few weeks." She crossed her arms, hoping he would just drop it. Breaking up with him was harder than she thought it would be.

"Why didn't you tell me?"

"What does it matter? I'm going."

Randall walked to her bedroom door. "Maybe I should have listened to my friends. All these years they said I could never make you happy, but I didn't believe it. When we made love, and the way we connected, I really thought we would be together forever. Looks like they were right and I was wrong. You're out for only yourself."

He had walked away and she hadn't seen him again, until last night. And when she had seen him, once again the world had stopped all around her. Her heart raced and she knew that moment that she had never gotten over him. Randall was the one who had gotten away. She was pretty sure it would stay that way. There was no way he would want to ever deal with her drama again. And she was no better now than she was in high school. In fact, she was probably worse.

Even if she did want to try and start something with him, most likely he was married with two kids at home.

* * * *

What a mess. Francesca had done some damage to her car. Had no one taught her anything about vehicle maintenance? The woman had almost no oil and what she did have was extremely dirty. And what a shame, because she had a top-of-the-line Lexus. The parts alone he needed to order just might break her bank. Hopefully she would call soon so they could discuss her price range.

Then again, knowing Francesca, she had some rich man who would either hand over his credit card for her to fix it or buy her a new one.

Turning off the sink, Randy dried his hands and tossed the towel on the counter. Even after all these years, he was bitter. Why couldn't she have gained fifty pounds or something? Instead, she was as perfect as ever and he wanted another taste. If he could be with her one more time, maybe he could convince her they were right together.

But they weren't. She never thought he was what she needed. He couldn't help but snicker. Little did she know, he had a lot of money. And he'd earned every damn penny. He was sure that if she knew he was rich, she would be all about him again. He had to stay far away from her, which was going to be hard seeing as he was fixing her car. Maybe he would get lucky and she would have some sugar daddy who would just buy her a new car and they could go their separate ways.

The shop phone rang. Caller ID showed a number he didn't know from a cellphone. But he knew who it was. "Hello, Randy here."

"Hi, Randall, it's Francesca." He could hear the hesitation in her voice.

"It's Randy. No one calls me Randall except you."

"I'll remember that. So, is my car ready?"

He laughed. Was she serious? "No, your car isn't ready yet."

"Later this afternoon?"

He rolled his eyes. She probably thought all he had to do was snap his fingers and it would be fixed. "I'm still assessing the damage. How about you find a way to get here in an hour or two and we'll sit down and talk about it so I can show you prices and so on."

"Shit."

He grinned. He couldn't believe he heard her pretty little mouth say a cuss word. "I'll see you in a bit."

Putting the phone back on the cradle, he wanted to kick himself. There was no reason for her to come to the shop.

He could have easily talked to her about it over the phone. He needed to get this car fixed and out of his shop fast.

* * * *

"Hi, Amy. Is there any way you can drop me off at Smith's Auto in an hour?" Francesca asked her future sister-in-law. "My car broke down last night, but it should be ready soon, I would think."

"Sure, but are you sure it'll be ready? If the car just stopped working it could be serious," Amy pointed out.

"It was probably low on oil. I appreciate it, really. I'll see you in an hour."

"Okay. Oh, one more question. Are you still a 'plus one' for the wedding?"

There was no way in hell she was showing up at her brother's wedding without a date. Of course she was still a 'plus one'. "Yeah."

"Adam wants to know who you're bringing."

"Tell Adam he has bigger things to worry about than me. See you in a bit." She hung up. Lately, Adam had been hounding her like crazy to settle down. She was tired of hearing about it. And it wasn't like she was purposely not settling down. She was just having a harder time finding the right person than the other people in her life had.

Francesca tossed her iPhone onto the bed and went to

finish getting ready. Today she was going to look her absolute best.

Just as she finished dressing, the buzzer in her apartment sounded, letting her know Amy had arrived. She hit the *accept* button that would let Amy into the complex and then went back to the bathroom. One last spritz of her pheromone-enhanced body spray and she would be complete.

Grabbing her purse, she gathered her things and headed out. She locked the door behind her and met Amy in the breezeway.

"You smell really good," Amy commented.

"Thanks." Francesca climbed into Amy's car.

Once Amy got in, she turned toward her friend. "You look spectacular too."

"Uh, you're not turning into a lesbian, are you?" Francesca wasn't sure what had gotten into Amy.

"No, I am completely in love with your brother. I ask because, while you always look beautiful, you have really outdone yourself to pick-up your car. Does this have anything to do with Randy, the repair shop owner?" Amy asked, with a big grin.

"Why would it?"

"Rumor has it he's one of the town's most eligible

bachelors."

"He's single?" She knew her voice sounded a bit too happy about that, especially when Amy raised an eyebrow at her. "I just mean, I assumed he was married. That's all."

"I take it you met him then and saw what a hunk he is."

"Me being this dolled up has nothing to do with Randall," Francesca said, hoping to convince herself more than Amy.

"Randall?" Amy paused a moment and then it was like a light bulb went off. "Wait a minute. Is Randy the guy your brother told me about? Your high school sweetheart?"

Francesca rolled her eyes. Of course her brother had to discuss her past with his fiancée. "Yes, it just so happens he is. So you can see why this has nothing to do with him. I've already been down that road. And the past should always stay where it belongs."

Amy didn't say anything else. She started the car and drove the short distance to Smith's Auto. Francesca knew she hadn't fooled Amy though. She was a smart girl. But perhaps Francesca could fool herself and really believe that she didn't still want Randall.

When they reached the shop Amy asked if she should stick around, but Francesca assured her there was no need and told her that if she needed her she would call. She was positive it wouldn't take long to get her car fixed. After Amy drove off, Francesca opened the door to the shop. She entered a small area with an old desk and even older computer setup. No one was there. A doorway was to her right, she went through it and found herself in the garage.

A radio played country music, and she heard a male voice singing. She followed the sound then stopped dead in her tracks. Randall was singing and bent over her car, looking at something under the hood. His jeans were tight against his ass. As if that wasn't bad enough, as he bent forward, he shook his hips with the beat of the music. Her gaze was locked on his ass and her hands hurt as they ached to reach out and touch.

She was so lost in her erotic daydream that she hadn't realized Randall had stopped dancing and had turned slightly, looking at her. As her gaze drifted up his body, she caught the look in his eyes she remembered. Lust. Licking her lips, she knew she was in trouble. She wanted one more romp with him, and as far as she was concerned, the sooner the better.

* * * *

Randy cleared his throat, hoping to break the tension between him and Francesca. The way she was looking at him, he was worried she was about to pounce. It was taking everything in him to not walk over there and kiss her.

Picking up a work towel, he wiped his hands on it and then directed her toward the front office. She walked in front of him and it was his turn to devour her ass. And hot damn, the jeans she wore were tight and molded to her butt perfectly. Her pants hugged her legs all the way down. She wore black boots that came to her knees. He wasn't sure what shirt she wore, because his eyes had yet to make it past her luscious ass.

Once in the office, he stepped around her, getting a whiff of a very tempting smell. He quickly sat and scooted under the desk as far as he could. His cock was hardening and he didn't want her to see.

Francesca took a seat in front of him and he now noticed her pink tank top that was cut low enough he got a hint of cleavage. Inhaling again, he wondered what perfume she used. It really was igniting his senses.

"I spent some time looking at your car today. When was the last time you had an oil change?" he asked.

"It's been awhile."

"I can tell. And how long has the car been leaking oil?"

She shrugged. "Not sure. I wasn't concerned since it was just little drops here and there."

"Those little drops here and there add up. You almost

had no oil in your car. And I hate to tell you, but you have torn up your engine."

"Well, can't you just pop a new one in and it'll be good as new?" she asked.

"I wish it was that simple. Here, look this over." He slid a sheet of paper across the desk. "The top portion has to be done, the middle is recommended, and the bottom is optional. The price is on there too."

Her eyes widened as she read over the paper. She then glanced up at him. "This can't be right."

"I'm afraid it is. You haven't taken very good care of the car."

"I get it washed and detailed all the time. I take very good care of it."

Randy shook his head. "There's a lot more to a vehicle than just its appearance. You've got to take care of the things people don't see too."

She was quiet for a moment and then finally spoke. "I don't know if I can afford this."

He raised an eyebrow at her. "Don't you have some rich man who can pay for it?" He regretted saying it the moment it left his lips.

Francesca's mouth fell open and he could see the shock on her face.

"I'm so—" he started to apologize.

"I can't believe you would say that, Randall. You of all people," she snapped.

"Me of all people," he repeated. "What the hell is that supposed to mean? If I recall correctly, you dumped me because you wanted a rich man to take care of you. Tell me, how is that working out for you?"

Francesca stood up, placed her hands on her hips, and leaned forward slightly. As much as he hated it, his focus darted in for a peek inside her shirt.

"I'll have you know that I'm not the gold digger you think I am," she argued.

"I bet you refuse to date any man whose income level doesn't meet your standards. Tell me, why haven't you married one of them yet?"

"Why aren't you married? Can't find a girl who will have you as a husband?"

Randy stood and stepped around the desk. "I haven't found anyone else who can start my engines the way you could." He rubbed the back of his fingers on her upper arm. "Haven't you found a rich guy yet who can kiss you breathless?"

* * * *

Francesca jerked her arm away. "And here I thought

you were going to be sweet."

He laughed. "Honey, I'm not here to make your life easy."

"Just fix my damn car so I can get out of here."

He stepped closer to her again, and she knew her cheeks were flushed. As much as he angered her, having him so close made her want to reach out, grab a hold, and kiss him.

He leaned into her and glanced out the window. "Do you have a ride waiting on you?"

"No."

"Well, you better call someone. Your car's going to be here for a few days or longer. Depending on how fast I can get the parts in." He stepped back and sat on the desk, crossing his arms.

"It won't be ready today?"

"No, didn't you hear me on the phone? You've got some extensive damage."

Francesca let out a sigh. "I guess I need to call about a rental."

"I've got a vehicle you can use."

"Really? Great."

"Follow me." Randall led her through the garage and out the back door where she saw some junk cars and a few that looked like they might be drivable. In the back of the lot, a vehicle sat with a blue tarp over it. He was headed toward it, and she hoped that since it was covered, it was going to be some fancy sports car.

She stood back as he pulled the tarp off. Once it was revealed, her mouth dropped open. It was his truck from high school. The truck where they had their first kiss, and where he made it to second base for the first time. It was the same truck where they had decided they were ready to move to the next level and give each other their virginity. Of course that didn't happen in the truck, but there were other times they had made love in there.

"Do you remember this baby?" He smacked the fender.

"Yeah. It still runs?"

"If you take care of your vehicles from the inside and out, they'll last a long time." He opened the driver's side door. "Climb in."

She hesitated, but did it anyway. He followed, causing her to scoot over to the passenger side. The key was already in the ignition. The truck started immediately and Randall smiled, rubbing his hands along the steering wheel. "I loved this truck."

He picked up the remote to the radio and touched the *on* button. The lights lit up and she heard a CD start to spin.

The next thing she heard was her and Randall's song come from the speakers. She looked at him and saw he was already inching closer. Before she knew what she was doing, her hands were wrapped around his neck, pulling him toward her.

She saw passion flood his eyes, and it took him no time to touch his lips to hers. She froze a moment from the intensity, but as the soft kiss began to heat up, she yanked his body into hers. His tongue thrust inside her mouth, and her world stopped. He could still take her breath away and make her feel complete with just a kiss. It had been so long since she had felt as whole as she did when Randall kissed her. As he pressed his body into her, one hand gripped her waist possessively.

"Oh God," she whispered against his lips, breaking the kiss momentarily.

"You taste better than I remember."

He gazed down into her eyes and as she stared back, she saw the only man she had ever loved. The one man who could make her want nothing more than to feel his arms wrapped around her each night before bed. Randall leaned in to kiss her again, but she stopped him.

"We can't do this."

He sat back in the seat and nodded. "You're right. It

didn't work out the first time. There's no way it will work this time."

She wasn't so sure about that. She had a feeling things would work out rather nicely between them.

"Anyway, if you want to use the truck, you're welcome to. I know repairs are expensive on your car, and this isn't a luxury car, but it will get you from point A to point B."

Could she really ride around in this truck? Every time she drove it, she would be haunted by memories and her nose would be attacked by his scent. But it was either this or a rental car—an expense she couldn't afford with her vehicle now in the shop.

"Thanks, it means a lot that you trust me to drive your truck."

He snickered. "I wouldn't call it trust. You break it, you buy it."

Francesca rolled her eyes. What the hell had she ever seen in him? "Whatever, just get my car fixed soon so we can be out of each other's lives for good."

Randall hopped out of the car. "That's exactly what I plan on doing. Call me mid-week for an update." He walked back toward his shop.

Francesca scooted over to the driver's seat. After buckling up, she put the truck in drive. A light flashed on the dash. It was the gaslight. *Seriously?* She should have expected no less.

* * * *

From inside the shop, Randy watched as Francesca drove off in his old truck. He hoped she stopped at the gas station right away, otherwise she wouldn't be making it far. Chuckling, he turned to order the parts he would need for her car and then he was getting the hell out of this place for the day. Without parts, there wasn't any reason to be there.

As he entered the office, the perfume she'd been wearing attacked his senses. The room was filled with her aroma and brought his mind barreling back to the kiss. Not only did she smell good, but she tasted absolutely decadent. Her tongue had been soft, but eager. Her hands had curled into the back of his neck, one finger lightly rubbing across the bottom of his hairline.

He wasn't sure if it was her or the memories in the truck that had made him kiss her. He would love to blame it on the truck, but he had to face it—Francesca was a hot woman. She had taken care of herself over the years. The way she dressed accented all the right areas on her body, and whatever that damn scent was, he had just wanted her. There wasn't a part of him that didn't want to be near her.

And now she had his truck. Which meant it was going

to hold her fragrance when he got it back. Then it dawned on him that her car reeked of her too. For the next week, he was going to be living with a constant hard-on.

But if he was feeling this way, there was a good chance she was too. Which meant, maybe they could have one final time between the sheets and just get it out of their system. Everyone was curious if their ex's had gotten better over the years. Then again, Francesca had rocked his socks back in high school. If she had gotten any better, he wasn't sure he would survive it. But there was only one way to find out. Now he just had to figure out how to do it.

Chapter 4

Francesca pulled the ancient truck into a parking spot at Hot Bods. As good as she looked today, she wasn't going to workout. She was looking for her wonderful friend Jane. She could really use someone to talk to. And over the past few months, she and Jane had become very close. Which was great, Francesca had never had many friends of the same sex.

Climbing out of the old red truck, she looked for a remote to lock the doors. Damn, this truck was so old she had to manually lock the doors. Laying her purse and keys on the seat, she leaned across the seat to push the lock button down on the passenger side. She grabbed her purse, pressed the driver's side down as well, and slammed the door shut. As she made her way into the gym, she scanned the parking lot for Jane's car. Once she spotted the silver Mercedes, she added a little pep to her step and was on the hunt for her friend.

It was a Saturday afternoon and the gym was busy. Which was usual. Everyone wanted to make up for their week of either forgoing exercise or overindulging on calories. The receptionist greeted her and Francesca smiled while she walked by and made her way down the hallway to Jane's office. She was so happy for her friend, who was now the manager of Hot Bods. Only a few months ago, Jane was the receptionist. Ever since Jane took over the gym, the place had really bloomed.

The office door was open and she found Jane sitting in her office chair, rubbing her pregnant belly.

"Hey, lady. How's the baby?" Francesca asked.

Jane looked up and said, "Kicking the hell out of me today. And not in a good way. I've been on the damn toilet all day. All she does is kick my bladder. That just might be too much information, but I'm a bit tired of almost peeing on myself."

"Uh, yeah. That's gross." Francesca sat down in a chair across from Jane's desk.

Jane laughed. "How are you?"

"I could be better. My car is in the shop after it broke down during that horrible storm last night. Now I have to figure out how to pay for the damn thing."

"How has work been?"

"Slow. Apparently nowadays people are doing decorating themselves. They don't need to hire interior designers anymore."

"It is spring. I bet a lot of people are moving. Maybe

you'll get some calls before long." Jane smiled.

"I hope. Otherwise I'm going to have to live up to rumors and get a sugar daddy."

Jane laughed. "Stop worrying about what everyone says about you."

That was easier said than done. Though, she hadn't stopped any of the stories all these years. She let everyone believe she was rich and had men just giving her money. Which wasn't entirely untrue, but it certainly wasn't how everyone thought it was. Rich men only showered you with money when you were servicing them, and she got tired of feeling like an overpriced call girl. She wanted to find love with one of those rich men. But it just wasn't happening. Maybe the saying 'money can't buy happiness' was true, because she certainly wasn't happy.

"How long are you without your car? I'm sure Ben has one you can borrow," Jane said.

Jane's fiancé Ben had a whole garage full of cars. Why hadn't she thought of that? "I might take you up on that. Right now I'm driving an old truck."

"I can't see you in a truck. I have got to take a picture."

"Shut up. It isn't like I'm driving the damn thing by choice. I just want to get my car back so I can be rid of Randall for good." Francesca crossed her arms and leaned back in the chair.

"Randall?" Jane looked at her with curiosity.

"He owns the repair shop and just happens to be my first love."

Jane leaned forward and propped her elbows on the desk. "Oh, this day just got better. My good friend, tell me about this guy. And did I hear right, you used the word love?"

"It was high school, don't get ahead of yourself."

"Does he have a big beer belly now, and already going bald?"

"God, do I wish. No, he is way hotter than he was back then. He's got that perfect shade of brown hair, kinda like an almond. With matching brown eyes. He's tall and built. The years have been good to him." *Yes, very good.*

"I see. Are you two going to rekindle?"

Francesca laughed. "I burned that bridge a long time ago."

"You never know, you just might be able to rebuild it."

"Doubtful."

The young receptionist poked her head in the door and let Jane know she was needed.

Francesca stood and offered her hand to Jane to help her up. Jane's belly seemed to grow bigger each day. Giving her friend a hug, Francesca said, "We'll talk soon. Don't work too hard."

"I try not to, but this place won't run itself," Jane said.

Francesca waved bye and as she made her way to the front of the building, she wondered what she was going to do for the evening. There was no way in hell she wanted to spend Saturday night eating take-out again.

As she left the gym, she dug through her purse, looking for her keys. Where the hell were they? Leaning against the truck, she started to empty the contents on the hood. She dropped the purse on the hood and peered through the driver's side window. Shit, her keys were on the seat. Pulling at the door handle, she hoped that maybe this damn thing was so old it didn't lock. But of course, luck wasn't with her.

She had two options—call Randall and hope he had a spare or call a locksmith.

* * * *

Stepping out of the shower, Randy heard his cellphone ring the ringtone that let him know someone was trying to get a hold of him at the shop. He ran through the house naked and answered his phone, out of breath.

"Smith's Auto, Randy here."

"Randall...I mean Randy. It's Francesca."

"What's up?" He walked back through the house to the bathroom and wrapped a towel around him.

"I have a problem."

"Forget to put gas in the truck?"

"Ha ha, no. Thanks for the warning, by the way. Actually, I locked the keys in the truck."

Randy started to laugh. Was this girl serious?

"It isn't funny. Please tell me you have a spare set and you can come unlock the door for me."

"I suppose I could do that." He smiled. "But I have a price."

"Are you kidding me? You know what, never mind. I'll call a locksmith." He could hear the irritation in her voice.

"I wasn't going to ask for money. I was going to invite you to dinner." He loved how things were working out. Maybe he could get her out of his system tonight, get her car fixed this week, and send her gorgeous self on her way.

"Is that a good idea?" she asked.

"I think it's a fine idea. Let me finish getting dressed. You caught me right as I stepped out of the shower. And then I'll be on my way. So just hold tight."

"Okay, I'm over at Hot Bods. Do you know where that is?"

"Yup." He hung up.

Oh yes, this was going to be much easier than he had imagined it would be. All he had to do now was convince Francesca to have dinner at his home. Could that really be so hard?

After getting dressed, he climbed into his fully restored 1972 Nova and headed across town. It didn't take him long to make it to the gym, and the first thing he spotted was a gorgeous woman standing next to a beat up ol' red truck. Back in the day, the truck looked as good next to her as she did it.

Parking, he climbed out and walked over to the truck. He had expected her to look a little grateful to see him, but instead she appeared angry. Digging the extra key out of his pocket, he unlocked the door for her. He opened his mouth to give her a smart alec remark, but she held her hand up to stop him. He couldn't help but grin. She still knew him.

"I don't want to hear it. While I waited I decided dinner isn't a good idea." She paused before continuing. "But since I know you're still going to beg me anyway, let's eat at my place. That way I can kick you out when I'm ready."

"How about my place, and you can leave whenever you please or if I decide to kick you out."

She shrugged. He'd expected a little more of a fight from her, but couldn't say he wasn't thrilled this wasn't going to turn into a drama fest. If there was one thing he remembered about Francesca, she loved drama and always had to win an argument.

"Deal. Don't get any funny ideas in your head." She climbed into the truck.

Randy leaned against the door and smiled. She still looked good in his truck. "My place is behind the shop. How about you come by in about an hour or so? Sound good?"

"Not really, but I'll be there."

He laughed and shut the door. "Try not to lock the key in the truck again."

As Francesca started up the vehicle, she shot him the bird, and then drove off. He wasn't sure what it was, but there was something about her that he couldn't help but love getting her riled up. She looked so darn cute when she was irritated. He had to get her between the sheets one last time. He didn't know how else to get her out of his system.

* * * *

Almost two hours later, Francesca pulled up to Smith's Auto. She noticed a small house next door to the shop. If she remembered correctly, that was his father's home. That must be where Randall was living. At first glance the house actually looked more like a small shack. It was in serious need of repairs and landscaping. It had been too much for his father, she was sure. But Randall was young, and surely his eyes worked and he could see what a mess this place was.

She knocked on the door, but no one answered. So she pounded louder and then turned the doorknob, finding it locked. What the hell? Was he here? Spinning around, she started to walk back toward the truck when she heard her named called.

"You're not leaving, are you?"

Turning, she saw Randall standing in the yard. He was dressed in a light blue button-down shirt with a pair of pressed khakis. "I knocked several times."

"Not on my door."

"I only see one house, unless you live in the shop."

"Follow me. My house is back here." He shook his head. "I think that house there needs to be condemned. You're lucky you didn't fall through the porch."

She couldn't help but agree with him. Randall disappeared between the shop and the small house. She sped up to see where he was going. Once she was on the other side of the shack she saw a clearing and stopped dead in her tracks. How could she not have seen this place earlier? A gorgeous home sat back away from everything. The lawn appeared to be professionally landscaped, and the house was a traditional brick two-story. Surely this wasn't his place. How could he afford it?

But he led the way to the front door then stopped and waited for her to catch up. As she followed him up the front steps, something washed over her and she felt like she was home. What a strange feeling.

After he opened the door, he allowed her to go inside first. While the outside looked gorgeous, the inside needed some help. The whole house looked like a guy lived there, no touch of a woman anywhere. There was no theme or order to the place.

"So, what do you think?" he asked.

"It's big. Is it yours?"

"Yup, had it built not long before Dad passed. I don't know how he lived in that other place."

"Well, he probably just didn't have the money to maintain it, being a mechanic and all."

He snickered and she wondered what that was about.

"You know, I'm an interior designer. We could trade services. You fix my car and I decorate your place."

"What's wrong with my place?" He glanced around,

obviously not seeing what she did.

"For one, you have these gorgeous vaulted ceilings but you have nothing in here that makes me want to look up. All your furniture is short. There is nothing on the wall. A few mirrors in the right places would make this room look even bigger."

"I'll think about it. And what do you mean my furniture is short? It's the same size as everyone elses."

"It might be, but in a room this big, it looks tiny. A big, gorgeous, hardwood entertainment center on that wall," she said, pointing, "would make all the difference."

"I'll think about it," he said again. "But for now, let's head out to the back porch. I was just getting ready to heat up the grill."

Francesca followed him through the house. She took note that the house had real hardwood floors. The walls were all painted a standard beige. The kitchen was elegant. The countertops were granite, and the appliances were top-of-the-line. She could get lost in this place decorating. Ideas flew through her mind and her fingers itched to touch.

As Francesca stepped outside onto the deck, her mouth dropped open in awe. The deck was...well...awesome. A lot of money and time had been spent on it. It featured an outside kitchen. In the back corner, a custom hot tub was set up, with plants all around it for privacy. Benches had been built into the railing, and a gorgeous glass table that could easily seat twelve was placed next to it.

How the hell had he afforded all of this? Maybe there was more money in the mechanic business than she thought.

"You must be doing quite well if you can afford all of this."

"I make it. But it also helps to know people."

Walking over to the railing, she looked out at the yard. It was overgrown and not as well taken care of as the front. The yard was wooded, private, and quiet. She liked it.

"I hope chicken's good. I marinated it in my special sauce," he said as he reached into the tiny outdoor fridge.

"That sounds great, but I'm surprised you're not a steak man."

"I am, but I know women like chicken."

She laughed. "I see now why you're the most sought out bachelor in town. You must really know how to get a lady into bed."

Her gaze locked on his, and her heart speed up as a grin spread across that gorgeous face of his. Before she knew what she was doing, she was walking toward him, closing the space between them, and her lips were pressed to his. She heard him set the bowl of chicken down and then his arms wrapped around her, pulling her close.

Francesca opened her mouth right away, letting his tongue dart over hers. There was a hint of mint as she felt her way around. Her hand massaged his neck and then slowly raked its way up through his hair. Lost in the kiss, she didn't realize he'd picked her up. The kiss broke as he lowered her onto a long patio chair. Randall nudged her legs open and positioned himself between them. She expected him to kiss her again, but instead he let his lips explore her neck, shoulders, down her arms. Letting out a sigh, her head fell back against the chair. His hand crept under her shirt and his fingers lightly brushed her stomach.

"I don't know what this scent is you wear, but it drives me crazy." Randall found her lips again before she could speak.

Francesca wrapped her legs around his waist. His erection pressed into her center and with her body, she urged him to grind into her. His cock was hard and she ached to feel it in her hand again. To run her fingers up and down his length.

As if he was feeling the same way, she felt his palm begin to rub her inner thigh over her jeans. She clenched her stomach in anticipation, but right as he found his way to her center, a loud burst of thunder shook the porch.

"Shit." Randall broke the kiss and quickly stood.

Straightening her clothes, Francesca noticed how dark the sky was. A storm was definitely rolling in. She hated spring time and all the bad weather. She expected Randall to reach out and help her up, but instead he was already over at his grill, turning it off, and gathering the food to take into the house.

Francesca let out a sigh and realized things had gone too far. That make-out session never should've happened. Standing, she made her way inside right as the clouds opened up and the rain started to fall. She found Randall in the kitchen pulling out what appeared to be a counter-top grill.

He looked up at her and smiled. "Give me a few and we'll be ready to eat."

She wasn't sure if she was hungry any longer. If it wasn't pouring rain, she would be getting the hell out of the place.

"How about you pour us both a glass of wine and I'll meet you in the dining room," he suggested.

She had to look in several cabinets before she found the wine glasses, and she grabbed two of them. From the wine rack on the counter, she picked up a bottle of white. She turned to ask where the bottle opener was, but found

Randall right there.

"I don't know about you, but the only thing I'm hungry for is exploring your body. Let's skip eating and do this one last time for the hell of it."

Setting the wine and the glasses down, Francesca placed her hands on her hips. "You're kidding, right?"

"I've never been more serious. Ever since I saw you again, I've wanted one more taste. Tell me you haven't."

"It's crossed my mind, but that doesn't mean it's something we should do."

Brushing the back of his hand down her arm, he asked, "How far would we have gone if the storm hadn't hit?"

"Well, a storm did hit, so I can't answer that."

He leaned in, his lips close. "Make love to me just one more time. After that, I'll fix your car and you never have to see me again. I'll even have the car delivered to your place so you don't have to come in to pick it up."

Could it really be that simple? As much as she hated to admit it, she wanted to get between the sheets with him one more time. Taking a deep breath, Francesca nodded. "If it's the easiest way to get you out of my life, then let's do it."

In one swift move, Randall picked her up and carried her across the house.

Chapter 5

Randy laid Francesca on his bed and gazed down at her. She was beautiful, and she looked perfect in his bed, gazing back up at him. Suddenly he felt nervous, the way he had the first time he'd been with her years ago.

Rubbing his hand along her arm, he made his way up to her mid-section and let his fingers lightly caress her belly button. She bit her bottom lip before she wiggled a little. Francesca reached out and wrapped her hand around his neck, pulling his mouth to hers. She kissed him with a hunger and he knew she needed this as much as he did. If this was going to be their last time together, then he had to make it memorable.

Leaving her lips, he trailed light kisses down her neck. He pulled her low-cut shirt down and licked all the way to her cleavage. Sucking on her breasts, he was able to free one. He swirled his tongue around her nipple before he drew it into his mouth.

"Oh God," she moaned.

She had always liked special attention in that area. Francesca was one of the few women who could come just from nipple stimulation. Smiling to himself, he decided to see if he still had the ability to get her to. He pulled the other breast free from her bra. As he flicked one nipple with his tongue, he lightly pinched the other.

Her hips squirmed and her breathing picked up. Continuing to play, he switched breasts and sped up his rhythm. Her body tensed and her back arched. She was on the edge. He rubbed the palm of his hand back and forth on just the tip of one nipple while he blew lightly on the other one.

"Oh my!" she cried out as her hands gripped the sheets.

Once she relaxed, he sat up and began working on removing her clothes. Her cheeks were flushed and she had a satisfied smile on her face.

As he pulled her boots off he said, "You're the only woman I've met who can release from that type of stimulation. It's hot."

She reached down and rubbed his cock through his jeans. "It certainly is."

Once her boots were off, he began working on her jeans. As he pulled them down, he went ahead and pulled her panties down too, leaving her aroused scent in the air. God, she smelled so sweet. He'd love to have a taste, but wasn't sure he could last. As Francesca's hand rubbed his erection through his jeans, he was worried he didn't have the self-control he'd spent years building. If she didn't stop, he was going to come.

He pushed her hand away. She giggled and then sat up. Along with him, she wanted his clothes off. She was less gentle about it. She tugged and yanked until he was naked. As she took in the sight of him, he began to unbutton her blouse. Once it was off, she unhooked her bra and let it drop. She looked up at him.

Licking his lips, he noticed the position they were in. He was on his knees and she sat with her legs to her side. His aching cock was in line with her big breasts. There was something about the softness of a woman's breasts that he liked on his dick. Taking it in his hand, he leaned forward and rubbed the tip into her cleavage.

At first she didn't move, only watched. Then she leaned forward a bit and cupped her titties together, creating just the right amount of depth for him. He only needed a few strokes before he had to be inside of her.

Randy shoved her down, forced her legs open, and climbed in between them. His fingers dipped into her folds, and he found her wet and ready. He needed her on the edge though, as he was. He wasn't going to last long. In a fast motion, he fingered her and thumbed her clit.

"Now!" she demanded.

He reached over to the nightstand and grabbed a foil package. In one swift move, he rolled the condom on and thrust his cock into her sweet center. Francesca cried out repeatedly. He'd forgotten how vocal she could be. He loved to hear the sounds coming from her mouth. She said his name, several times. Bringing his mouth back to hers, he picked up speed and began to thrust hard into her. He attempted to kiss her as his climax built, but hers tore through her first. Her entire body arched and her pussy tightened around his cock. Good God! How was she doing that?

He grabbed the pillow behind her and screamed out as his release hit him. He pumped into her, riding out his release and the pleasure he was feeling. It had been a long time since he had come this intensely. Finally, the vibrating pleasure slowed down and he was able to relax.

He rolled off Francesca and brought her into his arms. He knew he had a huge smile on his face. He was one hundred percent satisfied, the way he used to feel years ago.

* * * *

Francesca lay with her head on Randall's chest. Had she really just done that? Had sex with the only man she had ever loved? This had been a mistake. A very big one. But as she laid there, his arms wrapped around her, breathing in his musky scent, she had never felt more at home. They fit together like the right puzzle pieces. She couldn't remember the last time she'd had an orgasm so intense that it was as though each and every nerve on her stood on its end and vibrated. And yet, it was over. There was no way they could be together. There was a history there. And you never repeated history, at least not when things had turned out disastrously.

Clearing her throat, Francesca sat up. Randal was so handsome. His dark eyes stared back at her. More than anything she wanted to reach out and rub the back of her palm over his stubble and tell him she loved him. But instead, she said, "Well, that was fun. Guess I'll be on my way."

"It was fun." He lifted himself off the bed and slid on his boxers.

Letting her gaze follow him, she was surprised he left the room, leaving her there all alone. She sighed loudly and put her clothes back on almost as fast as they'd come off. After slipping her shoes on, she went to look for Randall. The storm had passed and through the back glass door she saw he was on the porch, in his boxers, staring out over the lawn with that look on his face that told her he was seriously thinking.

Making love had brought up feelings in each of them, she was sure. If she went out there now, they would talk, and somehow convince each other a relationship would work. But there was a reason she'd left him years ago. It was a selfish one, she'd chosen money over love, but it wasn't like she could go back now and change things. Randall would never believe she loved him. And the hurtful things she'd said years ago would always be in the back of his mind.

So she decided to leave. It was easier. Picking up her purse, she made her way out of the house and didn't look back. She walked in a fast pace. All it would take was for him to call her name, and she would turn around, go back, and be his forever.

Chapter 6

Randy slammed the hood down on the white Lexus. Finally, this damn car was fixed. All he had to do now was deliver it and he'd be done with Francesca. It was already done. She hadn't called all week, and he hadn't called her. They'd had sex—awesome sex. The only problem was she wasn't out of his system. That one last time between the sheets he thought would work, didn't. He wanted her again and again. He wanted to feel her warm breath on his skin, her soft touch as she caressed him, and her little murmurs as he pleased her.

But did she want him? Sure, he could tell her he was loaded, and she'd be knocking on his door. But he wanted her to want him for him not his money. It was hard to let her go, but somehow he was going to have to.

In his office, Randy picked up the phone. He needed to know where the truck was so he could swap out the vehicles. He dialed her and as he placed the phone to his ear, all he could hear was the sound of his heart pumping at a fast pace.

She answered on the third ring. "Hello."

"It's Randy. Your car's done. Let me know where my

truck is, and I can swap the vehicles out."

"I'm actually at the gym."

"You're always there. Do you live there or something?"

"No, it's customer appreciation week. They have free massages. I'm taking advantage of that."

"How long are you going to be there?" he asked, tapping his fingers on his desk.

"Another forty-five minutes."

"When you get done, your car will be there. Make sure you change the oil from now on."

"Leave the bill in the glove compartment and I'll send you a check," she said matter-of-factly.

He hated how formal this was. He wanted to know how she was, what she was doing, if her day was going well. Not this business talk. "Sounds good."

"Thanks, Randall."

He started to tell her once again, it was Randy, but she'd already hung up. Setting the phone down, he moaned. She'd given him what he'd asked for. But this certainly was not what he wanted. Damn, life had been so much simpler before that stormy night Francesca entered his life again.

* * * *

"How was your massage?" Skylar asked as Francesca

stepped out of the locker room.

"Heavenly," Francesca answered.

"Good, I'm glad to hear that."

Francesca started to walk away but then turned back toward Skylar. It was time to really put the past behind them. Amy's wedding was just around the corner and they needed to learn to like one another. "Want to hang out later?" Francesca asked.

Skylar raised an eyebrow. "Me? You know, we only have to get along for the wedding, not be best friends."

Normally Francesca would've said something in a snappy tone and been done, but she remembered Jane had told her one afternoon over coffee that she needed to be the bigger person. "I think it's time we put the past behind us. I'd like for us to be friends. Not best friends by any means, but friends."

Skylar crossed her arms. "What is this all about?"

"Look, Skylar, quit being so damn stubborn. I never wanted Drew the way you did. You're married to him. If that makes you feel better, you won."

"It does a little."

Francesca rolled her eyes. Maybe trying to be anything but civil with Skylar was a mistake. They were never going to be more than they were now.

"Maybe we can hang out in a group. Perhaps you, Jane, Amy, and I," Skylar suggested.

"I think that's perfect."

"We'll set something up before the wedding."

"Great. See ya around." Francesca turned and headed for the front doors. Progress had been made, and that was all that mattered. Maybe they would eventually get to the friend status, or they wouldn't. But if not, it wouldn't be from her lack of trying.

Placing a hand over her eyes to shield the sun, she looked for the beat-up red truck but didn't spot it. Then she remembered that her car was done and Randall had said he would drop it off. She skipped across the parking lot and quickly found her car.

Opening the door, she climbed in. She smiled as she rubbed her hands across the steering wheel. Breathing in deeply, she picked up a hint of Randall's cologne. For a moment she savored it, then reminded herself that he was out of her system. They had one last time between the sheets and now they were done.

Francesca leaned over and opened the glove box, revealing her keys. She snatched them out, slammed it shut, and then cranked up her engine. It was quiet…at least compared to that darn ol' pick-up truck.

The drive home was smooth, and she was thankful. It hadn't been long ago that she'd driven this same path in this car and had a much different evening. But not tonight. Francesca pulled into her usual parking spot in front of her apartment. She opened the glove compartment again to remove the bill and see what kind of damage the car repairs were going to do to her savings account. She found a medium size book. Pulling it out she noticed it was a calendar, but it wasn't hers. She flipped through the pages and saw Randall had taken the time to write in dates that maintenance was needed on her vehicle.

A warmth filled her chest, and for a moment she gripped the calendar tight against her and smiled. It was one of the kindest things anyone had ever done for her. She pulled the book away from her and opened it from the back where her bill was. She noticed a few other pieces of paper and saw that Randall had included coupons to local oil change shops.

She took a deep breath, it was time to look at the bill. She unfolded the yellow paper and glanced at the bottom right corner. That couldn't be right. She scanned the entire bill and saw that he hadn't charged her for labor and she was positive he'd given her a discount on the parts. But why? Certainly he needed the money. Was he just being nice, or was it more? Could Randall still have feelings for her?

Francesca laughed out loud. It was silly to think he had feelings for her.

Quickly, she folded up the paper and stuffed it in her purse. She climbed out of her car and jetted for her apartment.

* * * *

Randy set the empty beer bottle on the bar counter and cursed to himself. He'd come down here tonight with the intent of finding a woman to fill his evening with. Heck, he'd even had an offer from a very willing blonde. And for a moment, he'd thought about it. But then he remembered Francesca had blonde hair also and his mind replayed her soft locks brushing against his chest. He didn't want the blonde woman in his bed. Dare he say it? He wanted Francesca, again.

Standing up forcefully, he kicked the stool out from behind him, laid a bill on the counter, and made his way toward the front of the bar. *She* was supposed to be out of his system. He wasn't supposed to be thinking about *her* anymore. But ever since he'd had one more frickin' taste of her, he craved another. He had a suspicion that even if they hooked up again, it wouldn't be enough. It never was.

He was once certain he was going to marry that woman, but she'd wanted a rich man. Now he was that rich man. But he couldn't tell her that. Might be simpler if he did, but he'd be a fool.

Randy shoved the front door open and made his way across the parking lot to the old red pick-up. After getting his keys from his pocket, he climbed in. The damn truck smelled like her. She'd only had it a week, yet everything from the seat belt to the fabric on the doors smelled like her and that perfume she wore.

Just as he started the car, his cellphone rang. He pulled it from his pocket and saw it was her.

"What?" he answered.

"Not a good time?" she asked.

"Kinda." Randy leaned his head back against the head rest.

"Oh, sorry. I wanted to say thank you for the calendar. It was a nice touch."

"Hopefully you'll remember to take care of the car and change the oil every once in a while," he snapped. He wasn't really sure why he was directing so much anger at her, he just knew his emotions were out of whack.

"I will. I'm sorry I caught you at a bad time. I'll let you go."

He could hear the sadness in her tone. She hadn't called just to thank him. He was certain she wouldn't be calling him unless she had another reason.

"I'm sorry. I'm just having a rough evening," he said.

"You could come over."

"Really?" No, no he did not want to go over there. Her car was fixed. It was a clean break.

"Yeah, I had something I wanted to ask you anyway."

"Sure, okay. I will be over in a bit." He hung up.

* * * *

Francesca ran through her apartment, tossing anything that was out of place in a closet or drawer. Why had she invited him over? All she had planned to do was ask him a question over the phone, but then he sounded so angry. Was he mad at her? What had she done?

Before she had time to think about it further, the buzzer sounded, letting her know she had a guest at the gate. She hit a button by her front door to allow him in. She glanced over the apartment one last time. It looked tidy. She wasn't a housekeeper, that was for sure, but the place was acceptable. Not anywhere as neat as his place though.

Knock knock.

He was there. She straightened her shirt, cleared her throat, and opened the door with a smile. Holy hell, he

Page 354

looked hot. He still had a brooding expression on that made him look damn sexy. He wore a tight black t-shirt and a pair of light jeans that hugged all the right places. She licked her lips, and before she had time to think, he was inside, kicking her door shut and yanking her into his arms. His mouth pressed against hers and she immediately opened.

The kiss was filled with anger and need. She wrapped her arms around his neck and jumped up, her legs hugging his waist. Two firm hands gripped her ass as he carried her to the couch. Slowly he sat, placing her in a straddling position. He was hard and pressing right into her center. She couldn't wait to feel his thick cock inside her. He was just the right size that he could make her come as he entered her.

"I want to taste you," he said against her lips.

He toyed with her pants until he got them unbuttoned. Like a pro, he pulled them along with her panties off her hips and she lifted her legs so he could slide them off. A finger pressed against her clit and her breath caught. He kissed her neck, and she expected him to push her down, but instead, he pressed into her in an upward motion as he kissed his way down her body.

Before long, she was no longer straddling him, she was kneeling above him as he licked her belly button and then started a pathway to her pussy. Gripping the back of the couch, she braced herself, and boy was she glad she did. His tongue dipped in between her folds and lightly swept from back to front repeatedly. His mouth closed around her clit and gently sucked it.

Her knuckles were most likely white from how tight she held on as she leaned into his face. One of his strong and callused hands rubbed along her inner thigh while the other one found her opening and entered her pussy.

"Oh my God," she managed to speak.

"Are you enjoying this?" he asked.

"Yes."

He began fingering her in a rapid motion and his tongue teased. Her breathing was shallow and fast, and she could feel an intensity building. She was going to come and there was no stopping it.

"Oh my God, Randall," she called out as a wave of pleasure shook her body.

His rhythm slowed slightly and it kept her right on the edge. It was as though he was doing whatever he could to delay her orgasm. But she couldn't stop it. It felt too good. She had to come. Not knowing what came over her, she began to grind into his face and he rewarded her by picking the pace back up. His free hand urged her to continue her motion.

"Oh my!" she screamed as the orgasm raced through her. She continued to moan and cry out as she rode out one of the most intense forms of pleasure she had ever experienced.

Once she couldn't take any more, she stopped pumping her hips into Randy and felt herself begin to relax. She dropped down into his lap and laid her head on his shoulder. Taking in deep breaths, she hoped for the strength to return the pleasure to him that he had just given to her.

"That was amazing," she said.

Randall picked her up and laid her on the couch. She looked at him and then down his body to his cock. His rock hard cock wanting to break free from his pants. He unbuttoned his jeans and lowered them down along with his boxers. His dick was long and swollen. She found herself licking her lips again.

He took a condom from his pants, and as he rolled it on, she found herself wet and ready again. He nudged her legs open and leaned over her. Quickly, she grabbed the hem of his shirt and yanked it over his head, revealing his well sculpted chest. God, this man didn't hit the gym, but boy was he built. The six-pack on him was better than any she'd seen at the gym.

He placed his cock right at her opening. Francesca

wrapped her hands around his neck and kissed him. Right as her tongue found its way into his mouth, he entered her in one hard thrust. Her legs clutched his waist and with each pump into her, she felt the climax build again. She didn't think it was possible to be able to come so soon after the intense orgasm she had just had, but she was wrong.

She held onto him with a death grip. When his breathing picked up and he started to murmur into her ear, she knew he was almost there. She pumped her hips in an upward motion with force, and before she knew it, they were both calling out one another's names as the pleasure tore through her.

Randy broke the kiss to nuzzle his head into her collarbone. Francesca let her fingers dance up and down his spine as she gazed at the ceiling. Randall was an amazing lover. No one else had ever made her feel this alive. And even though he hadn't been back in her life for too long, she knew she was falling in love with him again. Then again, maybe she never stopped loving him.

Chapter 7

Shit! They'd done it again. Randy raked his hands through his hair as he waited for Francesca to return. She'd gone to get two glasses of wine, but he wasn't sure more alcohol was what he really needed.

"Here you go," she said as she handed him a glass.

He glanced up at her as she stepped around him and took a seat on the couch. They both had their clothes back on, which was a good thing. Taking a sip of the wine, he waited for her to talk. After all, she was the one who invited him over.

"That was a little unexpected," she said with a sweetness in her tone.

"Thought that's why you asked me here."

She giggled. "A booty call...really? I don't think so."

"So you actually have something you need to ask me?"

"Yeah."

Damn, usually when a woman called you late at night with some excuse they only wanted one thing. Or at least the women who called him did.

"My brother is getting married in a few weeks, and I wanted to see if you might like to go with me." She took a sip of her drink and then held the glass in her hand, slowly turning it so the red liquid swirled.

Was she serious? "You're kidding, right?"

"No. I thought you might like to see my brother get married."

"Yes, but you and me…together." It was music to his ears. Unfortunately, he knew they shouldn't go down that road again. "I don't think so. That would be taking whatever it is going on between us to something else."

Francesca set her glass on the coffee table, and he could see the fury in her face. She did not like to be rejected. Never had. "Obviously there is nothing between us. We are just two lonely people who needed the comfort of one another."

"Not me. I could have gone home with another woman tonight." Why did he just say that?

Francesca's mouth fell open before she replied, "Really? Then why didn't you?"

Because I wanted you. "I wasn't in the mood."

She laughed. "You're a man. You're always in the mood."

"That's such a stereotype. We can control it."

"Oh really?" Francesca stood up and let her fingers slowly raise her top. Damn would he like to see it keep going, but he had to stop her.

"It won't work. We aren't doing it again. Hell, this was supposed to be over. You got your car back."

She lowered her shirt back and crossed her arms. "For once, you're right."

"I'm sure you can call some rich man to take you to the wedding. Don't you have several in your back pocket?" He regretted it the moment the words left his mouth.

"You know what? Just get the hell out of here. Don't worry, I won't be calling you again for anything," she snapped.

Randy thought about saying he was sorry and that he was out of line. He didn't know what came over him when he was around her. He'd much rather be cuddled up with her on the couch watching a movie than fighting. But instead of responding, he just slipped his shoes on and headed toward her front door. He turned and looked back at her. He opened his mouth to say something, but was interrupted.

"Don't let the door hit you on the ass on your way out," she said.

He'd deserved it, but it didn't make it hurt any less that she wanted him gone.

* * * *

The next morning, Francesca was still fuming. She thought a good workout would help, but it only made it worse. She'd forgotten her MP3 player at home, so all she was left to while on the elliptical were her thoughts. And of course, her mind was on Randall.

It was silly to think he wanted anything more with her. She'd had a moment of weakness. Yes, Randall was the first and only love of her life, so far, but that didn't mean he was *the one*. The world was full of men. One of them was meant to be hers. She just had to find him. But right now, she had to work on finding a date for the wedding.

After she had showered and dressed, Francesca pulled her hair back into a wet bun. She had a full schedule today, and she needed to get home and get back to some clients. She'd left this place once not looking her best, she could do it again.

"Francesca," Jane called as Francesca was attempting to escape Hot Bods.

She turned to see her friend. "Hey, Jane."

"Skylar, Amy, and I are getting lunch. Come with us."

"Oh, I look horrible. I can't today."

Jane placed her hands on her hips. "I've gained thirty pounds. My legs are swollen, my face has broken out, and this beautiful shiny hair I hear about when pregnant, obviously didn't agree with me. You look as beautiful as ever. Your tiny ass is going with us…got it?"

Francesca laughed and glanced at her watch. She could probably squeeze an hour in for lunch with them. "If you're going to put it that way… Tell me where and I'll meet you there."

"The pizzeria one block down. I'm just waiting on Amy to arrive and then we're heading that way." Jane paused, looking over Francesca's shoulder out the window, and then said, "Here she comes now."

Francesca turned to see Amy walking in. Her normally short hair was now touching her shoulders. She'd decided to grow it out for the wedding. Something about wanting an up-do. Either way, her future sister-in-law was going to be gorgeous.

"Everyone ready?" Skylar asked as she walked around the corner. "After two kick boxing classes this morning, I'm starved."

"I'll meet you ladies there," Francesca said.

The ride was short. Once inside the restaurant, they made their way to a booth. Francesca glanced around noticing the décor which gave her a sense of home. It was one of those places where a candle was lit on each table that had a red checkered table cloth on it. The menus were on the table behind the salt and pepper shakers. She'd been there before, but it wasn't her usual type of place.

When the waitress appeared, she seemed to know Skylar and Amy right away. This must be a place they visited regularly. There was a cozy feeling to the restaurant. Francesca could see coming here with a close group of friends to have a few good laughs.

After they ordered drinks and decided on a pizza they would share, Francesca started to relax. The way Jane, Skylar, and Amy interacted with one another put her at ease. Maybe it wouldn't be so bad to open up and just be friends.

"I see you've gotten your car back. Does it feel nice to be driving it again?" Jane asked.

"God, yeah. The beat-up truck didn't have air conditioning."

"What's the story there anyway? Adam and I were wondering. Are you and Randy rekindling an old flame?" Amy asked.

"No," Francesca answered.

"You don't sound very convincing," Skylar chimed in.

"I don't really want to talk about him."

Amy nudged Francesca. "Oh, come on. You're among friends, and we want the dish."

"There is nothing to dish."

"Yeah, right. Give us something. I'm getting beat up from the inside, and the only thing Ben and I are doing these days is cuddling." Jane rubbed her belly.

Francesca took a deep breath and said, "Okay, fine. We did it one last time for old times' sake. But that's it. It's over."

"How was it?" Jane asked.

"Just because you're pregnant doesn't mean you can't be with Ben. Geesh." Francesca rolled her eyes.

"That's what got me in this situation."

"Yes, but you're already pregnant. It's not like he can knock you up right now."

"You never know." Jane shrugged.

They all laughed.

"So, just one time?" Amy asked.

Francesca nodded, looking away from everyone.

"She's lying," Skylar said.

Just as Francesca was about to argue, the pizza arrived. Thank God!

Soon, they were stuffing their mouths and talking about how good the food was. Jane kept giving her looks throughout lunch that clearly said she wanted to know everything. Francesca would fill her in later, but she didn't want everyone to know about her and Randall and the mess that had been created. Hopefully, however, they were really done.

But for some reason, the thought of that left her feeling sad. Did she really just want things over? She knew the answer and it was *no*. She'd like to get to know him again and see if maybe it could work. But he'd laughed at her and made it clear the sex between them had meant nothing.

And besides that, she'd never done the chasing. She was used to the man wanting her and doing everything he could to get her. She had no idea what to do if she had to pursue him. But she had a feeling that if she wanted to be with Randall again, she was going to have to show him that she wasn't who he thought she was.

Chapter 8

A week had passed since Randy had last talked to or seen Francesca. He had hoped by now she'd be free from his mind, but instead each night she was the last thought he had before drifting off to sleep. And when he woke the next morning, she was the first thing that popped in his head. And this was after she'd haunted his dreams.

But they were two different types of people, and he had to keep reminding himself of that. And tonight he had a date. A woman who was the complete opposite of Francesca. Dana had short, dark locks, and was on the sweet side. She was shy and quiet, unlike Francesca who was always up for an argument.

Randy knew Dana wasn't the one for him. But perhaps a few kisses could help him move on. Then again, maybe Dana was the one and he just wasn't giving her a chance. Tonight was her chance. In fact, this evening could be the best damn night he'd ever had. Yes, he had to stay positive.

Now, he had to shower and get ready for his date. He had seven o'clock reservations at one of those fancy restaurants. He'd never been one to want to pay twenty dollars for a steak but women liked those sorts of places. He preferred a burger and greasy fries from a drive-thru and watching a good action movie while wearing his favorite sweatpants on the couch. Randy chuckled, perhaps that was why his relationships never worked. Maybe one day he'd find a woman who wanted the same thing.

* * * *

The hostess led Francesca to the table she'd reserved. Taking her seat, she took a sip of the water already at the table and glanced around. Her dinner date should be arriving any moment. While she waited, she pulled out her folder with the designs she had come up with. She glanced through them quickly to make sure everything was there. This was a very important project for her on many different levels.

After she looked through the entire binder, she closed it and waited. It didn't take long for the handsome older man she'd been waiting on to arrive.

"You look as lovely as ever, Francesca," he said as he took his seat.

She smiled. "Thanks, Ben, and you look...well, tired."

"Jane isn't sleeping these days. She can't get comfortable. All she does is toss and turn all night. Then, like clockwork, every two hours she is up and in the bathroom."

"Poor Jane."

"Oh yes, the pregnant lady gets all the sympathy."

"Well, she is the one doing all the work."

"And for that, I am thankful. I don't think I could be doing what she is right now."

The waitress arrived and they ordered their meals. Francesca then handed the binder to Ben and waited to see what he thought. Ben was planning to send Jane away for a weekend of relaxation and when she returned, the nursery was going to be complete as a surprise. And Francesca was honored when he asked her to design it. So, this had to be perfect. And luckily, being good friends with Jane had helped her know just what she wanted.

Ben closed the binder and laid it on the table.

"Well?" she asked.

"It's wonderful. Jane is going to love it."

Francesca smiled. "I can't wait to start shopping for it. That is your copy." She pointed to the folder. "I've already shopped around and the prices are listed in the back. A few items could be bought at several places, and I listed them and the place that was the cheapest."

Ben held his hand up. "I don't care what it costs. You should know that by now."

"Jane is very lucky to have you."

"No, I'm lucky to have her."

It made her so happy to see these two so happy. She'd set them up, but hadn't known at the time that she was making a match made in heaven. Jane was getting out of a bad relationship and wanted to retaliate against the creep, to make him seethe with jealousy, so Francesca had set her up with Ben as a fake relationship. Only, it was never fake. They were destined to be with one another.

"Have you gotten Toby trained yet?" Francesca had met the yellow lab a few times. *Energetic* didn't even begin to describe Jane's dog.

"We're getting there."

Ben continued to tell her about getting the dog out of bed with him and Jane. And how the dog was still sneaking up in the middle of the night. Francesca had never owned a pet—she had severe allergies—however, she enjoyed hearing stories about other people's pets.

* * * *

Pushing the chair in for Dana, Randy glanced around the restaurant. It was a very nice steakhouse. The lights were dimly lit and music played at a quiet but intimate level, making it perfect for a romantic evening. The tables all had a candle on them, white table clothes, and dark hardwood chairs.

Randy took a seat across from Dana, and she smiled at him. She was impressed, and for that, he was glad. The girl deserved a nice evening out. And so did he.

Almost immediately, a waitress appeared to get their drink orders. He ordered a soda for now. He wasn't sure alcohol was such a good idea. Dana ordered a tea.

"This is a very nice place," she said. "Have you been here before?"

"No, it's my first time."

"Maybe this will be one of the many firsts we will have together."

He quickly grabbed the water that sat in front of him and took a sip. It was never good when a woman talked about a future right away. Or at least for him it wasn't.

"How was work today?" she asked.

"Pretty slow."

"Things were slow at the flower shop as well."

He nodded. First dates were always awkward, he reminded himself. As Dana continued to talk about her day, he did his best to pay attention. He was thankful when the server returned with their drinks and to see what they wanted to order for dinner. He let Dana go first and then he ordered a steak, baked potato, and grilled vegetables. He couldn't believe the prices. It wasn't like he couldn't afford it, but normally he'd never pay that much for dinner.

As they waited on their food, he looked around. A woman a few tables over with shoulder length blonde hair laughed, catching his attention.

Was that?

No, it couldn't be Francesca. There was no way they'd be at the same place. But he had to know.

"I'll be right back, I need to wash up." He excused himself.

As he got closer to the woman, she spoke and he recognized her voice. It was Francesca, and she looked to be having a fabulous time with an older man, one he assumed was rich. And to think, she'd just asked him to be her date at some wedding. And she wanted to see if there was anything between them. She was never going to change.

He cleared his throat to get her attention. She spun around in her chair and looked back at him.

"Randall. Wow, this is unexpected."

"It certainly is, isn't it?" he said with irritation in his voice.

"Randall, this is Ben. Ben, this is Randall." She introduced them.

"It's Randy."

"Sorry, I keep forgetting." Her smiled faded.

"It's nice to meet you." Ben put his hand out to shake.

Randy didn't take the man's hand. The older gentleman put his hand down and then excused himself to go to the restroom.

Francesca nodded at Ben as he left, letting him know she was fine. Once he was out of sight, she glared at Randy. "What's your problem?" she asked.

"You move on fast," Randy snapped.

"What?"

"Your date. He's just your type, huh? Rich and older. Aren't you tired of being someone's arm candy yet?"

Her eyes widened and he could see the hurt. "He's not my date. He's a client."

"Do you think I'm stupid?" he said loudly.

"Quiet down, you're making a scene." She reached across the table and grabbed a binder. "Take a look if you don't believe me. I'm designing a nursery for him and my friend Jane. He's surprising her."

Randy opened the binder and flipped through the pages looking at blueprints and nursery furniture. Oh fuck, had he made a fool of himself. He handed the folder back to her and didn't know what to say. He raked his hand through his hair and wished he could take the scene back.

"I'm sorry," he finally said.

She set the binder on the table, and just as she looked like she was about to speak, he heard a different female voice. "Is everything okay over here, honey?" An arm wrapped around his shoulder.

Dana. *Oh crap.* Randy studied Francesca and he could see it was taking everything in her to control herself.

"Hi, I'm Francesca," she said, holding her hand out.

"I'm Dana, Randy's girlfriend." Dana's tone was full of pride.

"Girlfriend? I didn't know."

"I wouldn't say girlfriend," Randy added. What the hell? The lady was about to ruin everything.

"It was nice to meet you. Listen, when Ben comes out of the restroom, let him know I got called away." Francesca grabbed her purse from the floor and before he could say anything, she was gone.

He turned to Dana and asked, "What was that all about?"

"You know, it isn't nice to ask a girl out when you're not really interested." She released his shoulder and then followed the same path as Francesca did.

This was not at all how he'd envisioned his evening. Not only had he hurt Francesca, but he'd hurt someone who was innocent in this whole situation. He had two women to apologize to now.

"You really screwed up, huh?" the older man asked as he came back to the table.

"Yeah."

"I don't know you, but I've know Francesca for a few years. And she's one of my fiancée's best friends. She isn't who everyone thinks she is. Francesca is one of the kindest people you will ever meet. She did so much for Jane and never asked for anything in return. Everyone seems to think she is only out for herself, but all the girl really wants is for Prince Charming to sweep her off her feet and love her," Ben explained.

Randy nodded. "I'm beginning to think you're right."

Ben chuckled. "Though, I'd hate to be on her bad side."

"Yeah, it's not my first time. I should be a pro at it by now."

"I think you know what to do though."

Randy wasn't so sure he did. But showing her how sorry he was would be the first step.

Chapter 9

He has a girlfriend! Francesca hadn't seen that one coming. Anytime she liked a guy, they were always taken. But wow, he'd slept with her and had been involved with someone all along. You didn't get girlfriend status with just a date or two.

Closing the door to her apartment, she walked through the dark room to her kitchen. Still not turning a light on, she opened the fridge and took out a bottle of wine. She started to reach for a glass, but then changed her mind. Pulling the cork out, she pressed the opening to her lips, lifted the bottle up, and took in a nice, long sip.

It wasn't like Randall had wanted a relationship with her. He'd told her the sex was just to get her out of his system. It was only meant to be a one night thing. And the second time, he'd assumed it was just a booty call. Nothing more. But in all that time, she couldn't believe he never mentioned the girlfriend. Even in his office, there was no evidence of her. What a creep! Men like that disgusted her. And she'd been stupid enough to sleep with him.

But still, that just didn't seem like the Randall she knew. When they had dated in high school, he was one hundred percent faithful. He hadn't even looked another girl's way. But it had been years since she'd seen him. People changed, and not always for the better.

Francesca took a long sip of her drink. She wasn't sure she had changed for the better either. She was the one who dumped him, telling him he could never be the man she needed. And for years, she had been living the high life with man after man, waiting on one of those rich men to steal her heart. It hadn't happened yet, and now she had a reputation.

Francesca took a seat on her couch, still in the dark. She set the bottle in her lap and decided that it was time to change. The life she'd been living wasn't getting her to where she wanted to be. The first thing she was going to do was get to know herself before she let anyone else in.

She stood and then finished off the bottle of wine. It had been close to empty when she opened it and now it was gone. She debated opening another bottle, but decided a long hot bath would be a better option than drowning her sorrows in wine.

After she got the bath started, she chose some music and lit a few candles. She kept the lights off. Once the tub was full of warm liquid and bubbles, she stripped off her clothes. As the water engulfed her, she began to feel better. Sometimes a bath was just what you needed. Leaning her head back against the tile, she closed her eyes and simply relaxed.

She finally felt at peace, as though the day was being lifted away. Things were going to be fine.

Knock knock!

Opening her eyes, Francesca gazed around. Had she heard someone knock? Then she heard it again. She started to get up but changed her mind. If it was important, they'd call her cellphone. And since she hadn't gotten a call from the front gate, she assumed it might be her nosey neighbor.

Letting her eyelids drift shut again, she ignored whoever was out there. She focused on the music.

"Fuck!" she heard a male voice coming from her bedroom.

Oh my God, there's someone in my apartment. She sat up, her heart beating rapidly as she looked for a nearby towel. She tried to pull herself out of the bath quietly so she wouldn't draw attention to where she was.

"There you are." Randall appeared in her bathroom.

Francesca froze. Part of her was relieved to see it was Randall and not a burglar, but the other half was pissed. "Get out!" she screamed.

He looked almost like a deer caught in headlights. "I just wanted to make sure you were okay."

"By breaking into my apartment?" Did he not remember her brother was a cop?

"It was unlocked and you didn't answer. I knew you were upset, and I wanted to check on you."

"But you don't just come into someone's house," she argued. "That's called breaking and entering."

"I didn't break anything, and you're the one who didn't answer the door. Your car is out front and I knew you were here."

Letting out a frustrated sigh, she said, "Did you ever stop to think I was ignoring whoever was there? I am, as you can see, in the bath."

Oh yes, he definitely knew she was naked. She hated that she noticed the bulge in his pants as he took in the scene in front of him.

"Can you please leave so I can get out and get dressed?" she asked.

"We need to talk."

"Fine, but not in here."

"I'm sorry about earlier. I never should have jumped to the conclusion I did about you and Ben. It was wrong and immature. And I know I said hurtful things. In fact, I've said a lot lately. I don't know what comes over me when I'm with you."

Francesca let out another sigh. "Look, I'll talk. Just please let me get dressed."

Randall's gaze swept over her again. Her nipples puckered and she was so glad bubbles were covering them. The last thing she wanted right now was for him to know how much he affected her. The longer he stood there and she could see the slight erection in his jeans, the more likely she was to lose herself in him and forget everything she'd just sat and thought about.

She cleared her throat, hoping to get his attention—in a different way.

"Okay, yeah, sorry. I'll wait for you in the living room," he finally said.

"Thanks, and close the door behind you."

He nodded and then left. Francesca moaned and sunk deeper into the water. After a few more moments of the bliss of her bath, she climbed out and dried off before covering herself with her favorite terry cloth robe.

In her bedroom, she found that door shut as well. She dressed quickly, all the while telling herself she would not fall into his spell again. Things hadn't worked out years ago for a reason. Randall and she were not the same people anymore. And holding on to the past would do no good. She had to let those memories go. And move on.

In the living room, she found the lights on now and Randall sat on the couch with his legs spread apart as he leaned against the side cushions. He watched her and she him. She took a seat on the opposite couch, keeping as much distance between them as she could. She had to stay in control of the situation.

"You know, I don't really know why you're here. You made it clear you weren't interested in me. You just had to get me out of your system. I would think I'm out by now. It's done. So why are you here and not with your girlfriend?"

"First off, Dana isn't my girlfriend. That was our first date. So just forget about her. It was stupid I even went out with her."

Francesca huffed. "Okay, let's pretend for a moment that's true. Tell me then, why did you care so much when you saw me with someone else? After all, it isn't like you want to be in a relationship with me."

"That's not entirely true."

"You're not serious, are you? Since I saw you again, you've repeatedly told me you didn't want to get involved. You keep reminding me I only like rich men and I couldn't possibly be happy with someone who isn't."

"Well, can you?" he asked.

"Can I what?"

"Be happy with someone who can't give you everything your heart desires. If I recall, that's what you wanted when you left me."

Francesca bit her lip and stared at her hands a moment. "I thought it was. But it hasn't brought me happiness. Money is good, but it isn't everything. I know that. I didn't only want a wealthy man, I also wanted someone who loved me as well."

They sat silently for a few moments. Glancing up, she saw Randall's gaze was intense and focused all on her. She didn't know if he just had nothing to say or if his mind was going a mile a minute like hers.

"Could you ever be with someone like me? I get my hands dirty every day. I don't like fancy restaurants. My ideal Friday night is a cold beer and a movie. I have no desire to live some fancy life and waste my money on stupid things like expensive cars or on a seventy dollar bottle of wine, when I can pick up perfectly good wine for three dollars at the local supermarket. Is that a life you could live?"

"I think so."

"I like you, Francesca, a lot more than I'd like to admit. But I don't want you to sacrifice things you want to be with someone like me who *might* be able to give you what you want." He paused a moment, then added, "What if I told you right now I could actually give you those fancy things? That I'm loaded."

"I know you're not."

"But if I was. Would I be perfect for you then?"

She smiled but didn't say anything. Randall stood up and her smile faded. "Are you leaving?"

"You gave me my answer."

"I didn't say anything," she argued.

"Exactly. You smiled, telling me my suspicions were true."

Francesca stood and placed her hands on her hips. "I'm sick and tired of you thinking you know me. I smiled because I was thinking when it came to you, money doesn't matter. Even if you were rich, I wouldn't care. No, I don't have the same desires for a Friday night like you do, but maybe we could have met in the middle and compromised. But you'll never see me as anything else." She paused and took a deep breath before continuing. "And I have no one to blame but myself. I dumped you years ago for that reason and have been living the rich life. And I like it. But for the right person, I could give it up."

Randall licked his lips, and for a moment she thought

maybe he'd grab her, press his lips against hers, and make love to her. God, she just wanted to feel him touch her. Whenever they connected, she felt whole and as though the world had stopped moving. He made her complete.

He took a step toward her, and she braced herself for the passion. But then he spun around and left. The door shut behind him and all was silent again. It was as though he hadn't even been there. She plopped back down on the couch. What a turn of events. He'd come here to apologize and when he left, she was now the bad guy.

Chapter 10

Sitting across from her brother Adam at Sweet Muffins Bakery, Francesca listened to him talk about work. The past week had been very entertaining for him. He'd had all sorts of calls from cats in trees to a woman who needed an alien arrested for abducting her. She knew Adam was just trying to make her feel better. He'd never been one to want to just sit and listen to her problems, but he did what he could to try and put a smile on her face. Right now, however, nothing was going to make her feel better until she figured things out.

She'd bumped into Randall a few days after their last fight. They'd both been at the same gas station. Neither of them spoke to the other. Just looked. She wanted to go over and talk to him but knew it was best not to. Until she sorted things out for herself, she couldn't try and work things out with him. He'd said a lot of things that made her think. And she needed to figure out if she could settle for the life he had to offer her.

Francesca hadn't seen him again. This could be the break she needed. But was it what she wanted?

"Francesca, you there?" Adam waved his hand in front

of her.

"Sorry. My mind is elsewhere."

"Shit, you want to talk, don't you?" He rubbed his forehead.

She laughed. "No, Adam. This is something I have to do on my own."

"Look, sis, you're perfect the way you are. You don't take shit from anyone. Don't sacrifice who you are for anyone."

"Even if I think I might love him?" She brushed a loose strand of hair behind her ear.

"If he loves you back, then you wouldn't have to sacrifice."

"Love sucks."

"So, you do love him?" He raised an eyebrow.

"I never stopped. But you're right. I suppose it's time for me to stop thinking about how I need to change and who I have to be and find out if he can accept me for who I am."

Adam sat back in his seat and took a sip of his coffee. "It's going to take a special man to put up with you. And I will say that I think *he* is the one who can do it. Heck, he's still around, that should tell you something."

Francesca sighed. "Maybe. I just need him to see me for me and not who he thinks I am. If money is such an issue now, won't it always be? How do I get him to understand I don't care?"

"If he can't see it, then it's his loss. Want me to play bad cop and pull him over and give him a talking to?"

Francesca burst out laughing. "God, no! Talk about embarrassing. I don't think I could ever look at him again, and I'd have to leave town."

"What's so funny over here?" Amy asked as she took a seat next to Adam.

"Your future husband. He wants to pull Randall over and give him a talking to."

Amy poked Adam. "You better not."

"I wasn't really. It was an offer," Adam said.

"I feel bad for our kids."

Adam pulled Amy close and wrapped his arms around her. "Let's skip the wedding and get started on those kids."

"Eeew, I'm out of here." Francesca stood, pushing her chair back.

"If you need some real advice, call me. I'm always here." Amy laid her head on Adam's shoulder.

"Thanks. Because he is no help."

"Hey! That story about the woman and alien thing had you smiling."

Francesca shook her head. "It's never a dull moment

with you. Glad you found a woman who can put up with
you!"

She began to leave when Amy called out. "I still have
you down for bringing a guest to the wedding. I expect a
certain someone to be there."

"We'll see." She pushed her way through the door and
out into the bright afternoon. She was happy that her brother
had found someone to be so happy with. Nothing else
mattered for Amy and Adam except one another. Perhaps
she and Randall could have that as well.

* * * *

Randy stood outside the shop and listened to Mr.
Arnold talk about the latest car he was rebuilding. Usually
he enjoyed hearing the man's stories, but today had been a
horrible day. If it could happen, then it did. And he had a
finger wrapped up to show it. He had been damn lucky it
hadn't been chopped off when the hood suddenly fell from
the car he was working on. There was still a chance his
finger was fractured.

He'd fallen several times in the shop over things out of
place. The phone had rung non-stop from customers calling
with questions. He had a full day ahead of him tomorrow,
and tonight he was on tow-duty. The guy he had hired
needed the night off for a school event for his kids.

Sometimes he thought owning his own business was one of the worst mistakes he'd ever made. All the pressure was starting to get to him.

He hoped tonight was uneventful. Since he couldn't relax with a six-pack, he planned to at least relax with a movie.

"Well, once I get her all shined up, I'll drive it up here for you to see," Mr. Arnold said.

"Awesome. I can't wait to see it. Sounds like you've got quite the project ahead of you though."

"Oh, I do. But all I've got is time." Mr. Arnold laid a hand on his shoulder. "Don't forget to take some time for yourself, boy. Life is short. Enjoy it."

"Thanks, sir. I'll try."

Mr. Arnold nodded and then went toward his vehicle to head home. Randy went back into the shop to turn everything off and make sure the phone was set to forward to his cellphone. Once that was all done, he went out the back door and walked up the hill to his house.

The first thing he did when he got home was take a shower to wash away the grime from the day. After that, he rummaged through the fridge before deciding on a sandwich and a whole bag of chips. Plopping down on the couch with his food, he turned the TV on and flipped through the channels. A movie that he hadn't seen was beginning on one of the movie networks. Finally, this day was starting to look up.

His phone rang. Grunting, he answered. It was someone wanting to know his hours of operation. He really needed to invest in one of those fancy answering machines at the shop where callers could press one to reach him and then he could include all that other nonsense people called about on the message.

His sandwich was gone and half a bag of chips before he was full. Randy kicked his feet up so they rested on the coffee table and did his best to concentrate on the movie. There was a blonde actress in the movie and each time he saw her from behind, his mind immediately went to someone else. Someone he was doing his damn best to get over and forget. He was sure things between them weren't going to start up again. They couldn't be in the same room without fighting. Some people just weren't meant to be together, no matter how much they wanted to be.

Randy's eyelids began to feel heavy and he decided a nap would be good. Just as he was about to drift off, his cellphone rang. "Fuck!"

He picked it up and saw it was a number he didn't know. "Hello."

"I'm looking for a tow. My car has broken down about a block from your shop."

At least he didn't have to travel far. "Okay. Can I get your name and a description of the vehicle I'm looking for?"

"Sure, my name is Skylar and it's a white Lexus."

He was beginning to hate white Lexuses. "All right, Skylar. Stay in your car, and I'll be there in the next ten minutes to help you."

"Thank you. You won't regret it." She hung up.

Regret it? What the hell was there to regret when it came to towing a car? Hopefully a serial killer hadn't just called him.

Chapter 11

Randy pulled up behind the white car. He couldn't see the woman inside yet. The whole drive over he'd had a weird feeling. He wasn't sure what was going on, but something seemed off. But he was here anyway in the event that this woman really did need help.

Leaving the engine on, he climbed out of his truck and started to walk toward the driver's side door. It opened and the first thing he saw was a pair of long legs. He followed those sexy legs up to a tight jean miniskirt, and forced his focus further up until he met a familiar face. What was going on?

"Francesca."

"We need to talk," she said.

"Couldn't you have called?"

She walked up to him and when he inhaled, he smelled that scent she wore that always drove him insane. Much like the woman in front of him.

"I'm so sick and tired of fighting with you." She yanked him by his shirt and pulled his face down toward hers. "Quit arguing with me all the damn time and let's figure this out."

He gazed into her eyes and did his best to resist her, but he couldn't. The need to taste her took over, and his mouth smashed into hers. He thrust his tongue in and couldn't believe how much he had missed the way she tasted.

Francesca's grip tightened on his shirt before she broke the kiss and pushed him off. Damn this woman!

"I need to know you can accept me for who I am. Yes, I like fancy things. And no, I can't settle for being curled up with you on a couch every single Friday night. I can eat fast food, but at least once a month, I need to be taken out someplace where we are going to overpay for our food. And if we live paycheck to paycheck, I don't care. Money doesn't buy the type of happiness that I'm looking for. Only your love can give me what I want. I am stubborn, and I make mistakes all the time. I am vocal, and I'm going to speak my mind—a lot. But that's who I am. And I'm not changing just so you will be with me. Take me as I am or don't take me at all."

Randy smiled. "There isn't a damn thing about you I want to change. You keep life interesting."

"I'll take that as a compliment, Randy." Francesca took a step closer to him.

"That's Randall to you."

Francesca threw her head back and laughed. He liked seeing her happy.

"What about that tow?" he asked.

She leaned up and kissed his neck and slowly moved toward his ear. Sucking on his lobe, she whispered, "Let's come back later, right now we have a lot of making up to do."

"I like the sound of that. Promise to sit next to me in the truck."

"Only if you promise to touch me the whole ride."

He wrapped his arms around Francesca and carried her to his truck. Opening the door, he sat her down, wishing they weren't on the side of the road, otherwise he would have feasted on her damn legs in that miniskirt all the way to her sweet center. Instead, she slid over as he climbed in.

Once he was inside and back on the road, Francesca grabbed his hand and placed it high up her inner thigh. "I'm not wearing any panties," she said.

He knew just what she wanted and he was going to give it to her. "Spread them open."

She did. He slowed the truck down but made sure to hit each and every bump he could. His hand found its way to her pussy. She was wet. Taking no time, he let his thumb roll over her clit and then thrust two fingers into her opening.

She laid her head back and let out moans of delight. Her breathing was quick. His parking lot was ahead and he knew the bumps of the unpaved road just might bring her over the edge. Thrusting in and out of her faster, he managed to make the left turn with one hand on the wheel and then with a thud, the truck jerked as he slowly crawled down the gravel road.

"Oh God," she called out.

"Come for me."

He pressed her clit a little more and she cried out. Her hips grinded into his hand. He did the best he could to get the truck up to his house. He needed to get inside of her.

Once she finished riding out her climax, he removed his hand and gazed at her. She stared back with nothing but pure passion in her eyes.

"Are we alone now?" she asked.

He nodded.

Her hands began to fumble with his pants.

"Wait, let's get inside."

"No, I want you in my mouth, right here. Just like old times." She winked.

Lifting up, he let her wiggle his pants down. She wrapped her hand around his cock and stroked him up and down in a slow rhythm. "You're bigger than I remember." She licked her lips. "I bet you taste better than my memory reminds me."

It was torture. He couldn't wait to feel her warm mouth on him. "Please, take me. I can't hold out much longer."

She smiled. "Impatient. Trust me, I can't wait to run my tongue up and down your long length and swirl my tongue around the tip and taste that first drip of cum."

She was trying to kill him. He had no doubt. He was going to explode just listening to her talk.

"How badly do you want me to suck?"

"Bad." He was so close to the edge he could barely think or form a sentence.

"Good, 'cause I don't think I could hold off putting you in my mouth much longer."

Francesca leaned over from the middle seat, and with her hand, guided his dick into her mouth. Randy groaned immediately. She sucked in the tip and let it pop out of her mouth, rubbing it along her lips, before taking it in again and letting her lips travel down his base as far as she could. Her soft tongue then slide up and down the backside of his shaft.

She brought her mouth back up his shaft and licked the head thoroughly before taking him farther into her mouth.

This time he could feel the back of her throat. She moaned in pleasure. He gripped her head and steadied her in place.

"I'm going to come. If you don't want it in your mouth, you better pull away now."

She didn't. She made sounds of pleasure as she began to move up and down his shaft in a faster rhythm. He couldn't hold out any longer. He lifted his hips up and felt his seed release. Francesca moaned in delight, and he could feel her swallow each burst that shot out. He rested his head on the head rest and did his best to catch his breath.

She sat up, wiped her mouth, and then reached for his keys, turning the truck off. "We're not done."

"No, we aren't."

* * * *

Francesca stood in Randy's living room as he went to get them some water. She looked around, feeling once again as though she was just where she was supposed to be. This house was one she could envision herself in. She could already see the place decorated for Christmas. Their stockings on the fireplace. Maybe she was getting a bit ahead of herself, but this time she knew it would work out.

Randy came around the corner and handed her a bottle. He'd already opened it for her. She took a long sip and then set the bottle down on a nearby table.

"I want to make one thing clear," she said. "This isn't a game. If we're going to do this, then we're doing it. Got it?"

"Honey, I've tried my hardest to get you out of my system, but I couldn't do it. This is happening. And everything that comes with it."

"Everything?"

He nodded. She didn't say anything. Surely they weren't talk about the same thing.

Randy took her hand. "You drive me insane."

"Hey."

He put his hand up to stop her from going any further. "For once, don't argue. I want to spend the rest of my life with you. There will never be a dull moment. I want to wake up with you every morning and go to bed with you each night. As much as we fight, I know the making up will always be ten times better. Francesca, will you do me the honor of being my wife?"

She covered her mouth. She couldn't believe it. It wasn't the big, grand proposal she always envisioned she'd get, but it was perfect. She jumped into his arms. "Yes."

"Can you be happy with me?" he asked.

"I'll be miserable if I don't have you. I don't want anything else in life but you."

"There's something I need to tell you."

She cocked her head to the side and lifted an eyebrow. He took her hand and led her toward the couch. Sitting down, she stared at him, wondering what he had to tell her.

"I hope you don't get mad," he said.

"I don't like where this is going."

"I'm rich."

Crossing her arms, she snapped, "Don't start this talk again. Why is this always about money with you? I told you, I love you. I don't care about money. Yet, you just can't let it go."

He chuckled and then knelt down, kissing her on the cheek. "Francesca, honey, I have money and a lot of it. I'm not joking."

"What? Are you serious?"

"Yes."

Tears formed in her eyes and she didn't know what kind of sick joke he was playing. Asking her to marry him and then this money talk. She pushed her way past him and wished her car was there now. She would have walked out. But she was stuck. She walked instead to his bedroom and paced his room.

He followed her. "Is it so hard for you to believe that someone like me has money?"

"No. But all we have done is fight, and you've called

me a gold digger. If you really have money, why did you hide it?"

"I don't tell people. And I guess I wanted to make sure you wanted me for me."

"Take me home."

"Why?"

"I'm so mad right now, that's why. I don't know if I'm angry at you or me. I keep wondering if this is a joke or if you think I am the joke."

He grabbed her and pressed her against the wall. "If we're going to get married, there is no running. We have to work this out. I know I hid this from you. And I know you're mad about it. I said a lot of things I regret, and I think you did as well. But there was no way I could not tell you that I had money. We're getting married, and we have to be honest with one another. I know you love me for me. And I love you for you. If it makes you feel better, I'll write a big check and donate all my money to some charity."

"You'd do that?" she asked.

He smiled. "Hell no. But if it makes you feel better, I'd say yes."

"Let's get one thing straight right now. I'm *not* marrying you for your money. If you ever say I did, I will write that damn check and get rid of it. Got it?"

He leaned forward and pressed his mouth to her neck. "Got it."

"Now make love to me," she demanded.

Randy trailed his lips from her neck down to her breasts. She didn't want this to be slow. Reaching down, she pulled her shirt up over her head and tossed it across the room. She then unclasped her bra and let it fall to the floor.

"I'm moving in soon and redecorating." She cupped her breasts as his mouth latched on to a nipple.

"I don't care what the fuck you do. Just as long as you always wear this perfume and you're in our bed every night."

He sucked in deeply and she moaned. Releasing one of her breasts, she worked her skirt down. Randy took a step back and looked at her standing there fully naked for him. "I'm way over dressed."

She watched as he got his clothes off as swiftly as he could. He then picked her up and pressed her against the wall. She wrapped her arms around his waist. His cock was hard and pressing into her pussy.

"I forgot the protection. We might need to take a quick time-out." He nibbled on her neck.

"It's okay, I'm on the pill." She captured his lips and thrust her tongue in. The kiss was intense and needy. As he forced his tongue deeper into her mouth, his cock drove into her. She jerked and cried out as he filled her. Her head rested on the wall behind her and he sucked on her collarbone.

Tightly she held on as he thrust deeply into her. Her arms gripped his neck, and she did her best to keep up with the rhythm. Her climax was building fast, and as much as she tried to hold it off, she couldn't any longer.

"Come with me, please," she cried out. "Now, please, now."

"Come, baby."

It hit her. Waves of pleasure shot through her body. She called out his name as she rode out the climax. Every nerve in her body stood on edge and she could feel Randall having his own orgasm. His grip was tight on her waist and he screamed out her name along with a few curse words as he pumped into her before firmly pressing her against the wall, using her as support to hold himself up.

"That was amazing," she whispered.

"Only because it was you and I together."

She giggled. "Let's lay down."

After he seemed to finally catch his breath, he took her hand and led her to the bed. She pulled the covers back and climbed in. He wrapped his arms around her, spooning her.

It was perfect.

"I have a question," she said.

"You better ask fast. I'm about to sleep so I can re-energize."

"I still need a date for my brother's wedding. How about it?"

"I'd better be your date."

She smiled and nuzzled her head against the fluffy pillow, letting sleep take her away.

Epilogue

"You may now kiss the bride," the preacher said.

Francesca smiled as she watched Adam and Amy embrace. Her brother, Mr. Commitment Issues, was married.

Skylar reached out and wrapped her arm around Francesca. "Isn't this great? They're going to be so happy."

Placing her arms around Skylar, she said, "They are going to have a wonderful life."

"We all are," Skylar replied.

"I'm just glad they're hitched, I've got to pee," Jane said from behind them.

They laughed.

"Only a few more weeks to go," Francesca reminded her. "You'll make it."

Standing back, they watched as Amy and Adam walked down the aisle to leave the church. It didn't take long for Ben, Drew, and Randy to make their way to them. She greeted Randy with a kiss on the cheek. Francesca couldn't wait for their big day.

Ben held Jane's hand as he helped her down the steps leading to the reception area. Drew whispered something into Skylar's ear. She giggled and then, with their arms wrapped around one another, they headed toward the doorway.

"You looked beautiful up there. I can't wait until you're the one in the white dress."

"Me either. If only I could narrow it down to one."

"Get two."

"You're insane. No, when I find the right one, I'll know."

"Well, hurry up so we can get hitched."

"Patience. We have our whole lives together. Now come on, let's go get some champagne and eat. I'm starving."

Randy took her hand and they made their way to the reception. When she walked into the room, Francesca smiled. She'd decorated it and it looked better than she imagined it would. She made notes to herself what she had to have at her own reception.

The reception went well. They all danced their hearts out, and Francesca had a good buzz going on. Her feet ached from her heels that she'd ditched some time ago under one of the tables. Her family was there for Adam's wedding and they couldn't wait until it was time for hers.

As the evening came to an end, Francesca found the

other girls all huddled together.

"Hey, are we exchanging secrets?" she asked as she approached.

Amy grinned. "We are."

"I hope you're planning on sharing them with me as well."

Jane nudged Skylar.

"Drew and I are expecting our first child."

"Really? Congratulations. I'm so happy for you two." Francesca leaned over and hugged Skylar.

"That's not all," Amy said with a mischievous smile on her face. "I'm pregnant too."

"I'm going to be an aunt!" Francesca clapped her hands together.

Amy nodded.

"Wow, that's great. I'm really happy for all of you."

Jane wrapped an arm around Francesca's shoulders. "You're next."

"Oh no, not yet. Remind me not to drink the water." Francesca laughed. However, the thought of having a mini Randy around wasn't so bad. One day, but for now she was happy just to have a man who loved her and three friends she could lean on.

About Lacey Wolfe

Lacey Wolfe has always had a passion for words, whether it's getting lost in a book or writing her own. From the time she was a child she would slip away to write short stories about people she knew and fantasies she wished would happen. It has always been her dream to be a published author and with her two children now of school age, she finally has the time to work on making her dream come true.

Lacey lives in Georgia with her husband, son and daughter, their six cats and one black lab who rules the house.

Lacey's Website:
www.laceywolfe.com
Reader eMail:
laceywolfe@live.com